FAERIE HUNT

THE CHANGELING CHRONICLES: BOOK SIX

EMMA L ADAMS

My office was still in one piece. A good sign, and given the business I worked in, not necessarily a guarantee.

Vance and I approached the two-storey building that had become the site of the business I ran alongside my best friend, Isabel, weaving through the crowds walking back and forth from the local shopping district. Mostly witches or plain old humans, though we did see a few mercenaries, recognisable by their scars and visible weapons. And the fact that they usually saw my sword and crossed the road to avoid me.

"I can't imagine why they keep doing that," I said to Vance after a mercenary had nearly walked headlong into an oncoming bus in an effort to keep from crossing my path.

"Nor me. You look so friendly and approachable."

"Look who's talking."

We made an odd pair, even I'd acknowledge that. Vance was nearly a foot taller than me and his tailored, expensive clothes made him stand out in almost any crowd. He'd left his long coat behind, but he carried a powerful aura which drew the eye even of those who didn't know him as the head of the Mage Lords. It was impossible to ask him to tone it down, because he didn't seem to realise the effect was there half the time. As for me, I lived in leather and denim and wore my sword, Helena, strapped to my waist at all times, even at Vance's cottage by the sea. Monsters didn't take holidays, after all.

"Number eighteen, right? There's blood on the porch."

"Of course there is." I rolled my eyes. "Someone couldn't wait to ruin my day."

Given that Vance and I had been away for two weeks, I'd half-expected to come back and find the place swarming with undead and other nasties, but the nice-looking brick building was in the same condition in which I'd left it. All the shitty jobs I'd taken over the last few years had finally paid off. Using a combination of savings and the money Isabel had inherited from the former witch coven leader, Francine, we'd purchased new premises on the upper floor of a converted Victorian house, with Isabel's new flat on the ground floor. It was twice as big as our last rental and a dramatic improvement in every department. Granted, the bar had been low, since our last flat had had holes in the ceiling and no working heating system. Not to mention the monstrous fae waiting to pounce as soon as a gap appeared in the iron wards.

While Isabel had been fine with running the business solo for a couple of weeks, I'd left a notice up in the window telling anyone with faerie-related problems to go to the mages for a temporary discount because the resident faerie killer was on holiday. Isabel could handle most cases alone, but I'd asked her to call me immediately if a Grey Vale-level threat presented itself. We'd had no calls, but Vance was right about the bloodstains on the doorstep. A small, feathered body accompanied them.

"Oh, someone left a dead crow for me. How considerate."

I'd bet my sword it was one of Larsen's cronies. My former employer wasn't best pleased with my change in fortunes, and Larsen's low-key resentment had led to several of his highest-ranked mercenaries attempting to take out our business. Unfortunately for them, they hadn't reckoned on the tripwire spells Isabel had built into the walls. I'd seen a pair of them hobbling down the high street shortly after one of those incidents, struggling to walk around the fist-sized boils they'd inconveniently developed in the crotch area. More's the pity.

Nobody intending harm could bypass the wards without being blown sky-high, but I guessed dead birds didn't fall into that category. I reached to remove the crow, but its corpse disappeared in a flutter of black feathers and a faint rush of wind.

"Where'd you send it?" I asked Vance.

"Larsen's porch."

"Ha."

Vance's ability to displace objects frequently came in handy for both of us. He could also move people, though his range didn't stretch as far as the other side of the country. We'd had a long drive home, made longer by the damage the faerie invasion had inflicted on the roads. Motorways had turned into swamps, country lanes had sprouted forests, and we'd had to take an hour-long detour around a sleeping giant that had decided to take a nap right in the middle of Spaghetti Junction.

That aside, I hadn't minded a few more hours in Vance's company. I'd been looking forward to seeing Isabel, but not so much to the frequent attempts on my life.

Erwin the piskie flew out the window as I dug in my bag for my key. "Ivy!" he screamed delightedly.

I unlocked the door. "Hey, Erwin."

"Missed you!" he proclaimed.

"You wouldn't have liked the coast. Too much sand."

I stepped into the hallway and wiped my boots. Amazingly, I'd only got a little mud on them, not blood. Well, that wasn't strictly true, but Quentin had insisted we take an entire suitcase of cleansing spells with us, correctly assuming that I'd maintain my typical habit of getting blood on my clothes at least once a day.

"Isabel's still using him as a security guard?" Vance stepped in behind me. "You should consider hiring someone to stand outside. I know your wards are strong, but…"

"But I have a lot of enemies, I know." I kicked off my boots and peered approvingly into the living room off the hall.

Gone were the days when we'd had our entire lives crammed into a single room adjoining two cupboard-sized bedrooms and an equally tiny bathroom. Now Isabel had the entire floor to herself and she'd moved all her witch paraphernalia into a single room she'd designated as her workshop rather than leaving them strewn all over the flat. Mostly. I still had to step around a chalk circle in the doorway in case it doused me in glitter.

"Maybe I'll try and lure away one of Larsen's people."

"Thought I heard your voice." Isabel, my best friend, came out of her workshop and smiled at me. She wore her usual bright, flowery attire that exposed the glyphs shimmering beneath her dark skin, designed to retaliate if anyone attacked her. Her arms were also dusted with the usual chalk stains from the time she spent creating spells, and bangles lined her wrists, lined with tripwire spells. As the leader of the local witch coven, she'd inherited her fair share of enemies to add to the faeries who wanted to ruin both our lives, but despite her unassuming appearance, few would underestimate her.

"How was your holiday? Wait, don't answer. It's written all over your face." She grinned at me. "It's been so calm I figured you took the monsters with you. Unless you want to tell me you made it through a whole fortnight without stabbing anything?"

"Almost." A smile tugged at my mouth. "Okay, I might have done it once or twice."

Isabel rolled her eyes. "Of course."

"Three times," Vance added.

"Traitor."

He flashed me a grin. You might think the mutual teasing would have got old after two weeks alone together, but that was how our relationship worked, and frankly, I'd never been happier.

"Is everything all right here?" I joined Isabel in the living room, taking a seat on the comfy new sofa. She'd inherited that from Francine, too, and two matching armchairs.

"Yeah," said Isabel. "Kind of. There's one thing, but you won't like it."

"As long as nobody's dead, we're all good."

"Well," said Isabel. "Yes. Someone is, actually."

"Damn. Really?" It wouldn't be anyone we knew, otherwise she'd have told us right away. "Shifter? Half-faerie?"

"Mercenary," she said. "Larsen called this morning. I think he wants to hire you."

"You're kidding. Right?"

Her mouth twisted. "From what I gathered, the case is too complicated for any of his mercenaries to handle."

"You mean complicated as in the solution doesn't involve stabbing someone?" More than that was beyond most mercenaries. "So it wasn't him who dropped a dead crow on the doorstep?"

Isabel grimaced. "Someone did that? Ugh. Probably Gregor."

"Fucker." Gregor and I had a longstanding animosity which would no doubt one day end with me pitching him headfirst into the canal. "Did Larsen tell you the name of the person who was killed?" I'd never been friendly with most mercs, but there were some I'd developed a tolerance for back when I'd raided trolls' nests on a weekly basis and occasionally needed a partner for backup.

"I think he said the mercenary was called Liam Harlow."

I'd hoped it wouldn't be a name I recognised. Liam had been one of the few good guys. "Murder?"

"Most likely, according to Larsen. He didn't give details. Said I was to tell you to call him back. Also, he doesn't want the mages involved."

"Figures." Larsen was under the impression that Vance had seduced me away from my former job taking on freelance cases for him. In reality, I'd quit because Larsen's mercs had screwed me over, and I certainly didn't miss always being given the shittiest jobs with the worst pay and the highest mortality risk. Now I split my time fifty-fifty between helping the mages and dealing with independent clients alongside Isabel, deflecting Larsen's attempts to sabotage us by lowering his rates and sending his mercs after our clients. After all that, Larsen had some nerve asking for my help. He must be desperate.

"What d'you reckon?" I asked Vance. "Want to head over there now? If a faerie is behind this, it's best to find out sooner rather than later."

"You're right." He sounded a little annoyed, probably because we'd been back all of ten minutes and already had clients queuing at the door. Or ex-employers, as it were. Really, a straightforward murder was child's play compared to some of the other crap we'd dealt with over the past few months. Our break had been sorely needed.

At Vance's command, the living room vanished, to be

replaced by the less appealing sight of the entryway to the local mercenary guild. The building was as dingy as ever, with the smell of stale cigarettes mixed with the coppery tang of old bloodstains nobody had ever bothered to wash out of the carpet. A short, balding man glared at me from the front desk, stubbing out his cigarette in the nearest plant pot. Its occupant was long dead.

"You," said Larsen. "Ivy Lane." His gaze shifted to Vance and his eyes narrowed. "Mage Lord."

"Larsen. I'm told you wanted to see me about a murder. Since most of your freelancers take on similar cases to the one you're offering, I'm curious to know why you think I'm the person for the job."

He discarded the cigarette. "Because the killer wasn't human."

"Neither is half your clientele." Larsen was part shifter himself, technically, but could no more turn into a wolf than into a tree. More's the pity for him.

"No, but a wild animal couldn't have got the jump on Liam. Not a normal one, anyway."

Put 'wild animal' and 'not normal' in the same sentence and I could see why he'd arrived at 'faeries'.

"Did you find anything else at the scene?" asked Vance. "Necromancy props, for instance?"

"Nothing. The manner of death was gruesome, but seemingly nonmagical in nature. That said, there's more to some deaths than the human eye can detect."

"Sounds delightful," I said. "I'll need more detail."

"If the Mage Lord steps outside. This is sensitive information."

Yeah, right. Now I got why he wanted me to do the job. I was, to my knowledge, the only person ever employed at the guild with the talent for seeing through faerie glamour. Although many of the guild's clients were half-bloods, none of the mercs were. Possibly, the half-faeries were put off by the collection of iron weapons in the guild or the number of dim-witted thugs present who couldn't tell the difference between the half-faeries and the sort of wild fae that turned humans inside-out for a joke.

"I'll wait outside," said Vance.

"Sure." The quicker I got this meeting over with, the better, and if Larsen thought he could get the best of me when the Mage Lord was absent, he was laughably mistaken.

I'd arrived at the mercenary guild as a penniless sixteen-year-old fresh from the trauma of spending three years trapped in Faerie. Survival had been my first priority, and Larsen had taken advantage immediately. My first case had involved extracting fire imps from someone's house, and he'd omitted to tell me the place was already on fire at the time. I'd toughed it out and came back to the guild with singed clothes and a cage of shrieking imps to demand payment, which he'd refused to give on the grounds that the whole farce had been a test. Which I'd passed. He'd been impressed enough to offer me a job that had ultimately turned into a ten-year-long stint of dealing with whatever bullshit Larsen saw fit to throw at me.

In his mind, I was still that kid, but he'd made a grave error in assuming my showing up here meant I'd take his attitude. I waited for him to speak, angling myself so that he had a clear view of the blade sheathed at my waist. Helena was no normal sword but a faerie artefact forged from the heart of one of their trees and imbued with magic that could destroy almost any enemy, living or dead.

Larsen's smirk told me he'd either forgotten all of that or didn't care. "If I knew what it'd take to get compliance from you, maybe I should have offered you a bonus on each mission in exchange for a night in my private rooms."

One twitch of my hand and my blade was at his throat.

"I'm not trading my skills for sexual favours, you perverted troll," I spat. "I picked Vance over you because he isn't an exploitative dick who spends half the guild's budget at the casino instead of compensating his employees. It's not rocket science."

"Jesus, Lane, I wasn't being serious."

"You're fucking kidding me, right?" I didn't remove my sword.

He coughed. "It was a badly judged joke."

"Yes, it was. And by the way, if I hear any rumours that you're coercing new recruits into a similar bargain, you'll get worse than one of Isabel's tripwire spells."

He shifted on his feet, a flash of guilt noticeably crossing his face. So he'd definitely been sending people to sabotage our business. Prick. I didn't think he *was* pressuring new mercs into trading blow jobs for bonuses—primarily because that would involve giving up some of his precious gambling budget that he thought nobody knew about—but I was doubly tempted to go ahead with Vance's suggestion to hire one of the mercs as a security guard for our business. It might also make Gregor think twice about dropping any more dead corvids onto the doorstep.

Maybe I'd be better off swiping Larsen's recruits than listening to him grovelling, but as far as mercs went, Liam had been a decent guy, and the circumstances of his death sounded weird enough that I wanted to learn more. "Back to the case. Did you have anyone administer a tracking spell at the site of Liam's death?"

"We tried. The spells' results were too muddled to see the killer."

Might be true, but I wouldn't take him at his word. "Does the victim have any surviving relatives?"

"No. Only an ex-girlfriend who hasn't seen him in years."

Not unusual for a mercenary. Most people joined the guild out of desperation, after all.

"And I can head there now?"

"If you accept the case."

I narrowed my eyes, debating. I could always back out if it turned out he was playing me again. "Fine."

"I'll let the mercs watching the place know to let you in."

How very considerate. The fact that he'd sent mercenaries and not called the police told me there was a less-than-aboveboard dimension to the case, but for someone who ran a guild ostensibly set up for the purpose of dealing with the city's most dangerous monsters, Larsen was surprisingly cowardly.

I made for the door, where Vance waited to meet me. Behind, I heard a thump and a gasp as Larsen stumbled against the desk; Vance had displaced the air and hit him on the back of the head.

"Did you lay a finger on her?" Vance asked in a low, dangerous voice.

"Christ, no. Mage Lord. Sir."

"Just a misunderstanding," I said cheerily, with a warning look at Larsen that told him he wouldn't get a second chance, and his next sleazy comment would be his last.

Once I was outside with Vance, I added, "He's being his usual dickish self. Want to go visit a murder site?"

As far as murder scenes went, Liam's was relatively neat. His first-floor flat was tucked away in one of the nicer areas of the suburbs outside of mage territory, neighboured by houses in a pristine enough condition to suggest they belonged to regular humans. Liam had probably wanted to distance himself from the other mercs. Not every mercenary was proud of their kill list.

I entered through the red-painted front door with Vance and Isabel close behind me. Up one flight of carpeted stairs, and the flat door lay slightly open. A baby-faced young merc jumped at the sight of Vance. He looked hardly older than eighteen. And Larsen had him guarding a murder scene. Dick.

"It's horrible in there," he said in a whispery voice.

"I figured. How long have you been standing there?"

"Only till you're done. Larsen told me not to let anyone else in." He glanced over his shoulder and swallowed nervously.

"No life forms." Vance pulled his pen-shaped detector out

of thin air and pointed it towards the door, then swapped it out for his custom-made dispeller. "No magical traces, either."

"Hmm." I saw no obvious sign of the faeries' magic anywhere either, and my sword's telltale blue glow remained muted. Still, I kept one hand on the hilt as the kid fumbled the door open and stood back.

The merc shuffled out the way. "I'll stay here, make sure no one else shows up."

"Sure."

I took the lead, Vance behind me. Isabel, who didn't handle this sort of thing well, hovered by the door with the mercenary kid instead.

Bloody smears formed a trail along the carpet, signs that the person who'd found the body must have run for the door instantly. The sofa bore the freshest stains, pale grey turned rust-brown in a pattern that suggested Lian had fallen backwards onto the cushions after being attacked, and darker stains fanned out on the carpet.

Liam's body had been sliced open with almost surgical precision, deep cuts exposing the innards, or what was left of them. Shards of ribcage stuck out at angles, revealing that whatever had attacked him had ripped out his heart, lungs, and possibly other organs as well. I couldn't be certain. Skin had been shredded and hung off in strips up to his neck. His gore-splattered face was stretched in a grimace of agony.

I closed my eyes and swallowed a couple of times, then made myself look at the rest of the body. No other wounds. He'd been sliced open by thick claws, not any I'd recognise at first glance. Shifter kills were messier. *Faeries* was the first thought that came to mind, but I couldn't immediately recall any that had a taste for human organs and not the flesh. Unless it'd been interrupted mid-feast.

I turned to Vance. "Any ideas?"

His brow furrowed. "It's worth trying a tracking spell again."

"In case Larsen's people screwed up, I know."

Why Liam, though? There were more vulnerable humans living in the neighbouring houses and apartments, but the monster had only targeted him. Which suggested it'd been following orders. Asking who he'd pissed off recently would be our next move, once we'd got this unpleasantness over with.

I moved closer to the sofa. Vance padded at my side, his footsteps muffled by the thick carpet.

"Still no magical traces." He held the dispeller out, his hand extended above the sofa. "Do you see anything?"

"No glamour," I confirmed, reaching for one of the tracking spells I carried in my pocket. "Doesn't mean the fae didn't do it, mind you. The wilder faeries don't need to use magic to cause that kind of damage."

I crouched down and laid the tracking spell on the carpet around one of the fading bloodstains. Isabel's handmade spells were typically shaped like ordinary bracelets that expanded to larger circles when activated. The tracker's green light flared up, and I lifted my palms, bracing myself. "Let's get this over with."

Reliving someone's murder was never pleasant, and Liam's blood would get me a front row seat. When my hands touched the circle, my vision darkened, the flat's walls patched in long shadows cast by the dying light streaming through the window.

It took a moment to get my bearings. From the angle, I was looking through Liam's eyes as he sat on the sofa. As there was no sound in a tracker vision, I had to brace myself for the moment without knowing exactly when it was coming. I held my breath.

My vision went black, then the green-lit circle swam back

into view. "Huh?"

"What happened?" asked Vance.

"I think the spell glitched." I removed my hands from the circle and the room came back into proper focus exactly as I'd left it. The spell collapsed into fine powder that mingled with the drying blood on the carpet.

"Got another one?" Vance asked.

"I can try," I said dubiously. "Larsen wasn't kidding, huh."

I activated another one, with the same result. The vision had scarcely begun before the spell cut off like a TV during a power cut. "How'd the attacker even get in here? The window's not damaged."

"Or the door," Vance observed.

"Right, yeah." I rose to my feet and examined the door frame, but there were no signs a clawed beast had ripped it open. No footprints or other markings on the furniture either. If not for the bloodstains, I wouldn't have believed the murder had taken place in this room at all.

"No use." I let the last tracking spell collapse into powder. "Trust Larsen to make a cockup of everything."

"He couldn't have meddled with the scene, to throw off our trail?" Vance suggested.

"Nah, he's not smart enough," I said. "Also, he's a dishonest lazy crook, but not a murderer. He wouldn't have reason to take out one of his own mercs, especially someone like Liam. Gregor, I'd understand. That guy could pick a fight in an empty room."

I made my way back over to Vance. If a cleansing spell had been used to erase the killer's traces, they hadn't touched any of the blood splattered on the floor, and the tracker likely wouldn't have worked to begin with.

The door nudged inward and Isabel's voice drifted in. "What's wrong with the tracking spells? Should I come in?"

"Probably not," I said. "It's not pleasant. The tracking

spells only showed a few moments before Liam's death and not the actual act. Does that mean magical interference?"

"Not necessarily," said Isabel. "Tracking spells can get muddled if it's been more than a few hours since the murder."

"Let's see what else we have in here." I'd avoided looking too closely at Liam's personal possessions, once I'd ascertained there were no magical props in the room. It was never fun sifting through the remnants of a life that had been brutally cut short.

I started with the living room, whose walls were bare aside from a generic landscape painting. Liam appeared to have been a neat freak and no discarded clothing or other items lay on the floor. I'd have said nobody had been in the flat for weeks if not for the TV remote lying on the coffee table, its light flashing, next to an open can of beer. Dusty shelves lined with books and older paraphernalia like CDs and DVDs stood on either side of the TV table. None of the typical mercenary trophies were on display, but he might have stashed them elsewhere.

Vance pushed open the door to Liam's bedroom, which was also neat enough to make me wonder if he had frequent visitors. Single bed, neatly made. More bookshelves. Half-full laundry basket. No magical accoutrements, nor any photos on display to indicate any special someones in his life.

With no family or partner to contact, we had one option remaining. I waited until we'd left the flat and Larsen's pasty-faced mercenary assistant behind before I told the others my plan.

"I'm going to contact his ghost," I said. "Ask for a first-hand account. Anything new with the necromancers I should know about, Isabel? No wandering undead or troublemaking poltergeists?"

"No," she replied. "Like I said, it's been quiet. I'll message Rick. He'll be happy to help you out."

"Are you sure?"

"No problem. What are friends for?"

"Summoning the dead, apparently." I flashed Vance a grin. "Want to come?"

"What about Larsen?" asked Isabel. "Will he want us contacting Liam's ghost?"

"I don't really give a shit, to be honest." I did need to tell him we'd checked the scene and found nothing of note, so I nodded to Vance. "Let's head there now."

Vance, not one for such mundane activities as taking the bus, transported us straight back to the mercenary guild—and right into the path of a hellhound.

I drew Helena immediately, swinging the blade into the beast's neck. The hellhound squealed in pain as its head was ripped free of its neck; its furred body slumped down onto the path, spilling blue-tinged blood all over Larsen's porch. Drool dripped from its jaws, burning hissing holes into the doormat.

Isabel raised an eyebrow. "That's one hell of a reaction time."

"Where'd that thing come from?" I ran along the front of the building, looking for more of the beasts. They tended to travel in packs, but I hadn't run into one in a long while. Much less on the guild's doorstep.

"There aren't any others." Vance met me on the other side. "Not around the back of the building, either."

"Weird." I sidestepped the puddle of drool and blood. "It can't be alone, surely."

"Maybe they got stuck here after you killed their master," Isabel suggested.

Technically, Calder had been their master and not Fionn, but I'd killed both, so the point was moot. I pushed open the door to the guild. "Or it wanted to hire Larsen. I'll call someone from clean-up to get rid of the body before it draws something nastier here."

Or before more of them showed up. Hellhounds weren't loners by nature. Yes, I'd killed the Huntsman who commanded them some weeks ago, before my long-overdue holiday with Vance, but it figured that some new depraved prick would have stepped into his shoes by now. Preferably their new master would have fewer world-destroying ambitions.

Larsen wasn't in the reception area. I knocked on the door to his office but didn't get a response, either.

"He's not here?" asked Isabel.

"Nothing new," I said. "Okay, I'm gonna see who's in charge of clean-up today."

Ten minutes and several arguments later, I left the guild to find Isabel talking to her necromancer boyfriend on the phone while Vance watched over the body of the fallen hellhound.

"I shouldn't have told them how lethal hellhound bites are," I said to him. "They're trying to bully the new recruits into moving the body. Larsen isn't in, so he'll be off at the casino again, gambling away the guild's money."

"That isn't allowed, is it?" said Vance.

I shrugged. "He's the boss. Nobody's gonna rat him out to the police, not if they want to keep their jobs. Larsen's people are as bad as he is, anyway. Most of them want the kills more than the money. Except people like Liam, and things didn't turn out so great for him, either."

"You aren't obligated to help," said Vance. "Did you even know Liam?"

"Not well, but he didn't deserve to die like that, and those tracking spells shouldn't have malfunctioned either. It's worth speaking to his ghost, at least."

Isabel ended her phone call. "Rick said the necromancers will help us. We can head there right away."

"Good," I said. "Better go before Larsen finds out we're planning to raise the dead behind his back."

———

"What can I do for you, Mage Lord?" Colby, a pale, skinny necromancer who wasn't a day older than twenty, answered the door to the depressingly soot-coloured building that acted as the necromancers' main headquarters. As per usual when he set eyes on me, his expression shifted to the resigned manner of someone contemplating the gallows.

"We'd like to speak to a mercenary who was murdered last night," I told him. "His name was Liam Harlow."

"Murder." Colby flinched. "Again?"

From his tone, you'd think I carried the Grim Reaper's scythe around with me, which was hardly fair. I wouldn't have anything to do with the investigation if Larsen hadn't dragged me into this.

"You're a necromancer. Surely you get more requests to investigate murders than to speak to people who died peacefully."

"You'd be surprised," said Rick, striding over. Compared to the other necromancers, he was a ray of sunshine with blond hair and a nice smile. As far as Isabel had told me, he was a gentleman, too, which made him a good guy in my book. "Most of our clients come here wanting to apologise for screaming arguments they had with family members before they died. Or resolve will-related disputes."

"Fair enough."

I followed the pair of them into the building. The main room in the necromancers' headquarters wouldn't win any decorating contests. Candles burned in sconces on the wide metal walls, offering no warmth in the draughty space. There was no furniture, and the solid metal floor was marked with a large chalk circle outlined with twelve candles. Why twelve was the magic number, I'd never thought to ask. Someone had already lit them, and a white flare of light shone from each candle, brighter than any natural flame.

I glimpsed more black-cloaked figures hovering curiously around the room as Isabel, Vance and I positioned ourselves in front of the circle. Rick and Colby stood on each side and began muttering under their breaths, speaking words that sounded vaguely like Latin. According to Vance, who knew several people who actually spoke Latin fluently, their mangling of the language would make a scholar weep. More-over, their display might sound and look impressive, but all the lights and chanting were purely for show. I could cross into Death with no need for ceremony, though I was a unique case, since I didn't have a drop of necromancer blood in my veins. The magic I'd stolen from a Sidhe lord enabled me to travel into Death with or without my body.

Grey smoke swirled within the circle, mingling with the pale light of the candles. My vision flickered, showing two worlds overlaid on top of one another. Death, formed of swirling fog without end, and the Grey Vale, whose endless silvery paths lay on the borderline between Faerie and Death. The Vale was a piece of the faerie realm torn away when the ancient Sidhe had exiled their gods, or so Frank the necro-mancer had told me, and even with a ring of candles in the way, the silvery path loomed close enough that I might have reached out a hand and touched it.

The Vale had become the home of any exiled faeries who slipped through the cracks of Summer and Winter or through the spirit lines dividing our own realm from Death. During events of turbulence when the veil between realms came under attack, the beasts of the Grey Vale had an annoying tendency to end up here in the mortal realm. Like hellhounds, for instance. Otherwise, the place was lifeless in a very literal sense. True fae didn't pass over the veil into the afterlife when they died, but I wasn't entirely certain on what happened to their spirits. They were too offended by the very concept of mortality to give me a straight answer.

I focused on the circle instead of the Vale, and the path faded into the background as an indistinct figure faded into view. Short in stature and balding, he wore a faded suit that looked threadbare even in death.

"Ivy Lane," said Lord Evander. "I wondered when you'd show up again."

"Still here, still causing trouble," I said. "We're here to speak to a ghost. Name's Liam Harlow, a former mercenary who was murdered yesterday."

"Mercenary," said Lord Evander. "I'll see what I can do." He disappeared in the way ghosts did, fading into the surrounding fog in the blink of an eye.

"Someone's not being chatty today." Not unusual for Lord Evander. We hadn't got on particularly well when he'd been alive, and death hadn't improved his personality in the slightest.

A second later, another person took his place, a blond man of around forty or so who was still in good shape from his mercenary work—apart from the *being dead* part. This was our guy. I sincerely hoped he knew he *was* dead, which wasn't always a guarantee.

"Hi," I said to him. "I'm Ivy. From the mercenary guild?"

His brow furrowed. "Ivy Lane? I thought you left Larsen's place."

"I did." He didn't sound panicked, more confused. Hoping that was a good sign, I pressed on. "Erm… do you remember what happened to you last night?"

His expression turned vague. "There was something I needed to do, but I can't recall what it was."

Nope, he doesn't know he's dead. Wonderful.

Rick stepped in. "Mr Harlow, I regret to inform you that you passed away last night. You have been raised from death so that these individuals may ask you some questions."

Liam's eyes widened. "I'm *dead*?"

"Sorry," I said. "You were murdered in your flat. It would be great if you could tell me everything you remember."

"I'm really dead?"

"Yes." Often, the shock of death caused the deceased to lose parts of their memory. Some even forgot their names, and the few ghosts that lingered for longer than a day rarely remained coherent. Odds were, he'd have zero recollection, but a single clue would be welcome. "You don't remember at all?"

Liam frowned. "I—I remember a noise. Like an animal screaming."

That might point to the faeries, but I needed something more concrete to draw any conclusions. "Did you leave your front door open?"

Whoever had got into the flat hadn't forced the door. Either they'd opened it without leaving any fingerprints, or they'd somehow teleported directly into the room. Which was impossible even for the fae.

"I'm sorry, I don't remember." His eyes clouded, and his body grew notably fainter than before. "I'm... I'm going, aren't I?"

I'd say yes. Fog swept in around him; when I squinted, the outline of a towering gate materialised behind his ghostly body. Nobody other than necromancers knew what lay beyond, when spirits moved past the first layer of the veil and into the true afterlife.

"If there's anything important you want to tell us, say it now," said Vance.

"Please." Sudden horror and desperation flitted across his face. "Help my daughter. She's in danger, horrible danger. I—"

Then he disappeared.

Well, crap.

3

———————

I stared into the swirling smoke within the candle's lights. Since when did Liam have a daughter? I hadn't known. Larsen sure hadn't mentioned her, and we hadn't seen any photos in the flat either.

"Sorry," said Rick. "It happens sometimes."

"It's fine." Isabel moved to his side, her face brightening as it always did when she saw him. It was kind of adorable.

I left them to talk while Vance and I made for the door. Though summer was on the way out, it was still infinitely warmer outside than in that freezing room, and I let the sunlight wash over me while I contemplated our next move.

"I'll have to check with the mercenary guild," I said. "Larsen kept a register of all the mercs and their next of kin. Can't say I want to admit we called up Liam's ghost less than an hour after we went to the crime scene, though."

"I have access to the entire register of mercenaries online," said Vance, who had his phone in hand.

"Of course you do." I rolled my eyes. "Okay, what've you got?"

"Liam is registered as unmarried, and he lived alone. No child is mentioned."

"Okay… maybe the kid's from a past relationship? Larsen's kind of sloppy when it comes to updating the records. Unless Liam didn't tell him, which doesn't make much sense. The kids of mercenaries get a payment from the guild if their parent is killed on the job."

I took Vance's phone and skimmed through the list he'd pulled up. "Huh. I didn't know they put on record if you're a supernatural."

There wasn't anyone else on the list under the name *Harlow,* and if Liam's daughter had taken a different surname, she wasn't linked with him on the register.

Vance took the phone back from me. "Liam was definitely human?"

"Yeah, he was." I lifted my head to the guild's door, where Isabel had just walked out to join us. "Hey, Isabel. Larsen didn't mention anything else when he asked you to call me, did he? I mean, having a kid nobody knows about is a pretty major oversight."

And he said she was in danger. That, above all, made this case worth pursuing.

Isabel shook her head. "No. I asked Rick if there might be any chance of finding Liam's ghost again, but he said the odds are low. Won't his daughter be on a birth register somewhere?"

"Yeah, I guess so," I said. "She might've been born outside the city, but I assume Liam would have left his daughter something in his will, at the very least."

"You're right," said Vance. "If the will hasn't already been unearthed by the mercenaries, I assume someone will be looking. Especially if there's no next of kin listed on the record."

"No." I scowled. "Might explain why Larsen kept the case isolated. He wanted to get his paws on Liam's valuables."

Isabel's mouth twisted in disgust. "Remind me why you're bothering with the slimy old troll again?"

"Because there might be a kid in danger." Isabel—and Vance, now—knew that when missing kids were involved, I couldn't back out in good conscience. I'd been one myself, spent three years as the terrified captive of a depraved Sidhe lord, and the memories and scars would never leave me entirely. This kid might be an orphan now, if Liam had been her only parent. Or she might be dead. My hands fisted. "You know what, screw it. I'm telling Larsen. Might as well know if we're looking for an actual person first. Some mercs don't want anyone taking their loot after they die, so I can see people like Gregor fabricating fake family members to pass on their haul to. Doesn't sound in character for Liam, but neither does not putting his child on the mercenary register."

Vance nodded. "If that's the case, then maybe the child is living with the mother. Or adopted, or in an orphanage."

"Or half-blood?" I stopped, my finger hovering above the phone screen. "Damn. That's actually a *good* reason not to have a child on record. If the other parent is fae…"

My gaze connected with Vance's, and he filled in the gaps. "Let's not jump to conclusions," he said. "Check with Larsen first."

Reluctantly, I clicked on Larsen's number. The phone rang a couple of times, then he answered. The noise level in the background made me suspect my guess that he'd intended to go straight to the casino was right on the mark.

"It's Ivy." I raised my voice over the clamour of voices and the clatter of coins from slot machines. "I have a question. Has Liam's will been found yet?"

"No." Larsen snapped. "Why?"

Less than a year ago, I'd have lied and then attempted to

muddle through alone. I'd learned the hard way that it was more straightforward just to tell the truth, however many headaches it might cause in the short term. "We communicated with Liam's ghost and he told us he had a daughter. He wanted us to find her, but he disappeared before he could give us any more information."

Larsen blew out a breath. I pulled my phone away from my ear as though the smell of cheap alcohol might come wafting out of the screen. "You had permission to visit the crime scene, not the necromancers."

"You weren't at the guild and there's only a limited time before spirits move on for good. I wanted to ask him if he remembered his death."

"And did he?"

"No, but he said his daughter's in danger. I didn't even know he had kids, but I assumed she'd be listed in his will. Right?"

"The will hasn't been found yet. And no, you aren't to go back to the crime scene. You had one chance."

Arsehole. "Is there really no trace of his daughter on record?"

"How the bloody hell should I know? I only update the records when people first join the guild, and I don't recall any kids in his file."

"Just checking," I said. "By the way, there was a hellhound on your doorstep. I sent in cleanup to get rid of it. You're welcome."

Larsen cursed. "Blasted creatures. You, Ivy, stay away from Liam's place."

As he hung up, a breeze brought the sound of rustling paper. I turned to Vance, who'd appeared a few feet away with a stack of pages in his hands that hadn't been there beforehand. "What are those?"

"From Liam's flat," he said.

"Did you just… go back in there?"

"I didn't touch anything."

Right. He must have used his abilities to open the cupboards and drawers until he found what he needed. "You're unbelievable."

"Or quick-thinking."

"I'll go with that. What are they?"

He passed me the papers. "These were in the desk drawer."

"Huh… they look like letters." I flicked through the pages and counted thirteen, all addressed to the same person. Roseanne Harlow. "I think they're for her."

Each ended with the same words: *from your loving father.*

I swallowed, a lump rising in my throat. "I don't know if I should be reading these."

"What are those?" Isabel, like me, had grown used to Vance's habit of disappearing and reappearing by now.

"Letters. To her." The opening line of the first leapt out at me: *I remember the day I first saw you. Your mother never told me the date of your birth, but it was a spring morning when I found you, lying in a basket on the doorstep with a single feather from her as a gift. You looked just like your mother.*

"He found her on the doorstep." I lifted my head. "In a basket, with… a feather? Pretty sure that means her mother was fae."

"Abandoning a child in a basket certainly sounds typical of the faeries," Vance agreed. "Why did Liam then abandon her in turn?"

"No idea." I flicked through the letters and found they all had the same date. The anniversary of the day Liam had met his daughter. None of them had been sent, and most were short, the ink smudged by spilled drink or tears. I blinked my own eyes clear and lowered my hand. "I'll read them later.

There might be clues pointing to why he believed her to be in danger."

"Yes, and perhaps the cause of his own death." Vance took the letters from me and they vanished, most likely to the desk in his office.

Had Liam believed the killer would target his child next? I'd have to go by the assumption that someone had given orders to whatever monster had been responsible for Liam's gruesome death, but the bizarre nature of the attack continued to bug the crap out of me. Not a single trace had been on the door or windows. Other than Liam's mutilated body, the flat had been undisturbed. I hadn't looked for wards, but Liam had almost certainly used some kind of iron barrier at the very least. He wouldn't have survived so long as a mercenary by being careless.

"Perhaps," said Vance. "We need to find the child, and I can bring her under the protection of the mages if she doesn't live on half-blood territory."

"Assuming she's interested."

"Based on the letters, she turned thirteen years old a few months ago. Surely, she would accept our protection."

"Yeah, well. You never know with half-bloods, especially ones who weren't raised by humans." Based on stories I'd heard about humans unsuccessfully trying to assimilate stubborn half-bloods into their lifestyles, this could go either way.

Who'd raised this girl, if not her father? Faerie parents rarely took their children with them when they departed this realm, though few other than the Sidhe were capable of passing between worlds whenever they liked. If her mother was of lesser fae origin, she'd still be somewhere in this realm, I assumed, but there were no guarantees she'd have accepted a half-human child.

As for Liam? From the letters, it was clear he had loved her, but did she even know he existed at all?

"I think I'll need to read the letters in more detail," I said. "Wouldn't mind knowing why he gave her up to the faeries. A mercenary life isn't easy, but most people would choose that over being raised by the fae. Unless he made some dangerous enemies." That was possible, though it'd take a particularly vindictive sort to go after a kid.

Thirteen years ago… damn. I hadn't even been here. I'd been in Faerie.

Vance, who'd been typing into his phone, looked up. "Roseanne's name doesn't come up on the official register of half-bloods."

"There's a register?"

"Those who wish to live amongst humans can apply for official documents," Vance explained. "It's easy to tell who is likely to be half-fae, because they usually don't know their birth date. It's an imperfect system, but being on the register is a guarantee that they'll be able to get a proper ID and other vital documents. Unfortunately, the Chief has been less than successful at convincing half-faeries living in poverty and danger in the wilds that they would be better off coming to live and work amongst humans."

"Must be a tough choice." Registering would grant them access to our schools and jobs, but at the cost of being seen as betraying their heritage and giving up any chance of going back to Faerie, even if it was only a pipe dream. And if they didn't choose the Chief, the single alternative was living wild and potentially falling prey to the more powerful outcasts. Hell, even the mercenaries sometimes hunted wild fae for kicks. "Bet the banshee isn't on there either."

"No, she isn't, but if you want to find Liam's daughter, we can try asking the Chief."

"He always says he doesn't know who lives on his territory," I reminded him. "Which would explain why people keep getting murdered or starting illegal underground fighting rings."

"Last I heard, he's no longer being so cavalier, though he refuses to admit it's because of his own failure to keep his people safe that he was forced to take my advice."

"Pity." Served him right, too. "This won't be easy, though. Some of his people live underground or in the woods and don't have addresses. I don't see the Chief getting off his arse and searching the whole territory."

Which, as usual, left the job to me. Yet if Liam's ghost had told the truth, I couldn't ignore his warning. Instinct demanded that I do everything in my power to find and protect the child.

The trouble was, the same resolve had got me into sticky situations more than once. I had no evidence of Roseanne's existence but the word of a dead man who'd known his days were numbered. A man who'd kept his child at a distance for a reason, however well-intentioned that might be.

I wasn't particularly keen to speak to the Chief again, either. Our last encounter had ended in a bitter argument when he'd found out that a group of ambassadors for the Seelie Court had shown up at the manor and hadn't bothered to pay a visit to half-blood territory during their brief time in this realm. He didn't seem to care that they'd come to threaten me over a talisman they'd misplaced—and that I'd thrown into an endless abyss inhabited by a giant deity, *not* that I'd told them that part—but their departure had proved above all doubt that the Sidhe gave zero shits about their part-human offspring.

I'd become all too familiar with the Sidhe's loathing of anything mortal during my three-year captivity in the Grey Vale, and it said a lot that the worst punishment a faerie could suffer was having their magic stripped before being sent to a realm which sapped away their immortality until they expired. With that in mind, I didn't believe for a minute that Roseanne's fae mother would have taken her in. She'd have been sent to an orphanage instead, most likely.

"If you're heading there now, I can stay here and wait for Rick," Isabel offered. "Let me know how it goes?"

"Sure." I waved goodbye.

Vance transported us to the road across from half-blood territory. Hedges surrounded the area which had once been a normal-sized human park before a giant forest had sprung up out of nowhere, courtesy of the twin spirit lines that intersected above this part of town. The faeries had settled here shortly after and had expanded their territory into a wide space that should by rights have been a city all on its own. Faeries had a questionable relationship with the laws of nature, but the same could be said of the witches who made their home in the forest and who'd been here long before anyone had known this was anything other than an ordinary park.

The Chief's armoured guards gave me a cursory glance as we passed through the gate. Half-blood territory had shaken off the brightness of Summer and moved into September, with grey skies similar to the sky outside, a distinct chill in the air, and autumn leaves dappling the paths in shades of red and amber. The flowers that usually filled the air with their fragrant scent drooped and exuded the scent of slow decay, and most of the faeries wandering around were fully clothed, except for the group of half-nymphs who waved at Vance from the shallows of the river, baring their breasts. I glared at them until they dived underneath the water.

We walked past the apartment blocks that were home to the half-bloods who wanted to stay in more human-style accommodation. Beyond lay forested lands that belonged to those less inclined towards imitating their mortal neighbours, but our target was a clearing just inside the forest where the Chief spent most of his time. The half-bloods' leader sat on a makeshift throne that resembled a cheap prop from a stage play and his wooden staff didn't look much more impressive after I'd spent so much time around genuine talismans from Faerie itself. The Chief was supposed to have the strongest magic of all the local half-bloods, but he'd got the position due to his half-Sidhe heritage and not through any merit.

Right now, he looked downright miserable. It was difficult to tell age when it came to the faeries, because if their magic was functioning as it should, they had a permanent glowing, clear-skinned appearance which made them look like they were barely out of their teens. I'd assumed the Chief was early twenties at most, but he might as well have aged a dozen years since we'd last met. His green eyes were glassy, his black hair oily and straggling to his shoulders, and not so much as a wisp of green magic stirred around his staff. Strange. It was the end of summer, but he still ought to be running at full power, at least until autumn began in earnest.

"Hey, Chief," I said. "Bit run-down, are you?"

"Ivy Lane," he said. "What are you doing here?"

"Seriously, man, have you been spending too much time close to iron?" Iron was the fae's one true weakness. It burned away a faerie's very essence and had even helped me kill Lord Fionn, the leader of the Wild Hunt. Given that, you wouldn't think the fae would thrive in one of England's most industrialised cities, but they were stubborn bastards and half-bloods had some level of resistance to iron's effects. Not much, but their inability to travel into Faerie themselves meant they had little choice but to live alongside humans.

"What do you want?" The Chief's voice held a strained edge. "I have a territory to run, and the needs of my fellow half-faeries take priority over yours."

I don't see anyone who needs you. There weren't many people around at all, in fact. Even his ogre bodyguards seemed to have taken the day off.

"I'm looking for an unregistered half-blood who might live on your territory. Her human father was murdered, and he believed her life might be in danger too."

"An unregistered half-blood? Non-registered ones don't want to be found."

"She's a thirteen-year-old kid. Abandoned."

"Why didn't her human father take her in?"

"No clue. He was a mercenary. I assume he made some enemies and didn't want her dragged into it. His life wasn't easy."

Maybe Liam really had callously abandoned his child, and the letters were fabricated, but I had my doubts. Regardless, I wanted to get the full picture before I made any decisions. This case had hit on all my weak points, and in fact, if I went down the cynical route, I'd wonder if someone was trying to lure me into a trap.

"Your lives and ours are vastly different," the Chief said. "If the child doesn't want to be found, you will never find her."

"The child's life is in danger," I shot at him. "And with how Liam died, the killer doesn't screw around. It was brutal."

I could see the internal war waging on the Chief's face as his curiosity did battle with his instinctive need to avoid the very subject of death. Half-bloods didn't like to examine their own mortality closely at the best of times, and frankly, the guy looked to be halfway into the grave already.

"How did he die?" he finally ground out.

"He was savaged by something with sharp claws. Organs removed and probably eaten. Definitely not a shifter. I'd say it's a wild fae's work, but they didn't leave a mark on the doors or window. Any ideas?"

His mouth twisted. "Shapeshifter?"

"Could be." If they'd been in humanoid shape when they'd entered… but again, why would a shapeshifter not show up on a tracking spell?

"That method of killing doesn't sound like any creature I know." He coughed, a rattling noise that mildly alarmed me. Faeries didn't catch colds, did they?

"Is your magic acting up again?" I asked.

"My magic is fine," he said.

Yeah, sure it was. Out of curiosity, I called on my own magic. Blue light sprang to my palms, confirming it was working just fine. Of course, my magic wasn't the same as the sort the Chief used, nor the other half-faeries either.

"What are you doing?" asked the Chief.

"Just checking my magic's working."

He coughed again. "If you've nothing more to say to me, get off my territory."

Charming. I hadn't exactly expected a red carpet to unfurl before me, but he still hadn't so much as offered a thank-you for saving him and his people from being devoured alive by the all-consuming deity slumbering in the liminal space between realms directly on top of his territory. It spoke to his sheer stubbornness that he'd refused to move his people elsewhere after I'd dropped *that* bombshell on him, but the territory's odd emptiness indicated that some had made that choice without me needing to tell everyone about the world-devouring monster sleeping beneath their feet.

"If you learn anything, call the mages or me." I didn't expect an answer. Without waiting for his response, I turned my back and left the clearing with Vance.

The Chief's attitude was nothing new. Ruling over half-bloods was a thankless task, and he, like all the others living on his territory, wanted nothing more than to go back to Faerie. Unfortunately for them, the only part of the faerie realm open to outcasts was the Grey Vale, and everything they'd been told about Faerie was mostly a lie. They'd never be immortal like their faerie kin, and only death waited on the wrong side of the veil.

"Does it seem quiet to you in here?" I murmured to Vance.

"Yes," he answered. "I thought so, but there's been a marked uptick in people parting ways with the Chief since the recent upheavals."

"I'd have thought they'd at least stay on the territory." Most supernaturals were drawn to one another and faerie magic had an amplifying effect the more of them were in a single space. Loners got eaten alive, often literally. "He didn't tell them...?"

"No, I made it clear that the forest's existence was to remain confidential," he said. "There's been quite enough disruption here already."

"True." The one part of the story we'd omitted was the fate of the ring, which I'd tossed into the abyss to join the sleeping beast. The Chief had already been pissed off with me for nearly causing an evacuation of his entire territory when Fionn had left the ring in the middle of the forest. As a talisman that destroyed any magic it came into contact with, the ring had swiftly begun eating away at both the half-bloods' own magic and the spells that kept the godlike monster between realms from escaping. I'd been forced to get rid of the ring via the only route open to me, but permanently losing one of the Summer Court's most valuable possessions was not the kind of crime the Sidhe forgave, and the Chief would doubtless share the same opinion.

"You have to tell him eventually," Vance said, as if he'd sensed my thoughts. "You mentioned the ring to him before the battle. He'll wonder what you did to stop it destroying his territory."

"You're giving him too much credit."

The Sidhe, though, were a potential problem. A group of Summer's ambassadors had shown up on Vance's lawn the morning after the battle to demand I hand over the ring, and I hadn't been able to give a proper explanation before they'd buggered off back to Faerie. I'd made it clear that Fionn was the person responsible for unleashing the ring's power in the first place, but his demise left me open to any potential retaliation. I was banking on the Sidhe assuming that no human could ever be capable of destroying one of their all-powerful talismans, but since the same human had killed three of their number, that assumption held little weight.

One of those Sidhe was Fionn himself. Since his job had once been to ferry the souls of faeries killed in battle to the afterlife, part of me had wondered if death truly applied to Fionn in the usual sense, but I'd seen his body and talisman disintegrate before my eyes. When I'd employed the ring's destructive power against him, his own magic had fled, allowing me to poison him with iron. Not that the Sidhe had asked me for the details. They cared nothing for his aborted attempt to destroy humanity, only their Erlking's precious ring.

"Probably." Vance's gaze swept over the bare-branched trees and the leaf-dappled paths. "Did you want to go to the witches' forest now? Or should we wait?"

"Better wait, I think." After Larsen, the necromancers and the Chief, I didn't have anything left in the tank to deal with the coven of ancient and terrifying witches and their mind-warping forest. I hadn't visited the Hemlock Coven since we'd narrowly saved them from destruction, figuring that they needed time to rebuild their defences, but they'd given me a hell of a lot to think about in the meantime. Like, for instance, the source of my talisman's power.

"I do need to have another chat with Cordelia," I added. "But I figured I should sort out my list of questions first."

"I have a fair few of my own," he said. "Your magic…"

I looked around in case anyone was listening in, but the forest remained quiet, the trees stark, almost abandoned. "I know."

Vance might have used his power to transport us out of half-blood territory, but walking to the gates afforded us the chance to have another look around. I didn't see anything awry, but no vibrant displays of magic leapt out at me either. At the gates, I waylaid one of the Chief's guards, a pale Unseelie knight who wore armour covered in so many spikes that it must be a real pain—pun intended—to put it on without stabbing himself in the hands. Which might explain why he had an ugly-looking cut on his forehead. "Hey, Bob. Did the Chief's ogres go into hibernation?"

"What makes you say that?" he said in an unusually hostile tone.

"They weren't there." What was with his attitude? "Nobody was guarding him. Seems strange, given… recent events."

"That's none of your concern, human."

"I'm the one who warned you about said recent events," I said testily. "C'mon, Bob, I thought we'd established a rapport here."

"Your attitude will be your undoing, human."

"You need to look into taking a course in effective communication. You might get into fewer fights that way."

I made for the gate before he snapped and tried to run me through, which would end worse for him than it would for me. When I heard his footfalls behind me, I drew my blade from its sheath an inch or two, just enough to expose its vibrant blue glow. I didn't need to turn around to know he was retreating.

Vance eyed my sword as we walked out, his gaze lingering on the hilt. "It's worth asking Cordelia Hemlock for clarification on what she meant when she implied your talisman's magic originally belonged to a creature similar to the one in the forest."

"Yeah." I'd firmly shelved that in the category of 'shit to deal with later' when we'd left for our holiday, but now we were back home, I had no choice but to stare that monster in the eyes. "It's like when faeries store part of their magic inside a talisman. Doesn't mean the god has to be awake or even alive for me to use its power. Remember the life-drinker sword functioned just fine while its master was sleeping. In another realm, even."

"That's right." He watched me push the blade back into its sheath, though the blue glow remained visible to anyone with the Sight. "It would, however, be prudent to learn if its original owner still lives."

"Owner?" I echoed. "You mean the deity? I mean, they might not be thrilled to see a human running around with their power, but neither are the Sidhe. I'm used to that shit. I doubt the gods want the *Sidhe* using their power, either, given what the Courts did to them."

I'd told Vance more or less everything I knew about the Sidhe and their deities, which was both more than I wanted to know and yet much less than I needed to. When he didn't look convinced by my casual tone, I added, "Trust me, I don't know how to feel about it either, but honestly, part of me had already guessed. I can leave my body behind and travel into Death. Not sure the Sidhe can do that."

He arched a brow. "Has anyone asked them?"

"And lived to tell the tale? Unlikely." I shook my head. "There's also the fact that my talisman gets a boost from pain and suffering. That's not typically a side effect of Winter magic."

Winter magic drew strength from the presence of death in the same way that Summer was drawn to life. While both were stronger in their own realm, the changing of seasons in the mortal realm empowered those in a position to benefit. By contrast, my own power didn't grow any stronger in winter than in summer. My power was born of the Vale, and of those who'd been exiled there.

"No," Vance said, "but it would help to know the parameters."

"It seems to be different for each deity," I said. "The life-drinker feeds on life force. Like a twisted reversal of Summer's magic. Usually there's a balance. Life flows into and out of Summer faeries in equal measure."

"And yours is a reversal of Winter, in a way. Instead of gaining strength from being around death, your talisman…"

"Feeds on the pain of the deceased." A cold sensation grew within my core. "I can also draw on the pain of the living, so I'm not sure it's an exact match, but it's pretty close."

I could tap into the relentless agony of the restless dead and even destroy them, shattering their ghostly forms like glass. It gave me no joy. Unlike its previous wielder, Avalin, I didn't get a kick out of the suffering of others.

"There can't be many talismans of the sort," Vance said. "The ring was one, too…"

"Probably," I said. "And… shit, I hope there isn't a portable version of that giant god in the forest. Nobody needs that."

The ring destroyed all magic it came into contact with, but that deity had the power to obliterate… well, everything. At least according to Cordelia. Very luckily, the mortal realm had been spared from finding out how far the beast's limits stretched, and I sincerely hoped that it would sleep on in the forest for the rest of its unnatural existence.

"Especially if that talisman fell into the hands of the exiles," Vance added. "Which seems to happen on a regular basis."

"Unfortunately." To my knowledge, we'd encountered three talismans of the gods and all had been in the possession of the exiled Sidhe who lived in the Grey Vale. "I can see why those exiles are the only people who survived the Vale. They were stripped of their original magic, and to a Sidhe, magic is a part of their very soul. When I had that vision through Avalin's eyes, I felt it. The Vale wasn't just draining his will to live. It was sucking out the very essence of him."

Damn. Was that what was happening to the Chief? I'd wondered if his territory's dismal state might be Summer's punishment for losing the ring, but maybe I ought to have checked to see if killing a death god like Fionn came with side effects for the other fae in the vicinity. Maybe I was wildly off with my estimation, but unlike the exiled Sidhe, I was immune to the effects of the Vale. Being human, I didn't depend upon magic to keep myself alive. In a way, I had the best of both worlds, while the half-bloods had the worst of each. But it didn't mean we weren't *all* in deep shit if I really had irreversibly damaged the faerie magic in this realm by killing the leader of the Wild Hunt.

So much for a relaxed and easy return to work after our holiday.

4

I didn't mention my theory to Vance. I'd spent the bare minimum of time dwelling on the potential side effects of Fionn's demise, and the Sidhe's vague threats over the ring were concerning enough on their own. I had zero desire to achieve the dubious honour of being the first human to be arrested by the Seelie Court for annihilating a priceless artefact, nor to find out what the price for that crime would be.

"What now?" I asked Vance. "We could go back to see Isabel, or the manor. Or rearrange Larsen's face."

"If you like, we can check on the storeroom," he suggested. "I meant to go there as soon as we came back."

"Me, too." It'd slipped my mind altogether thanks to our decision to go straight to Larsen after our return. "Good call. Let's see if everything's where it should be."

Vance transported us to the road across from the magical depository where the Mage Lords kept their own most valuable and dangerous possessions. We took a quick detour to the nearby cemetery to check that no more undead had decided to wander out and play, then made our way to the small brick building in an otherwise uninhabited part of the city. The mages' depository held an unassuming air both on the inside and the outside, its dimly lit hallway lined with old-fashioned torches which made it look more like an underground passageway than a house. Doors lined the hall, each covered in in shimmering wards, the only clue as to the power that lurked within the rooms.

Vance and the Mage Lords alone had the ability to walk in and out of those rooms without meeting an invisible wall. Even for me, an unseen pressure pushed against my skin when he opened the door to the room we needed. Gold light emanated from the glass cases within the room, and power thrummed in the air, cold and forbidding and seemingly designed to make me want to flee in the other direction.

Inside one of the cabinets was the source of my disquiet: a long roll of parchment inscribed with every Invocation known in this realm or in Faerie. Vance had told me the mages had held the parchment in their possession since long before the invasion, though he wasn't clear on where they'd originally obtained it. Only a person with Sidhe blood—or magic—could read the glyphs, let alone speak the words. Each was a command, a concentration of raw power, and the first time I'd used one, I'd been ripped out of my body and had nearly taken a one-way trip into the permanent afterlife.

"Nobody's touched the wards," Vance observed. "That reminds me… I should teach you how to undo and reset the wards on the door in case you need to come here alone."

"I'm already on the manor's wards." Since I'd moved in to live with Vance, the first thing he'd done was teach me how to undo and redo the security wards and activate extra layers in an emergency. Vance's grandparents had been prepared for any scenario. Except, of course, for the Sidhe, though the invading faeries had made swift work of any wards they'd come across and only now did I suspect that they'd done so using Summer's ring. Whatever the Seelie Court might think, as far as I was concerned, we were all better off without it.

"These aren't the same," Vance said. "If I add your blood to the spell, all the wards on this place will obey you the same way they do me and the other Mage Lords. You won't end up in another scenario like…"

"Like when Lord Carlisle got possessed, I know. You trust me that much?"

"Of course I do." He slipped an arm around my waist. "Besides, you can read those glyphs better than I can."

"I wouldn't call it *reading*, exactly." The glyphs on the parchment were unreadable, generally, unless there was a specific one I needed. With one exception. As my gaze passed over a specific line, a familiar tingling sensation rose to my tongue, and I turned my head away, chewing the inside of my cheek as the words tried to force its way out of my mouth. "Except that one *really* wants to be spoken, but I don't know what the hell it says. It might be harmless like the faeries' equivalent of Isabel's glitter spell, or it might be trip-wired to turn me into a goat."

"The Chief would probably be able to fix you, but I think I prefer you as a human." His eyes glittered with amusement.

"Me too. It's annoying that there's no translation."

Not even in Vance's extensive collection of magical theory books. They were an all-mage family aside from the shifter blood on his father's side, but a family that old had surely met the Sidhe at some point or other. I'd spoken three Invocations aloud, all in similar life-threatening circumstances and aided by the talisman I carried acting as a kind of portable translator. Otherwise, I might as well be looking at a foreign language.

"Where'd these Invocations even come from, anyway?" I asked Vance.

"Faerie, I assume," he said, then as I raised an eyebrow at

him, he added, "They've been passed down through my family since at least my grandfather's time."

"And nobody knows all the symbols, including the Chief."

"He claimed to know most of them," said Vance. "Certainly he's familiar with the one you used to seal Calder's magic."

"And that one means *forget*." I pointed to the glyph that I'd used to defeat Calder for good by making him forget his very identity—and that had also, I suspected, erased the memories of those who'd witnessed the invasion. "And—"

I cut myself off as the glyph on the line below filtered through my mind, telling me the meaning. *Break.* "Huh. That one just revealed itself to me. Means *break*. I'll use it if Larsen gives me trouble again and break his kneecaps."

"You don't need a spell to do that," he reminded me. "Remember how dangerous it is to speak those words in this realm."

"I know, I know." I didn't plan to make it a recurring habit. "I also usually need to have the symbols directly in front of me to be able to say them, which kinda limits the practicality of the whole thing."

My gaze strayed to the life-drinker sword in the cabinet on my right, sheathed in green light. Glyphs swirled up and down its length, and the blade at my waist tingled in synchrony.

"Directly in front of you?" he echoed. "You weren't carrying them when…"

"When I sealed the god away and erased Calder's memories." I gestured to the cabinet that contained the second talisman I'd claimed. "Can you see the glyphs on that?"

"On the blade? No, nothing."

"I thought not." The hairs on my arms stood on end. "They're always there, but they shift and change around a lot, and I can't always read them."

Concern furrowed his brow. "I do wish someone could teach you more."

"Yeah." My hand dropped to the blade at my side, fingers tracing the hilt. "Not like I can ask whoever put the spell on the dragon shifter god and buried it underground. Or whoever bound Fionn. They buggered off a long time ago."

In the case of the shifter god, a *very* long time ago. Perhaps the dragon had been around in the time of ancient civilisations where giant shifter gods were par for the course. Considering how ancient the Sidhe were, I could believe it.

Vance gave me a sideways look. "When we speak to the Sidhe directly, they should be able to give you guidance."

When, not *if.* Vance knew as well as I did that the Sidhe had a lot to answer for. The invasion, I was convinced, was due to a mass incident of irresponsibility on their part, though Fionn had been the orchestrator who'd brought every other exile in the Grey Vale along for the ride. The rest was a mystery even the Hemlock Coven didn't have the answers to.

"I doubt they'll consent to giving a human magic lessons," I said. "Also, you know, I kinda lied to them." Not that they'd given me much choice, and after my experiences with the Grey Vale, a jaunt over to the Seelie Court didn't seem nearly as daunting.

"I can at least give you ward access for now," he said. "I'll need a drop of your blood."

"No problem."

I withdrew an iron dagger from my pocket and pricked my fingertip while Vance drew a pen-shaped device out of the air. He gently tapped my bleeding finger and transferred the blood to the wards drawn on the cabinet. They glowed red, then went back to their usual colour.

"Neat trick."

He smiled and the device vanished, to be replaced with a healing spell.

"It's a tiny cut, Vance." I sucked the blood from my finger. "I don't need a healing spell."

"I respect your wishes, but I'd prefer it if you took better care of yourself. I'm quite attached to you." His lips brushed my ear and his hands slid up my hips, lazily tracing circles on my skin through my shirt.

"*Vance.* We're in public."

"No one can see us." His lips moved down to my neck. "I hoped we might get a little more time alone when we returned."

"As opposed to running around murder scenes and chasing wayward half-bloods. I know. Is it the full moon, by any chance?"

"Yes, but I want you every day of the year."

"Now you're being unfair." Two weeks alone in his company had only made me crave more of him, as well he knew.

His teeth snagged on my lower lip as his tongue traced the outline of my mouth before slipping in and exploring the inside just as thoroughly. He smelled good and tasted even better. As a quarter-shifter, he claimed not to be affected by the week surrounding the full moon, which forced most shifters to take on their animal forms and lose all sense of humanity during night-time hours. Vance had as much remarkable control over his shifter side as he did over his mage powers and he rarely shifted accidentally, but the full moon brought out an impulsive side to him. His hands moved over my breasts as a cool breeze caressed my skin, seductive, wanting.

"Vance, I'm pretty sure this isn't the place for—" I gasped as his body pressed against mine.

"My ancestors won't mind."

"What, you think their ghosts are judging us right now?"

"Quite a few of them are buried in that cemetery, actually."

"I knew I felt someone watching me." That, and our previous visits to the depository had involved battling undead and skin-eating faeries. Not to mention the spells trying to wriggle into my head and possibly turn the pair of us into goats. "As much as I like living dangerously, I don't want either of us to end up cursed. I vote we finish this back home."

"If you like," he murmured into my ear. A cool breeze swept around us, and the next second, we were in his room at the manor. "You're not usually the sensible one."

"One of us has to be."

He grinned and pushed me down onto the bed.

———

Thinking of the manor as home had taken me some adjusting. I'd lived in a tiny flat since I was sixteen, at first saving money on rent by sharing with a dozen others and sleeping on the floor, then going through a series of flatmates from hell before I'd lucked out and found Isabel. Now, I lived with Vance, in one of the biggest properties in the city. The manor's security made it one of the safest, too, meaning that if we found our missing half-blood, here would be the most secure place for her to avoid whatever nasties might be on her tail.

Vance woke me early the following morning to spar in the back garden. After yesterday's frustrated trail of dead ends, I needed the chance to blow off steam, and giving my magic a refresher didn't hurt either. We took our post-workout shower together, and by the time he'd made us breakfast, I was feeling pretty damn good. At least until I returned to our missing half-blood problem. I'd read through the letters the night before but got them out again at the table, scowling at Liam's cramped handwriting.

"He's frustratingly vague." I tapped a finger on the first letter. "He says a few times that he regrets 'having to give her up'—Roseanne, that is. But he doesn't say *where* he sent her. I did find a couple of passages that hint she might have been left with humans."

"That's more likely than the alternative," Vance agreed. "We're limited by the few places that might have a register of half-bloods, and we're working on the assumption that the child remained within the city itself, aren't we?"

"Yeah, but… good point." If he'd sent her halfway across the country, our chances of finding her dropped below zero. "Maybe Liam didn't send the letters because he didn't know her current location, but if he was the one who sent her away in the first place, you'd think he'd have kept track."

That didn't mean anyone else had, however. Post-invasion, it was all too easy for someone to disappear without a trace, even a child. Finding an individual half-blood was like looking for a pin in a mound of troll dung, and we might find ourselves mired in just as much shit if we poked any further.

"No." Vance had read the letters, too, and had wasted no time in reaching out to his contacts. "He might have worried the letters would be traced."

"By whom? The mother?" I flipped through the letters and shook my head. "He doesn't imply *she's* the source of danger, but he also doesn't give her name or describe her except superficially. Doesn't say much about how their dynamic worked either. Whether he went with her willingly or was… coerced."

Many faeries made seducing humans into a game. Often one that the human thought they'd won, until the claws came out. Liam, I was convinced, had had a lucky escape, but why had he kept his daughter at arm's length, too, when he'd clearly loved her deeply?

"Back to work already?" asked Wanda, walking into the kitchen. She was Vance's assistant and had helped keep the place running smoothly while we'd been gone.

"We're looking for a half-blood who isn't on record," I explained. "Her human father was a mercenary who was recently murdered, and he wants us to find his daughter. Except we don't know anything about her other than her name and age. She's thirteen and might be any kind of faerie, Winter or Summer."

"A murdered mercenary?"

"Yeah. He knew she was half-blood, but I've no idea why he gave her up. She seems to have disappeared off-grid."

"The girl might be living on half-blood territory," Wanda suggested.

"We tried. The Chief couldn't find her." I sipped orange juice—freshly squeezed, one of many perks of living with the mages—and surveyed the topmost letter again. "Abandoning a child isn't exactly in character with the guy I knew. Even mercenary work's better than living on the streets."

Unless she'd had magic that was hard to hide or that would make it unsafe for her to live amongst humans, but nothing I'd read in the letters would indicate that that was the case.

"Maybe," said Wanda. "How did he die?"

"Something clawed and nasty," I said. "Possibly fae, but we couldn't get a clear picture with a tracking spell, and we can't figure out how it got into the flat without leaving a mark on the door or window either."

"Shapeshifter, the Chief suggested," Vance said. "Might be worth looking into."

"Shapeshifter faeries are more likely to live wild than most." I sighed. "All right. I have an hour before Isabel and I open for clients, so I guess we might as well have another look around Liam's place. I know Larsen said not to, but screw him."

Vance inclined his head in agreement. "I picked up those letters because they were at the top of a pile in one of the desk drawers, but there might be others hidden away. I didn't check every corner."

"We can do that before I head to the office. I'd prefer not to be late. Isabel's been holding the fort the whole time we've been away."

I checked my weapons were in place before we left. Twin daggers in my pockets, made of reinforced iron, which Vance had bought for my birthday this year. He'd also had them engraved with tracking glyphs in case they went missing, though I'd joked that if I wanted them to stay in pristine condition, I should have shut them in one of the Colton family's cabinets. I had to admit they were pretty snazzy. Helena was strapped to my waist in a decorative sheath—another present from Vance, since my old sheath had been damaged in one of many fights with Faerie's creatures—and I had an array of spells stashed in my pockets, too.

Speaking of Faerie, I'd forgotten to check up on the Vale the previous day. We hadn't figured out where the hellhound at the mercenary guild had come from either, whether it'd been a weird anomaly or a sign of trouble to come. Given Faerie's tendency to warp the passage of time, abandoning Isabel to go into the Vale to look for hellhounds would be a dick move. I'd have to save that one for later.

"Ready?" Vance waited, dressed in his knee-length black coat but not visibly armed, courtesy of his ability to grab a weapon out of thin air at any moment.

"Yep." I stepped up to his side. "Hope Larsen's left the place alone. I don't want him sticking his nose into this case any longer. I realise a runaway monster slicing people open *is* mercenary business, but he doesn't give two shits about getting actual justice for his employee."

Vance wrapped an arm around my shoulder and pulled me against his warm body. He didn't need to be touching me to transport us both, but there was a comforting note to the gesture which I appreciated.

At least, until we landed at Liam's flat door, right in front of a group of mercenaries.

"What're you doing here?" said Gregor, who held what looked like a pile of troll's fangs in his arms.

"Are you raiding Liam's flat?" Anger spiked through me. "Get the hell away. All of you." I waved my sword for emphasis, and wisps of blue magic sprang to my arms in response to my rage.

The mercenaries scattered. Mostly. Gregor, too dim-witted to flee, stood his ground. "Liam didn't leave a will. It's every man for himself."

"Or woman," added Elaine, a merc who I was half-sure was part ogre somewhere. She was the size of a tank and wore a necklace made out of knobbly bones. "You snooze, you lose."

"You'll soon be snoozing in an early grave if you don't put that shit down." I pointed my blade at the pair, making a conscious effort to tone down the magic flowing over the surface so it didn't rip their heads clean off. I didn't need to leave a mess in here for Liam's already traumatised neighbours to clean up.

For his part, Vance glared at them but didn't intervene. The Mage Lord was intimidating enough to most people without needing to lift a finger or pull out a weapon.

"Go on," I ordered the mercs. "Whatever Larsen told you, that shit isn't yours to take. Put it back. All of it."

I fired off a quick text to Isabel explaining the situation in case I ended up coming into work late and then got on with wrangling the mercenaries into returning their contraband. Twice, I had to give them a modified taste of my magic when I caught them slipping trophies into their pockets, and after the mercs finally cleared off, I set about hunting in every crevice in the flat.

The mercenaries had left no stone unturned, and for all I knew, someone else had come in the night and stolen away the evidence regardless. Either way, no will materialised, nor any evidence of where Liam's daughter might be. There were no letters aside from the ones Vance had found, no correspondence with her mother, and no photos. Had he ditched her as a baby outside a hospital or even on half-blood territory? Why ask me to protect her and make it all but impossible for me to find her?

As I left, fuming, I put down a tripwire spell in front of Liam's flat door in case anyone came back, and resolved to go back to my usual routine of avoiding the mercenaries as soon as humanly possible.

5

Scheming mercenaries turned out to be the least of my problems. All the local clients from hell had apparently waited until I was back from holiday to come into the office and make trouble. By the time Isabel and I had sent away two of the whiniest wannabe-witches I'd ever had the displeasure of encountering, I found myself daydreaming longingly of the sea. And Vance. My phone buzzed with a message around midday asking me to join him at a cafe for lunch. The moment I said yes, he appeared behind the desk.

"I'll be back in an hour," I said to Isabel, who arched an eyebrow when the air current from Vance's arrival knocked a stack of paperwork over.

"This place was so quiet without you here," she said.

"Yeah, it probably was," I admitted. "But didn't you miss the excitement?"

"Of course. Try not to get into any more trouble. I'm meeting Rick, so I'll close the office for an hour."

"Try not to get distracted."

"Same to you two."

Vance transported us to the café. The local shopping

district was busy enough that few people noticed us appear out of nowhere, and anyone who did would see the Mage Lord's coat and know not to ask too many questions. He'd already ordered lunch and reserved a table at the back.

"How's work?" he asked me as we took our seats.

"A bloody nightmare, but this makes it better." I smiled at the waitress as she delivered the hot chocolate that Vance had correctly remembered was my favourite. "The clients are all being extra dickish to make up for my absence. How's yours?"

"Nothing too strenuous." He waited for the serving staff to depart before saying, "I had some time between clients and obtained the details of three former orphanages or institutes for abandoned children that all existed thirteen years ago, at the time of Liam's daughter's birth."

"Only three?"

"There were very few places that would accept half-faerie children until less than a decade ago when my predecessor changed the laws to prevent half-blood orphans ending up on the streets."

"Huh. I didn't know. I guess I wasn't around thirteen years ago." And I hadn't exactly paid attention to the laws on half-bloods when I'd returned. It'd been difficult not to see them as a reminder of the life which had been ripped away from me, but now, the thought of this kid out there alone made my chest tighten. Had she even known she had a human father who was still alive?

"I left a message on the phone for the first orphanage, but the other two have changed addresses or shut down since then. I'll have to research further."

"I can do some poking around between clients, too."

Our food arrived and I took a bite of chicken salad sand-wich, mulling it over. Orphans of the invasion already had a shitty start to life, but being half-faerie would have made their situation a hundred times more dire. Most supernaturals usually looked out for their own, but half-bloods were often unwanted by both sides of their heritage.

"Thirteen years… that's before the Chief's time."

"Yes, and there wouldn't have been enough adult half-bloods present to look after all the orphans left here after the invasion. Most would have been left to their own devices."

True. The first half-bloods to set up their territory had already been living in hiding before the invasion forced them out into the open, but they hadn't been present in huge numbers until then. Most of the people who lived on the territory now had moved there in the years following the invasion, either having left their human families behind or been ditched by one parent or the other. The latter was less common with the human parent than with the fae one, but invariably, the Chief's connection with the Seelie Court lured anyone in who wanted a fighting chance of making it back to Faerie.

"Also, faeries had a habit of switching out human children with their own offspring," I said. "There's a chance that's what happened with Roseanne. She lived with her fae mother, who then dumped her here without telling her who her father was."

Again, though, that didn't explain why he'd never tried to find her. None of his letters had mentioned any search attempts, and he'd seemingly never set foot on half-blood territory either.

"It's a starting point," said Vance. "I'll see what the staff at the orphanage have to say."

"Yeah."

My phone buzzed on the table, and I picked it up.

"Ivy," said Isabel. "Sorry. There's a half-blood here asking for advice on getting lice off a kelpie."

Oh. It was one of *those* days, apparently. "Tell them to ring the vet. Assuming there's one who works with faerie pets. I'm *not* combing a kelpie. The last one I met tried to bite my foot off."

There was a long pause. "He told you to do something unhygienic."

I sighed. "Better go back to work."

———

Six more disasters later and I finally had a free minute to run a web search on the other two possible places Liam's daughter might have been. One had merged with the local foster system years ago. The other had been set up the year of the invasion to deal with the rising tide of abandoned or orphaned children and had been shut down seven years prior. When I read the name, a chill ran up my spine. I'd *been* there. When I'd worked for Larsen, a couple of years after my return from Faerie, I'd been hired to find a kid who'd gone missing from that very orphanage. The case hadn't ended happily.

"The first orphanage I spoke to said they'd never admitted any half-bloods in that year," said Vance later, when Isabel and I had shut down the office for the day and I joined him in the manor's living room. "As to the second, I can't find anyone who has the records from the old place. But the third—"

"Yeah. It shut down when your former Mage Lords brought in the new rule." I blinked, tears stinging my eyes. I hadn't wanted to go poking into that area of my past. "I worked on a case at the place, years ago. Kids were going missing, and… it was them. The faeries."

The night I'd hunted them down occupied a dark corner of my memories that still arose in my dreams sometimes. I'd never forget the satisfaction as I ended the kidnappers' lives on the point of my sword, but I'd been too late to save most of the kids. I'd been a wreck for weeks afterwards.

Vance put an arm around me. "I'm sorry."

"Never mind me. Those kids… dammit. I wish I could remember if anyone there was called Roseanne." The place had dropped off my radar altogether, and while I'd heard secondhand that the orphanage had eventually closed its doors, I hadn't known the mages were responsible. "I guess it's too much to hope that you can find someone who used to work there?"

"I might be able to, but I doubt they'll remember the names of every child who entered their doors over the years." He squeezed my shoulder. "It's okay, Ivy. You don't need to put yourself under pressure to remember."

I tugged at my hair, thinking hard. "I'm pretty sure it was near the council flat where Calder grew up."

Not just him. There had been kids living wild there. Half-blood children.

"The banshee, too." Vance released me. "There were others?"

"Yeah, there are loads of them living in those broken-down old flats. They have their own territory there, from what the banshee told me."

"She's not there herself anymore," said Vance.

"No, not unless she followed us back and has been avoiding me the whole time." I'd accidentally left the banshee behind when I'd departed the Grey Vale after killing Fionn. She'd worked with him—against her will, admittedly—when she'd planted that magic-destroying ring in the Hemlock Coven's forest, and while Fionn was no longer around, she was far too unpredictable to be trusted.

Another unpleasant possibility hit me. "Damn, I hope Roseanne didn't meet *her*. Or Calder. If she's been lured in by that *immortality can be found on the other side of the veil* crap and Fionn and his brainwashing, I won't have a hope in hell of getting through to her."

"It's a place to start," Vance said. "Want to go and look around?"

"Might as well." I was all out of any better ideas, and the banshee was a loose end that had gnawed at me since I'd woken up from nearly bleeding to death at the end of Fionn's sword. I didn't expect to run into her again, but if I did, I could expect to be serenaded by a funeral dirge at the very least.

Calder had lived in one of the abandoned zones that had been left to ruin after the invasion. Half the city was in a similar state, and since approximately the same percentage of the human population had been wiped out, there wasn't enough manpower or funding to fix the damage. Even the mages couldn't work miracles. The end result was that like with all evacuated areas, the faeries had swooped in and made the place their own. Thick clusters of trees had sprung up in the middle of roads, inhabited by wilder faeries of the inhuman sort, and vines crept up the exteriors of any building that still stood.

Blue light gleamed from my sheathed blade as Vance and I walked towards the block of former council flats. Even the more intact ones bore shattered windows and holes in the brickwork, either from the invasion or from people raiding the place when the original inhabitants had fled. Now, the whole area was home to half-blood kids who didn't want to obey the Chief's laws but refused to lower themselves to living alongside humans.

Heads popped out of the bushes growing thickly at the roadside, vibrant eyes fixating on the glow my sword emitted even while in its sheath. When we neared the first council block, a pair of half-bloods came out to meet us. One was a teenage boy with dark skin and curved horns—half-satyr, I'd guess—and the other was an ivory-skinned girl with soulful blue eyes and delicate gossamer wings.

"Hey," I said to them. "My name's Ivy. Do any of you know someone called Roseanne Harlow? I'm here to talk to her."

"You're not from around here," said the satyr boy. "You're human."

"Yeah, I am. I'm here to speak to Roseanne. Do you know her?"

The winged girl nodded so vigorously that her feet left the ground. "I know her. She goes by Splinter, usually."

Splinter. The name rang a bell. *Oh, no.* I was almost positive I'd heard the name at some point in the first round of the Trials.

"Where does she live?" A wary edge entered my voice, though I forced my shoulders to relax and my hands to stay at my sides and not near my blade's hilt. My priority was to ensure Roseanne's safety, not jump to conclusions before I'd even met her.

All the same, the mere thought of the Trials brought up a slew of unpleasant associations. The Trials had been a contest of brutality set up by Calder as a ruse to convince half-bloods the winner would be granted immortality. In reality, they'd been pawns in his bitter scheme to open the gates to Faerie. As if that wasn't depraved enough, Calder's ghost had stuck around after his demise, together with the spectres of some of the half-faeries he'd tricked into doing his bidding. If anyone here recognised me as the person who'd killed him, twice, I'd have a kelpie on my tail any second now. *Please don't let Roseanne have fallen for the ruse. Please.*

"Splinter lives over at number eight," said the satyr boy. "She doesn't like humans."

That figured. "Well, I need to talk to her."

The winged faerie beckoned. "This way."

Vance and I followed her zigzagging path. She hovered half a metre above the ground but didn't seem to be able to fly higher, which was common enough in half-bloods. Reaching an apartment block, she opened the front door—like most fae, they didn't bother with locks—and entered a dimly lit hallway.

Rapping on a door on the left, she called, "Splinter, there's two humans here to talk to you."

The door opened a crack. A pale black-haired girl peered out, chewing gum and wearing a sullen expression.

"Hi," I said, feeling vaguely ridiculous. I hadn't expected to find her right away. She didn't look anything like Liam and hadn't even inherited his blond hair. Her faerie blood had clearly won out, and with porcelain skin and bright-blue eyes—Winter—she'd be stunningly beautiful if it wasn't for the claws that came out when she saw my blade. Tensing, she raised hands that reminded me more of an eagle's talons than anything else.

"I'm Ivy." I lifted my own hands to ensure she got the message that I wasn't going to draw my sword. "I need to talk to you."

"Ivy Lane?" She looked me up and down, and her claws turned back into human appendages. The banshee had probably told her who I was. Or Calder. Oh, boy.

"Yes. I have a message for you." I gave the winged faerie a pointed stare until she flitted away, then turned back to Liam's daughter. "It's from your father. He—"

"I don't have a father." She spat out the gum at my feet. "And you'd better stay away from me, human."

"You're half-human. Your father—"

"God, shut *up*. Why can't you people leave me in peace?"

That's a bit of an overreaction. "What, has someone else been here?"

Her eyes narrowed. "Fuck off. I don't have to talk to you."

Yeah, someone had definitely riled her up. Teenage attitude problems didn't account for *this* level of belligerence. "Your father thinks your life may be in danger, and I've seen proof that he's probably right. You want to listen to me."

"Dunno who he's talking about, but it's not me. I don't have a mum or dad."

"Your mother was a faerie, right?"

"Gone, ain't she? You humans are stupid."

Play nice, Ivy. I attempted a placating tone. "Your father... I don't know why he abandoned you, but he loved you. And you were the last person he wanted to give a message to before he died."

Now she looked up. "He's dead?"

"Yes." I ploughed ahead. "I have a bunch of letters he wrote to you. If you come with me, you can read them."

She took a step back. "No. You're trying to trick me."

"We aren't." Vance lifted a hand, displaying the letters.

Roseanne made a compulsive movement forward and then halted, folding her arms across her chest. "I don't want them."

"You can decide later," Vance said, "but this place isn't safe for you. The mages would be happy to provide protection, as well as any resources you need."

"I don't need anything from you," spat the girl. "Or you. Ivy Lane. Don't they call you the faerie killer?"

"I kill rogue fae who break the laws and hurt humans, not innocents. So does Vance. We'll help protect you."

"Yeah, right. You humans are all the same."

"You're dead wrong there." I lifted my hands to show her the dazzling blue glow of my magic. "I'm no ordinary human, and I can help you."

"No, you can't." Her voice rose in pitch. "I don't need your help, or anyone else's. Why can't you leave me be?"

"Someone *has* been here, haven't they?"

"I told you to fuck off and die."

"Lovely." I levelled her a stare that mirrored her own contempt turned up to max. "For the record, I'm not offering you help out of charity, but because a horrible monster might be trying to kill you the same as it killed your father. I don't *want* to be here."

She didn't even blink. "So? Humans die all the time."

"You're half of one." I hadn't expected her to renounce her human side altogether, though it shouldn't have surprised me that she had, given the company she kept. "It's your choice. Come with me and I'll show you the letters your father left for you. Stay here, at your own risk."

"Nobody can touch me," said Roseanne. "I'm gonna be immortal. Soon."

I groaned inwardly. "That's a lie. No mortal can become immortal, unless you count wandering around as a ghost for the rest of your eternal existence. All the times I've heard that rumour, everyone who believed it ended up dead."

"Why should I believe you?" She jutted her chin out.

"Your father was murdered by a creature I've never seen before, and I've been killing faeries since before you were born." Technically true, thanks to my time lapse in Faerie. "Trust me, you want me on your side."

"Stop lying," she said. "Calder would have given us immortality, and thanks to you, he's gone. Fuck you."

She slammed the door in my face.

I waited thirty seconds, then knocked. No answer. I knocked again, and she screamed more obscenities at me. I hadn't expected instant cooperation, but the idea that she'd believed Calder over me made me want to keep prodding until she gave in. Would the rumours he'd stirred up never die?

Glimpsing the winged fae hovering outside the building

behind me, I reminded myself that I was the adult in this situation. Maybe it'd been too much to expect her to accept our protection right away.

"I'll come back when you've calmed down," I told the closed door, and left the building.

Vance stood outside. He carried his hand and a half sword, but it didn't look like he'd needed to use it. Shimmering glyphs caught my eye, etched onto the door frame.

"Wards?" I guessed.

"They'll alert us at the manor if anything dangerous gets into the building."

"Good. The girl has a death wish—literally." The worst part was that I entirely understood where she was coming from. Kids forced into desperate situations formed protective gangs for survival's sake, and while I couldn't dismiss them as harmless, they didn't deserve to be turned into playthings for Faerie's most depraved monsters either.

"She won't go with you." The winged half-faerie flitted into view, feet skimming the ground. "She hates humans."

"Her father was brutally murdered by a monster. He told me Roseanne's life is in danger."

The half-faerie shrugged. "Nothing new."

"Has she always lived here?"

Another shrug. "No, she came in 'bout seven years ago. Lived in one of those human places. That's right."

"Orphanages." I swallowed. "The place was shut down."

She eyed me suspiciously. "How'd you know so much about us?"

"Roseanne's father wanted me to find her. I don't know why he never got in touch, but he said her life was in danger."

"Might be 'cause she's the Morrigan's daughter."

My heart skipped a beat. "The Morrigan?"

"The Morrigan is a death faerie," said Vance, to my surprise. "Have any of you met her in person?"

"Faeries don't come here. Duh."

"But you think being the Morrigan's daughter might be why her father was killed?" How would they have been able to identify him when Roseanne had no idea who he was? I didn't see the connection, but evidently, I didn't have the full picture yet.

"Dunno. Maybe. Why are you still here? Nobody wants you around."

"Ouch," I deadpanned. "I'm trying to help your friend—and all of you, by extension. And yes, that includes protecting you from yourselves. I can say right now that anyone who tells you they can offer you immortality or to take you back to Faerie is lying through their teeth."

"Sidhe can't lie, stupid."

"They can mislead. They love to mess with mortals. You might hate humans, but the pure faeries think of you as the same. Playthings. Expendable."

She snarled. I flung a shield up before her fist could make contact with me, and she recoiled, the fight in her eyes already dimming. "You're not one of us. You shouldn't have—"

"Magic? You're lucky I'd prefer not to use it against you," I told her. "I meant what I said. If anything attacks you, I'll be back to save your miserable hides."

And on that unceremonious note, I turned and left the tower block behind.

6

As I prepared to walk into Faerie, my human instincts screamed *danger*, while my magic stirred in restless anticipation. It'd been weeks since my last visit and I'd reluctantly concluded that dropping in on the Vale before work was easier than trying to get a spare moment between clients to check on the potential end of the world.

The field bordering the manor's back garden was empty, but when I reached the point where the realms touched, grey mist crept outward and wrapped around me. Vance had stayed behind, though we'd agreed that I'd stick to visiting the faerie realm only within sight of the manor. That wouldn't change anything if I ran into trouble over there, but it saved me the bother of walking. The whole city was covered in spirit paths, currents that controlled the ebb and flow of magic between realms, so it didn't really matter where I crossed over. While the Ley Line was the biggest and dominant connection to Faerie, any line was a potential entry point to the faerie realm.

Now the process was as easy as breathing to me, though I

did have to concentrate hard to avoid accidentally leaving my body behind. Magic encased me from head to toe within seconds as my surroundings turned to grey smoke, and I moved swiftly through Death and into the Grey Vale.

The Vale's default setting was a path framed by rows of silver-leafed trees. The sun—or the illusion of one—shone dimly, creating an eerie twilight atmosphere which was nothing like Summer's vibrant gardens, nor like Winter's icy forests either. In the Vale, everything seemed to exist in a state of transition, neither beginning nor ending. Except its inhabitants. The realm sucked away their very life-force, with the result that being exiled from the Courts invariably ended in an agonising death.

Likely, more Winter than Summer faeries survived here, because the former drew on death for their source of power, but it was still a miserable place to endure. Avalin had been unhinged, undoubtedly, but a fair part of his penchant for cruelty to humans had been fuelled by his need to draw on the pain and suffering from others to keep himself alive.

At first, even thinking about setting foot in this place again brought me out in a cold sweat, but I'd forced myself to do so the day after I'd killed Fionn to ensure he hadn't lingered as a ghost. While the Vale's habit of preserving the dead was all too familiar to me, I'd found no traces of him nor the banshee he'd coerced into aiding him.

Helena gleamed bright and hummed in my hands, and a rush of icy energy surged through my body in response to returning to its realm of origin. Where Avalin had originally obtained the talisman, I had no idea, but it drank up the energy of the place like a person dying of thirst in a desert. My body moved faster, my senses were sharper, and the Vale itself responded to my thoughts.

"Take me to the nearest faerie." I didn't have to speak aloud, but I found it helped to clarify my intentions. I didn't quite know *what* I was looking for, but I began to walk, counting seconds in case time slipped away from me. Through experimentation, I'd learned that spending up to ten minutes here didn't affect the way time passed in the real world, but once I passed the half-hour mark, up to seven hours might slip away in the mortal world without my knowing. Vance couldn't contact me from Earth, so I had to rely on my own timekeeping abilities to ensure I didn't lose hours or days while walking the Vale's paths.

I had no intention of spending longer here than I needed to, but my encounter with the Chief had brought the nagging urge to look for anything that might have changed in recent weeks. Whenever the faeries in our realm lost their power, it was usually the precursor to something worse, and my triumph over Fionn had come with suspiciously few aftereffects. As the master of death, I wouldn't have put it past him to have hidden a sting in the tail of my victory that I hadn't been aware of at the time.

I walked, humming under my breath to hide my jumpiness. The occasional wisp drifted past but didn't try to entice me into a trap. I'd grown wise to most faerie trickery, but it would have helped to have someone to explain how this place actually worked. I'd figured out what I knew via trial and error, and frankly, my encounter with those Seelie nobles had made me wonder if most existed in a state of complete ignorance of the domain that had been ripped away from their own realm so long ago. No matter how vividly I imagined the forests of Summer-infused half-blood territory bursting to life with green-tinted energy, I was unable to conjure a path into Summer from here, nor Winter either. For whatever reason, this was the only part of Faerie accessible to me.

Not just me. Exiles had no way home, and though not a soul disturbed the silence of the path, I'd learned from experience that the Vale's occupants had an annoying tendency only to show themselves when they *wanted* to be found. After several minutes of quietness, I rounded a corner and found a hellhound waiting for me.

"Knew you wouldn't let me down, Faerie." I stalked forward, but the hellhound didn't move an inch, not even when I raised my sword. When it lifted its head, I averted my eyes, but I felt none of the chilling fear-effect that its stare unleashed on its human prey. When I lifted my sword, the hellhound turned and sprinted away into the trees.

"Hey!"

Wandering off the path was a suicidal idea for most people, but not for me. I pictured a new path forming and sure enough, the trees parted to expose a clear route after the hellhound. I jogged through, my feet pounding against the silvery leaves. *Is it taking me to its new master? Or a whole pack of them?*

The hellhound vanished around a corner, and when I followed, an empty path greeted me. A tittering laugh sounded, and my gaze fell on a long-limbed faerie with dark-green, bark-like skin peering out of the undergrowth.

"Human... your magic tastes familiar."

Ew. "Lovely to meet you, too. I don't suppose you know why that hellhound didn't attack me?"

The faerie gave no reaction to my apparent lack of fear. "The hounds are searching for their master."

My heart sank. "I killed the leader of the Wild Hunt. Not to mention the dickhead who woke him up."

Another laugh. "The Wild Hunt always has a leader."

"What does that mean?" Was Fionn still alive in some sense, or would another Huntsman rise to take his place? He'd been stuck in an enchanted sleep for twenty years, so clearly the Hunt didn't *have* to exist with a leader, but then he hadn't been dead, only sleeping.

For centuries prior to the invasion, Fionn's job had been to harvest the souls of the dead and presumably help them move on to the next world. I didn't know if the Sidhe actually had any concept of an afterlife, but without someone to help them move on… I could see how that would cause some issues. Though since the fae were supposed to be immortal, I hadn't the faintest idea what those might be.

"When one soul passes, another rises," said the faerie. "Always must there be balance. Like Summer and Winter, Seelie and Unseelie."

"You're saying the job passes onto someone else? How does that work?"

Shit. I hadn't accidentally inherited that role myself when I'd killed Fionn, had I? The ring had been blocking both of our powers at the time, so I might not have known if any faerie vow had come into effect. Being forced to take his place as head of the Wild Hunt was not on my list of life goals.

"Would you bargain with me for that information, human?"

"Nope." I pointed my sword at the bushes. "I'd rather kill you instead."

A growling noise answered, and the hellhound's huge, furred body leaped at the other faerie. The beast fled, screeching, deeper into the forest.

"Hey," I said. "We were talking."

I wasn't particularly scared of hellhounds anymore, but I instinctively tensed when the beast padded closer to me.

"Stay back."

The hellhound let out a distinct whine, but it did as I asked, sinking back onto its haunches.

What the hell? "Erm… down, boy."

The hellhound's head lowered, and it dropped to its front. Whoa. Had Fionn trained them that well, or was the creepy faerie right, and they were looking for a new master?

"No," I said firmly. "Absolutely not. I'm not your master. Go home."

The hellhound whined, tongue lolling, its eyes regarding me soulfully. I glared back, refusing to let myself forget its terrifying stare or its deadly bite.

"Go somewhere else," I commanded. "Find a new master. Maybe try to stop snacking on humans. Leave me alone."

I turned my back and shifted through Death back into the human world. The crossing was so smooth that my feet slipped on the wet grass, and when a growl came from near my shoulder, I damn near slid onto my back. Arms pinwheeling, I faced the hellhound who'd apparently followed me *out* of the Vale.

"What do you want?" Damn. While I'd known hellhounds could walk between realms, they weren't supposed to tail after me like a house pet. "Go back to the Vale. You shouldn't be here. If any of the mages sets eyes on you, they'll fry you alive."

I lifted my blade, but my heart wasn't in it. The beast didn't present any more threat than a fangless snake. For a hellhound, this one was on the small side, more the size of a cow or bull than some of the menaces I'd fought. Moreover, its behaviour was so disconcerting that I didn't have the heart to stab it in cold blood.

Given that I'd stolen my magic from someone who'd commanded an army of hellhounds, I'd wondered if I might possess the same affinity, but all the ones I'd previously encountered had been following someone else's orders. Now that wasn't the case. Come to think of it, maybe the one I'd run into at the mercenary guild hadn't been hostile at all. I'd reacted on instinct when I'd sliced off its head without waiting for it to bite me first.

"Fine," I muttered. "Just don't attack any humans. Now, go."

The hellhound whined, but it obeyed and slunk away across the field.

"Ivy." Vance came striding over, his sword in hand. "Was that a hellhound?"

"Yep," I replied. "I've officially reached my quota of weird for the week and we've only been back in the city a day."

I filled him in on the way back to the manor. I'd misjudged the time by half an hour, but that didn't bother me nearly as much as the oversized hound that had seemingly attached itself to me.

"I have no idea if I can control hellhounds because their master died and needs a replacement or if they were actually cuddly puppies deep down all along," I remarked to Vance as we entered the manor's garden via the back gate. "I bloody hope it's that and not that it's my fate to collect faeries' souls for eternity. Because if the Huntsman's job is anything like a vow, I'm screwed."

"There haven't been any other signs, right?" asked Vance. "Your magic might react to hellhounds because—"

"—they both have the same source. Death energy. That and Avalin had command of an army, so it stands to reason that I can give them orders, too. Don't you find that weird, though?"

"No more so than you travelling into Faerie or Death. Which you do on an alarmingly frequent basis."

"Guess you're reached your quota of weird, too. Nothing surprises you anymore."

"I beg to differ." He kissed me lightly on the lips. "You never fail to surprise me, Ivy."

"Hope you meant that in a good way." My light tone faded. "Seriously, though. After what I saw on half-blood territory yesterday, I know something is *off*, and I can't shake the feeling that killing Fionn might have had… well, side effects."

"Ivy." Vance's warm gaze offered comfort, reassurance. "It'll be okay. None of this is your responsibility to fix. If the faeries' magic is fading, it isn't your fault. There are also people you can ask for advice."

"If you mean the Hemlocks, I assume we're using the term 'people' loosely." He was right, though. I'd put off my visit to them for long enough. "All right, I'll go there today—"

The manor's back wall flashed red once. I jumped, my hand flying to Helena's hilt, and Vance pulled his hand-and-a-half sword out of the air.

"It's the alarm outside Roseanne's flat," he said. "I set it to trigger the manor's wards."

Something's attacking her? "Let's go."

We did. In the blink of an eye, we stood in the entryway of the apartment building, and in front of us was a monster.

Oh, lovely. Its body was covered in suction cups, while its face was dominated by a hoover-like mouth. A skin-eating faerie. Roseanne's door had been wrenched off its hinges, so she must have hidden herself, but the scent of her magic would have drawn the beast's attention right away. Our arrival had startled the monster, but it soon recovered, shuffling towards me with a revolting sound like a plunger stuck in a drain.

I conjured up a shield and drove my blade into one of its suction-cup-like protrusions. The beast flailed, its mouth emitting a hideous shriek. A glance inside the flat confirmed the presence of a second monster making its way across the floor. Sniffing out its prey.

"Run!" I shouted at Roseanne, spying her cowering in a corner, her clawed hands wrapped around her knees. "These fuckers will tear off your skin and wear it as a coat."

She whimpered and didn't move. Vance ran in to fight the

second beast, while I continued to stab and swipe at my own opponent. Skin-eating faeries also drained the energy of any human who got too close, and sweat soon ran down my face as I fought to maintain my magic-enhanced speed. The presence of two monsters had twice the effect. Even Vance fought at a slower pace than usual and didn't use his typical tactic of throwing weapons out of thin air.

I snarled, stabbing another suction cup. Spots intruded on my vision and my legs felt like sacks of concrete. "Just die already."

A thud from inside the flat warned me Vance was down, and the second beast was swiftly gaining on Roseanne. I gasped when its suction cups locked onto her legs and pulled her towards its gaping mouth.

"Help!" she screamed. "Help me!"

"If you get me killed, I'll haunt you forever." I left my own opponent and ran into the flat, urging my magic to draw on any fear and pain in the area to boost its strength. In a place like this, a layer of misery and despair lurked beneath the surface, and I tasted its echo on my tongue as the blue glow around my blade heightened.

The flood of magic momentarily banished my exhaustion, and I swung Helena in a wide arc at the suction cups on the monster's side. *Feel their pain, you bastard.*

The beast let go of Roseanne, who fell head over heels with a shriek. Dazzling blue light exploded from my blade, still buried in the monster's side, and it let out a piercing cry as my magic burst through its flesh from the inside. Dead skin flew in all directions as it sagged like a deflated balloon.

Behind me, Vance was back on his feet and had taken over fighting the other monster in the doorway. I checked on my terrified companion, who lay where she'd fallen, whimpering.

"It's dead," I told her. "You're safe."

Lifting her head, Roseanne pushed a flap of dead skin from her face. "You saved me."

"You're welcome." I ran to join Vance, who'd already dispatched his opponent in a flash of iron and steel. As the beast crumbled into a mass of decaying skin and flesh, Roseanne came creeping out of the flat behind me.

"I was gonna thank you," she mumbled. "I didn't think you'd come back."

"I always keep my word."

"These things killed my dad?"

"No," I said. "Something worse."

Paling, she stumbled out of the building and threw up in the bushes. Air buffeted me from behind, indicating that Vance had displaced the corpse out of the doorway.

"I hope you put that somewhere they won't attract more of them," I said to him. "We can't leave death fae lying around."

Roseanne groaned. "They've never come here before."

Vance strode in behind her. "I'll send some of my mages to clear the area. We need to get you out of here."

She uttered an incoherent noise of protest.

"Trust me, it's for the best," I said to her. "Can you think of any reason those monsters showed up now? I mean, they're drawn to powerful magic, but yours has always been there, right?"

She lowered her gaze. "Yeah, but… but the charm's gone."

"The what?"

She fidgeted. "I used to have a lucky charm, but it disappeared two days ago. Think someone stole it."

"What did it look like?"

"Just… a necklace. They found me wearing it when I showed up at the orphanage."

"Did your father…" Maybe her father had given her a witch charm to protect herself, but if it was a blood charm, it might have only worked as long as he was alive. *That might be why he wanted me to find her. The protection ran out.* I'd have to ask Isabel if that was possible, but I'd definitely heard of similar charms passed among witches. And the fact that her protection had disappeared at the same time as Liam's death was worth noting, too.

"Come with us," said Vance. "It isn't safe to stay here."

"But…" Sudden suspicion flitted across Roseanne's face. "How'd you know I was being attacked?"

"We used a security spell that warned us when someone attacked you."

She scowled. "You knobheads were spying on me?"

"We saved your neck."

"I already said thank you."

"Yes, and I'm saying that you'll be far safer if you stick with us." I tried to keep the impatience out of my voice. "Until the death fae have gone."

"Don't assume I've nowhere else to go."

"The streets aren't a safe place," I said. "Trust me, I know. I've been there myself. Not long ago, I was in the same position as you are."

Her lip trembled. "I didn't *ask* for this shit."

"Neither did I, believe me."

"Decide quickly," added Vance. "We need to clear these creatures away and destroy the bodies."

Roseanne sucked in a breath. "I'll play nice, if you do me one favour."

"What?" I asked warily.

"Take me with you to Faerie."

7

"No," I said, not missing a beat. "Absolutely not."

"You *can* go to Faerie." Her eyes had lit up like beacons, bright iridescent blue. "Take me with you. I know you can do it. Calder *wasn't* lying."

"Yes, he was. Being immortal has nothing to do with being able to travel to Faerie. I'm a hundred percent human, and trust me, you wouldn't last five minutes in the Grey Vale."

She made an indignant noise. "You're underestimating me, you are. I belong there."

"You really don't." Of that I was certain. "The Grey Vale's not at all like the Courts. It's a soul-sucking death trap created as a punishment for faeries who committed the worst crimes. You know what happens to the Sidhe who are banished there? They have their magic ripped away, then the realm sucks the life out of them until they're nothing more than husks. Sounds fun?"

"Sure."

Teenagers. Actually, that was unfair. I was sure I hadn't been this obnoxious as a teen, even pre-Faerie, and the centuries-old Sidhe were stark proof that age was no guarantee of maturity.

"Did Calder tell you *why* I can travel back and forth from the Vale?" I enquired. "When I was the same age as you, I was captured and imprisoned by the Sidhe Lord Avalin. He tortured me, and all the other humans he held there, for three years. Then I killed him and escaped. My ability to cross realms isn't a secret I'm withholding from you, it's proof that I survived something that nobody else should ever have to suffer through."

She exhaled. "That's what Calder meant when he said you stole from his father. You stole Lord Avalin's magic?"

At least she believed that part. "Yes. I stole it by accident while trying to escape. My point is that being able to go into Faerie is no guarantee of survival. The half-faeries who believed Calder will certainly be dead by now. If you die in the Vale, you end up trapped between life and death forever. That's not the sort of immortality you want."

"Calder didn't say that," said Roseanne. "He said that he'd be given a new body, same as the rest of us. He would have, if you hadn't destroyed him again."

She means Fionn would have given him one. "Yeah, he wanted to permanently possess someone, but it's not possible to do that. He was lying."

"*You're* lying. You've met the Huntsman yourself."

My expression froze. How did she know? Calder had already been dead, his ghost on the brink of eternal banishment, and I'd surely remember seeing her on the battlefield.

"I'm the daughter of the Morrigan," added Roseanne. "Means I know all about death fae. More than you, I bet."

"How do you know your faerie parentage? Did Calder tell you?"

"Does it matter?"

"Well, the only other person who could have told you is

Velkas. He was Calder's mentor, did you know? He was the one who started this immortality crap."

"Lord Velkas *was* immortal," she said. "Before you killed him."

"Which is kind of the opposite of immortal, isn't it?" I shook my head at her. "Velkas was originally from Summer, before he was exiled. Avalin came from Winter. Once you're exiled, there's no going home. I can't walk into Summer or Winter either. I'm not part of either Court. Neither are you."

Pity, because they might have been able to take her off my hands, but I knew better than to expect the Sidhe to offer a helping hand. No pure-blooded faerie, Sidhe or not, would ever accept custody of a half-blood.

She jutted out her chin. "Don't care. Going into the Vale doesn't kill you. It makes you stronger."

"Velkas and Avalin preserved their lives by stealing magic from other faeries. That's not strength. It's eternal suffering."

"I don't need to," she said. "I have the death goddess's magic. I don't need anyone else's."

"Doesn't mean you'd survive the Grey Vale," I said. "The only reason *I* can survive there is because my magic keeps the bad guys away, and because I'm not fae, so I don't get the downsides to being exiled."

She gave me a belligerent look. "Don't talk to me like I'm five. My magic's probably stronger than yours."

But you can't cross realms. Or could she? Probably, it was unwise to make assumptions when it came to the death fae.

"What can you do, then?" I asked her.

"You don't get any more of my secrets."

"Has anyone ever taught you?" I continued, undeterred. "I don't think so, somehow. Same with me. I had to figure out how to use my magic on my own."

"Really."

"Yes. It was only in the past year that I learned I can go

back to the Vale at all." Seeing a gleam in her eyes, I added, "It's not fun. You have to travel through Death to get there."

"So? I can already hear the dead."

"You can… hear the dead?" That was the power she'd inherited from the Morrigan? No wonder part of her was drawn towards the veil. We had that much in common.

"Yeah, and the last few weeks, they've been really angry."

The last few weeks. *Since I killed Fionn. Ah, shit.* "Angry how?"

"Shouting and screaming. Does it matter?"

"Yes. If the spirits are restless for whatever reason, it might mean another attempt to break the veil."

"Good." Her eyes lit up. "That's what Calder wanted to do, and it has to happen for all of us to go back to Faerie and become immortal."

"Look, the only way to become immortal is to be *born* immortal." I was being cruel, but she needed to know the truth. "If anyone knows how to put a mortal soul in an immortal body, they probably don't exist. And if they did, is it worth giving your life up for?"

"Yes."

It was like talking to a brick wall. "It means dying. Assuming your spirit isn't dragged through the gates of death right away, you're stuck there without a body until you move on. I'm here to protect you on your father's orders, which means keeping you alive. I told you I have your father's letters, didn't I? Maybe you'll feel differently if you knew how much he cared about you."

"Go to hell," she whispered, turning her back on me.

Dammit. I was back to square one again, and it'd be much easier to walk away than to make another failed attempt to bridge the gulf between us. Our lives were worlds apart, literally, and meeting Calder first might have killed any part of her that might have been open to hearing me out. But I hadn't spent years trying to spare kids like her from Faerie to give up when I found someone who didn't want my help.

I looked to Vance pleadingly. He was generally better with small children than I was, but Roseanne was miles past the adorable kid stage and had likely never been compliant in her life.

"It's your choice," he said to her. "You'll be much safer at the manor and you'll have a roof over your head."

"*Manor?*" Her eyes grew wide, then narrowed. "You're try'na bribe me, aren't you?"

"It's not bribery if it's free." Aha. "There's a massive TV, a garden bigger than your house, a weapons room…"

"Weapons room?"

Maybe not the best thing to mention to a thirteen-year-old. "No offence, but you need clean clothes and a bath, for starters. Then you can explore the manor."

Roseanne pouted. "Bribery."

"Then feel free to stay here with the dead." I indicated the discarded skin left behind by of one of her attackers and the blood splatter on the walls. "Or come to a nice, clean manor full of everything you could ever want. Up to you."

"I've changed my mind," she announced. "I'll come with you."

———

Roseanne took one look at the long, carpeted corridor of the manor and lost her shit, pelting towards the conservatory and screaming like her hair was on fire. Doors slammed as she peeked into every room, uttering cries of delight. With an exasperated sigh, Vance took it upon himself to chase her around while I pulled out my phone.

"Hey," I said to Isabel. "Really sorry, but I'll be an hour or so late to the office. Vance and I ran into a… situation."

After I'd explained, she said, "Ivy. You don't do things by halves, do you? You took one of them back to the manor?"

"I'd rather babysit Erwin the piskie in a roomful of Vance's family's antique china," I muttered. "She's a literal nightmare. Convinced Calder was right and she can have immortality if she goes into the Grey Vale. Because *that* always ends well."

"Oh, man," said Isabel. "Be careful. You know how slippery some of those half-bloods can be."

"I know. By the way, I was wondering if it's possible to make a witch charm that keeps someone safe as long as the person who gave it to them is alive. Roseanne said she had a lucky charm that disappeared two days ago, around the same time Liam died."

"Sounds plausible," said Isabel. "Her father might have hired a witch, sure. Did she say he gave it to her?"

"She said she doesn't remember, but it'd explain why nobody attacked her until now."

"True," she agreed. "From what I remember, those charms fell out of vogue because they have a dampening effect on the magic of both people wearing them."

"Might be why nobody detected her magic before, too." I nodded. "Anyway, she's the daughter of the Morrigan, a powerful death fae. I haven't been able to get any more details out of her."

Ahead of me, Roseanne ran out of the weapons room with a howl worthy of a banshee.

"I told you not to pick up anything," said an irate Vance. "They're all made out of iron."

"You knobheads tried to poison me!" shouted the half-faerie.

"Yeah, she's charming," I said in an undertone.

"Don't worry," said Isabel. "I'll tell the clients you're busy with full-time bodyguard duty. That's what it is, right?"

"Debateable. I might end up stabbing her myself."

"She's a kid," said Isabel. "And you saved her life. She'll worship you by the end of the week, trust me."

"Sure she will. As long as her death fae mother doesn't show up."

If she did, I might get to offload my problem child onto someone else, but I doubted a death faerie would have any interest in her half-human offspring. The Morrigan herself was something of an enigma, at least to me. She was known by her title rather than her name, but all Gerry—the old man who'd saved my life during my captivity in Faerie—had told me was that she was one of the most ancient and powerful beings in Faerie. He'd called her a death goddess, but not in the same sense as the ancient gods the Sidhe had banished. More in line with... Fionn.

Dammit. It looked like I might have to pay the Hemlock Coven another visit. That is, if I ever got a moment's peace. The second I ended the phone call, the doorbell rang.

"Ivy?" Wanda called down the corridor. "It's for you."

Please be someone from Summer. Or any other faerie who can take her off our hands. Please.

The universe answered my prayers for once. The Chief of the half-faeries stood on the doorstep. "Ivy Lane."

My mouth dropped open. "Hi. What are you doing here?"

"It's come to my attention that you've taken custody of a half-blood. I want you to return her to my territory."

"Hardly custody. More like bodyguard duty. She's being pursued by death fae. Didn't I tell you one of them tore open her father?" Why had he dragged himself all the way here? He was in terrible shape, leaning heavily on his staff, and hardly a hint of Summer magic glowed from his washed-out green eyes.

"It's not appropriate for any of my kin to be kept inside the mages' headquarters."

"There are other fae on staff." Okay, one: Quentin the brownie, who I'd gathered had worked for the Colton family for generations. "Why, is it because her mother's the Morrigan?"

The Chief backed away so swiftly that he nearly fell off the doorstep. "The queen of the death fae had a child? I don't believe it."

That's a no, then.

"Care to explain a little?" said Vance, who'd walked up behind me. "Queen? I was told she was a harbinger faerie, more like a banshee."

"The Morrigan is the ruler of the Death Kingdom," said the Chief. "She is known as the mother of all death fae, and she would never consort with a mortal."

"Don't be so sure," I said. "Someone I know also called her a goddess. Is she the same as the ancient ones you exiled?" Not exactly a subtle approach, but I'd squeeze every piece of information from him possible before he clammed up again, especially if her parentage was the reason Roseanne was being targeted.

"If you're thinking of sticking your nose where it doesn't belong again, you're mistaken, Ivy Lane."

"I need the facts if we're to keep her alive," I retorted. "I'm guessing she was abandoned by her human family due to her mother's status, but she's gone unnoticed by Faerie for this long. There has to be a reason someone has targeted her now."

"Then she got lucky," said the Chief. "Most would see any offspring of the Morrigan as an ill omen. *If* it's true, which I very much doubt."

"Have you forgotten all the other times you've assumed I was lying and it backfired in your face?" I asked. "Also, haven't we already met one death god recently?"

He flinched. "*That* one is dead, you told me."

"Oh, he is," I said. "Out of curiosity, how many gods *are* there? There seem to be a lot around."

The Chief ground his teeth together. "There is a difference between the ancient beings that predate the Sidhe and such beings as the Morrigan and the Huntsman. Human languages are woefully limited, but a different term for each is used in the faerie tongue."

"Good to know." Though it begged the question of why the death fae would try to kill the daughter of their queen. "What about the leader of the Wild Hunt? Does there *have* to be a leader? What happens if he dies?"

"How should I know? I belong to the Seelie Court, and the death fae are exclusively allied to the Unseelie—those that claim allegiance to anyone at all."

"Then the Morrigan isn't the same as the Unseelie Queen?" Man, Faerie and its divisions made my head spin. "Why would someone try to kill her daughter? To steal her magic?"

"Perhaps. Few other Winter faeries have access to that particular realm of magic, aside from banshees. Furthermore, I believe most of the Unseelie nobles find death fae somewhat… distasteful."

"Why's that?" Roseanne came sauntering up behind us. "Also, if you wanted to know what my mum can do, you could have asked me, you know."

"You yelled at me for interrogating you," I pointed out.

"It's fun to wind you up." She shrugged. "The Morrigan commands an army of crows and can transform into one herself. Also, she can remove your soul with a touch, but only if you annoy her. I can't do that, though, don't worry."

The Chief took a startled step back, then covered up the motion by leaning on his staff. "I am Chieftain Taive, leader of the faeries in this realm, and I wish to invite you to take up a new home on my territory."

"Thought you were scared shitless of us." She lifted a hand, the skin bubbling before reforming into feathers. Ugh.

"If you choose to live on my territory, you will speak to me with respect. I am the son of Lord Daival of the Summer Court."

"You've never been to Faerie," she said. "They came here twenty years ago. You're older. Did they dump you here and never come back?"

"That's quite enough cheek," said the Chief. "If you don't wish to accept my invitation, you are nevertheless subject to the same rules as every being with faerie blood in this realm."

"Bollocks," she said. "Living with you'd be the same as these humans. Go away."

The Chief looked affronted. "If that's the attitude you've decided to employ, you won't be welcome on my territory."

He turned and walked away with as much dignity as he could scrape together, which wasn't a great deal. I watched him leave, torn between dissatisfaction and surprise that he'd come here at all.

Roseanne snorted. "He doesn't want me on his territory anyway. Knobhead."

"Yes, he is." I closed the door. "You know all about your mother. Did you ever meet her?"

"No." Her claw transformed into a hand again. "I won't tell you my secrets."

"You just said a bunch of them straight out. Besides, I've already proved I want to keep you alive."

For now. As much as I enjoyed the sight of the Chief sloping off with his tail between his legs, now we were saddled with babysitting the daughter of a death goddess. And to think I'd assumed a bunch of annoying clients would be the least of my problems this week.

"If you wish to stay here," Vance said to her, "you'll be

subject to *my* rules, as well as those affecting half-bloods such as yourself."

"The hell I will—" Roseanne sputtered to a halt when Vance turned the full power of his most intense Mage Lord stare on her. The air crackled, and the fear effect of his shifter blood combined with the brewing storm in his eyes sent Roseanne into retreat. Casting him a frightened stare, she ran down the hallway and out of sight.

I raised an eyebrow at Vance. "Too much?"

"Perhaps, but she needs to know where we stand."

"Yeah, you're right. I never know if I'm being too harsh or if she needs someone to shake some sense into her. You'd think her narrow brush with death would have helped."

"It's not your fault," said Vance, striding down the hall. "Compassion isn't a crime."

"No, but she's already driving me out of my mind." I groaned. "She's either going to break something important or compromise our security. And what if she's not on our side after all?"

"What is going on?" Quentin the brownie walked out of one of the side doors and addressed us in his gravelly voice. "Why is there a death fae here?"

"Because we're protecting her, unfortunately," I said. "And we had nowhere else to put her."

"She will not stay in the manor."

Vance frowned at Quentin. "It's a temporary arrangement. Death faeries are threatening her life."

"Then she'll stay with her own kind. We don't offer shelter to dangerous Unseelie."

"We've had half-blood employees staying here before. Why not her?" Sure, I was all but looking for an excuse to make her leave, but maybe she'd grow on me if we got to know each other. Or maybe Gregor and I would become BFFs.

"She is the daughter of the Morrigan. She has no need of our protection."

"Doesn't she?" I frowned. "She's a kid. Also, you've never had anything to say about the death gods before, including the one who I killed a few weeks ago. Why's she suddenly an issue?"

An unidentifiable emotion passed over the brownie's face, but before he could speak, someone rapped on the front door.

"It's Drake," said Vance. "Quentin, keep an eye on our guest. If you see Wanda, ask her to take over at the door for the day and tell clients to come back at another time."

"Why?" I asked. "A tracking spell won't work on those creatures. There's no way to find out who sent them. If anyone did."

"The Hemlock Coven might know," said Vance. "This is—"

Another, louder knock. "Vance Colton!" Drake bellowed. "Open the damn door. It's an emergency!"

"What now?" I ran after Vance to the front door.

On the other side, Drake leaned against the door frame, his face pale and his hands covered in blood.

"Someone's attacked Wanda," he said. "I think she's dead."

8

Vance and I ran after Drake around the manor's side to the neighbouring street. Thick blood spattered the ground where Wanda lay with her eyes closed and her body lacerated by deep wounds. Claw marks. My mind roiled, and bile burned my throat.

Vance carefully lifted her into his arms and disappeared. I veered back around the corner and sprinted back to the manor, Drake close on my heels. We found Vance in the main room, standing over Wanda with a healing spell in his hand. She lay still and pale on the sofa, her wounds already healing despite the blood soaking through her clothes. Something with razor-like claws or teeth had torn her open. If the healing spells had worked, she must still be alive, but her eyes didn't open and she showed no signs of alertness.

Footsteps came from the doorway. Roseanne had crept into the room. When I turned to her, she shrank away.

"They were looking for me," she whispered. "I was their target."

"Who's *they*?" Not expecting an answer, I asked Drake, "Did you see?"

"No. I heard her scream, and I found her like this." Drake had gone as pale as milk, his hands still streaked with Wanda's blood. "I don't know why she was outside the wards. The other guards didn't know either."

"Go and find them," Vance ordered. "Search everywhere around the scene of the attack, and don't let anyone go off alone until we catch whoever was responsible for this."

"Got it, boss."

He ran from the room. Roseanne had gone, too, and though I knew I should probably follow her, my attention was fixed on Wanda. She was too still, too pale, like a necromancer who'd got too close to death. My nails bit into my palms, wearing crescents into the skin.

I took in a shuddering breath and lifted my gaze to Vance. "Is she…?"

"The healing spells aren't strong enough to heal the internal damage." His mouth pinched at the corners. "I don't know what else to do."

Dammit. My own healing ability had even brought me back from near death, but it barely functioned here in the mortal realm and didn't work on other people besides. "There has to be a way. She can't be…"

She can't be dying. The stark devastation on his face was all I needed to see to know it was true. He'd known Wanda all her life, and she was like a younger sibling to him.

"Let me through," growled a quiet voice.

Quentin crossed the room, moving swiftly on his short legs. He reached for Wanda, green light spilling from his palms and enveloping the sofa where she lay until her skin glowed with vibrancy.

"What the hell are you doing?" I made to grab him, but Wanda gave a sudden loud gasp. Her eyes flew open, and then closed again, her breathing calming as the light began to dim. Her wounds, too, faded, sealing before my eyes. *Impossible.*

"She will live," growled Quentin. As his hands dropped, the dazzling green light faded, revealing that every mark on Wanda's skin had vanished. She might never have been attacked at all.

I gaped at him. "You can heal. Since when?"

Vance leaned over Wanda. "She's breathing normally. Her injuries… they've gone."

Thank god. She's okay. I wiped tears from my eyes with the back of my hand, resting my elbows on the back of the sofa. My legs trembled with relief.

"Thank you, Quentin," Vance said softly. Then, a moment later: "Why did you never tell me you were able to heal others?"

"My instructions were to only reveal my true nature if one of your lives was threatened," said the brownie.

"Your… true nature?" Suspicion stirred inside me, and I lifted my head. "This isn't the first time our lives have been threatened. What about when Vance was stabbed with thorns?"

"I planned to intervene in that case," he growled, "but you removed the thorns before I had to. As to the other injuries, none of them would have been as certainly fatal as this one."

"The other injuries? You mean all the times I've nearly died?" My suspicion, at first a trickle, became a fast-flowing river. I'd come in here with life-threatening injuries at least twelve times since I'd started working with Vance. I'd been shot, stabbed, left to bleed out. How many times I'd returned from missions one healing spell away from death? I'd known the brownie wasn't my biggest fan, but this was one revelation too many on an already emotionally taxing day. As my shock faded, it was replaced with a current of unexpected rage.

"Who exactly gave you the orders?" I pushed away from the sofa, my hands curling into fists. "Well?"

"My parents?" added Vance.

"Your grandfather gave me the instructions."

"Then why didn't you use those skills in the invasion?" The air chilled and a breeze stirred, though Vance's grey eyes showed more sadness than anger.

"Because they told me not to interfere," he said. "I was ordered to hide in the shelter with the other servants and return to the manor if your parents did not survive the battle."

My heart gave a stutter. The river of suspicion inside me became a torrent. "You fucking *what?*"

"You're not bound by law," said Vance. "Not like a faerie vow."

A faerie vow.

My sword was in my hand in two seconds flat and pointed at Quentin's throat. "He's a spy for Faerie. I know you are, Quentin. Admit it."

"Not a spy," said Quentin indignantly. "I report to my Court, yes, to ensure the Mage Lords are not targeted by another attempt at an invasion of this realm."

My hand trembled on the blade's hilt. I stopped short of stabbing him, but magic leaked out in a surge that sent Quentin staggering back several feet. The brownie caught his balance, eyeing me with reproach.

"You lying little shit. How many times did you nearly let me or Vance die? Was *that* on Faerie's orders, too?"

Quentin had saved Wanda's life, but the idea of one of the faeries spying on the mages for *months* awakened an instinctive loathing that burned my throat like bile. For all we knew, he might have reported all our secrets to the murderous pricks who'd killed both our families and countless others.

"You mistake me, human," said Quentin. "Master, Lord Colton, I have always served you loyally."

"Yes," said Vance. "As you served my father, and my grandfather before him. Did either of them know about your bond to the faeries, or did you lie to them as well?"

My breath caught. I clamped down on the unspoken words I wanted to say. This was Vance's argument, and he had more cause to be angry with the brownie than I did. Quentin had been the Colton family's trusted servant for three generations.

"Your grandfather knew. It was on his instructions that I kept the truth from you."

Wanda made an indistinct noise. "What's going on?"

Vance was at her side instantly. "Are you okay? Don't move."

"Yeah, I'm fine. My head feels strange…"

"Do you remember the attack?" I asked. "You—you nearly died. Some huge beast attacked you."

"What?" She pressed her hands to her face and then stared down at herself. "Is this blood mine? I don't remember anything at all."

"You don't?" Vance gave her a searching look. "Do you remember why you left the manor?"

"There's a spy from Faerie." I couldn't help myself. "In the manor. Did you see Quentin before the attack?"

"Quentin? He was just there." She pointed.

I whirled around to see the brownie had disappeared. "The lying little bastard."

"I'll find him," Vance said, and vanished, too.

"I'm fine," said Wanda, when I moved to her side. "Better than fine, actually. Did someone use a new healing spell? I've never seen that kind of light before."

I didn't have the heart to drop the bombshell. Not yet. "Get some rest. You lost a load of blood."

My mind reeled, my relief at Wanda's survival warring with a renewed surge of anger towards whoever had been behind the attempt on her life, and towards the faeries in general for their endless deceit and trickery.

"Hey!" Drake walked in. "Wanda—she's alive. Look, she's alive!"

A half-dozen mages swarmed in, including Bailey and Rod, a mage couple I'd become friendly with over the past few months. While they exclaimed over Wanda's recovery, I went looking for Roseanne. I was far from in the headspace to deal with her attitude, but she wasn't hiding in any of the nearby rooms, and Quentin was nowhere to be seen either. I checked for him in the kitchen, including under the table and in the cupboards, but all I found was a box of Isabel's cookies I'd forgotten I had. I took one, hoping it'd improve my mood, but even the taste of cinnamon deliciousness didn't quell my urge to get my hands on Quentin and throttle him.

"Fucking faeries." My fist clenched, scattering crumbs on the table. "They can't just be honest with anyone, can they?"

"Why are you murdering that cookie?" Drake walked in and began washing the blood from his hands in the sink.

"Hey! Quentin will be pissed off at you for getting blood in the—" I cut myself off. "Never mind."

"Never mind what?"

"Vance and I found out Quentin's a liar and a spy for Faerie." I shoved what was left of the cookie into my mouth. "You haven't seen him, have you?"

"No." Drake turned off the tap. "Quentin, a spy? Did I hear that right?"

"He healed Wanda using faerie magic and then confessed that he was sent here to watch us on behalf of—I assume the Summer Court. Has he always lived here?"

"Huh?" Drake frowned. "I think Vance said the brownie's been here as long as the house has existed."

"Makes sense, since their magic ties them to one place," I muttered. "Their *magic*. He's never used any. I didn't even question why, nor why he was so loyal to a family of humans."

I'd asked, when I'd first visited the manor, but Vance's unquestioning trust in the brownie had all but stamped out my own misgivings. I'd put the feeling down to old paranoia around the fae and nothing more.

"Neither did Vance. Quentin has served the Colton family forever, and if he healed Wanda, surely he's on our team."

"Nobody who spies for Faerie is on our team."

Quentin *knew* what the faeries had done to me. I'd discussed the subject with Vance often enough in the house that the brownie was bound to have overheard us. He'd have heard every word of our discussions on Calder, on Fionn, even my talisman. And if he'd told the Sidhe…

They knew everything. All our advantages, and all our weaknesses, too,

"Whoa there," said Drake. "Don't skewer anyone just yet. How do you know he's a traitor? People can be on more than one side."

"Not if they're telling our secrets to the Seelie Court."

"I don't know." Drake's mouth pulled into a frown. "I know for a fact Quentin saved Vance from attempts on his life at least four times when he was a teenager. He can run circles around most human bodyguards, but I swear he's never used magic. Not where I've seen, anyway."

"Faeries have their own rules." Bitterness spilled out of my mouth. "They put their own species first, no matter what. Think of how many times he could have used that healing power on someone else. How many died in the invasion? He claims Vance's grandfather ordered him not to interfere, but shit, I can't even wrap my head around that. If I were Vance, I'd never forgive him."

Drake shuffled his feet. "I… don't know. It seems kinda unlikely that Vance's family would have kept him around if they knew he was spying for the faeries."

"Yeah, I'd like an explanation, but he's buggered off. Probably to his other home." I ground the heel of my boot into the floor. "Why did I ever trust one of them? They're all fucking psychopaths."

The words had scarcely escaped my mouth when my gaze fell on Roseanne peering through the doorway. She flinched, hurt stark in her eyes, and fled into the hallway.

"And now I've insulted our guest." I leaned my head against the wall. "Great."

"Whoa there," Drake said. "If you need to punch someone, I'll join you for training."

"I wouldn't mind that, actually, but someone attacked Wanda right outside the manor. What if they're still here?"

"I sent people to look out, but you can join us on patrol if it makes you feel better," he said. "If you promise not to sling insults you don't really mean at anyone else."

"Who says I don't mean them?" My voice held little heat. I didn't think all faeries were the same. I even felt for them sometimes, including Roseanne, but that was precisely why Quentin's betrayal cut so deep. He'd never given me cause to doubt his loyalty to the Colton family despite his open dislike of my attitude towards the faeries in general. That someone had got so close to me and then thrust a knife into my ribcage only accentuated how thoroughly I'd let down my guard.

Saving Wanda wasn't the act of a traitor, but why spare her and not anyone else who'd nearly died in the last few decades? He'd lived through the *invasion.* Hundreds of mages had died in the fighting and countless others had been killed when the invaders had hunted down the safe houses where the more vulnerable mages and their children had been sheltering. Vance's survival had been down to luck and being buried so deeply in the ruins that the Sidhe had thought him dead.

Quentin owed Vance an explanation, first and foremost, so I left him to chase down the brownie and helped Drake organise the security patrols outside the manor. I ended up on a team with Bailey and Rod, and their good-natured banter as we walked somewhat soothed my frazzled nerves. At least until we passed by the spot where we'd found Wanda bleeding. Already someone had put down a cleansing spell, but faint traces of blue light lingered in the air, remnants of faerie magic visible only to me. Blue meant Unseelie, but the traces weren't substantial enough for me to identify their owner.

I squinted. *Or are they?*

"One minute," I told the others. "I'll meet you back at the manor."

"Where're you...?" Bailey trailed off, muttering something to Rod along the lines of 'weird faerie magic'.

Spotting another wisp of light further down the road, I ran that way and was rewarded by another flicker of light. The traces formed an erratic trail until I came to the field where I'd crossed into the Grey Vale that morning.

Oh, shit. Wanda's wounds hadn't been inflicted by a hellhound, but what if something else had followed me out of the Vale? I hadn't checked. Hadn't known I needed to.

Chills racing down my spine, I went to search, but nothing remained inside or outside of the field except for the faint glow of magic. Death magic. I gave the area a thorough comb and then rejoined the others. Bailey and Rod eyed me warily but didn't ask any questions, for which I was grateful.

When we returned to the manor, I spied Vance walking out of the conservatory and strode to meet him. "Did you find Quentin?"

"No." He met me halfway down the corridor. "Either he's left the manor, or he's using some kind of magic to conceal himself."

"Do you really think he's working against us?" I asked. "I mean… he did save Wanda's life."

"No," said Vance. "The wards keep out anyone intending harm. However, he's undeniably concealed the truth from me."

"Has he really never used magic in front of you before?"

"No… doesn't your sword react to faerie magic?"

"He never used magic at all, did he? He fooled both of us."

"You're right." He closed his eyes and inhaled as though trying to calm himself down. "Wanda is fine for now. Without Quentin here, I'll need to assign someone else to keep an eye on Roseanne while we try to determine what attacked Wanda. We also need to ask the question of whether she was the intended target or if they came for Roseanne."

"Probably our half-blood friend." I grimaced. "Dammit. I kinda scared her off by insulting the faeries in general when she could hear me."

"I don't blame you." He wrapped his arms around me. "I'm sorry I ran off."

"It's fine. You needed to find our spy." I rested my head against his chest, drawn into the comfort of his embrace. "I can't believe it. You don't think he went to *Faerie,* do you?"

"I didn't see him leave the manor, but it's a possibility." Anger burned in his grey eyes, and his grip turned rough; I caught a glimpse of black scales on his hands when he let go of me. "He had full access to all of our resources and strategies. If he *is* an enemy…"

"He saved Wanda, but what about all the times we nearly died on missions? I can't believe he's lived here for so many years and never met someone in a near-death state before. That's at least one war he's lived through."

"Yes, but he's also been confined to the manor the entire time," said Vance. "Perhaps his instructions were specific in that he was only allowed to use his abilities in certain circumstances."

"Knowing the faeries, they probably were," I said. "Like 'you're permitted to use your healing power only on members of the Colton family while at the manor on a Tuesday afternoon.'"

Vance considered this. "Actually, I think Wanda is a distant relation of mine. We might be second cousins a few times removed. Mage family trees tend to get complicated."

"Huh. You learn something new every day." I took in a breath. "You should know I found a trail of faerie magic near where Wanda was attacked that led to the field behind the manor. The same place I last went to Faerie. For all I know, I brought the enemy out of the Vale myself, same as that hellhound."

"You didn't. I was watching when you came back from Faerie and I only saw the hellhound. Whatever attacked Wanda didn't follow you here."

I wasn't convinced. "And if it was glamoured?"

"Still not your fault."

Whatever the cause, Wanda had damn near died. Until we could determine who her attacker was and where they came from, no more trips into Faerie for me.

9

My phone buzzed from the bedside table, waking me from sleep. I glared at it. The buzzing continued, but Vance didn't stir. He'd been restless all night, probably worried about Wanda and how Quentin was still absent, and I didn't have the heart to wake him up and make him help me deal with whoever was hounding me at this ungodly hour. I threw on a dressing gown and slippers before carefully pushing open the glass doors to the balcony and stepping outside with the phone pressed to my ear.

"What now, Larsen?" I hissed.

"There's been another attack similar to Liam's death. No survivors."

I cursed under my breath. "When?"

"About midnight, in the middle of mercenary district. Three victims with the same injuries as Liam had."

"One of the mages was attacked yesterday, too," I said. "Can't you assign someone else?"

"You agreed to do this job for me," said Larsen. "Don't think I didn't hear about that half-blood."

"You have people spying on me? Seriously?" I nearly ended the call there and then.

"The will has not yet been found. Liam's possessions—"

"Will stay where they are until someone finds it. Don't pretend you didn't give the go-ahead to your mercs to raid his flat, Larsen."

"Liam left no instructions behind. I heard you decided to go chasing after a half-blood instead of pursuing his killer, so I assumed he'd ceased to be a priority for you."

"Don't talk bollocks," I snapped. "And don't pretend you even knew the names of the mercs who died without having to look in your files."

Silence. A guilty silence, at least.

"I'll be there later this morning. You're welcome." I clicked off the phone, cursing again when I saw the time. Five thirty. Bastard. If the mercs had been killed last night, there was no reason for him to call me this early. The attacker would be long gone.

I found Vance sitting up, his hair rumpled from sleep. "I heard you yelling."

"Sorry. It was Larsen again." I kicked off my slippers and slid into the bed beside him. "He called me early because he's a dick. Another mercenary—more than one, by the sound of it—was killed in merc district last night. Larsen thinks it's the same monster that got Liam. Not sure if he's right."

"That strikes me as worth looking into."

"But what about Roseanne? We can't leave her here alone, especially with Quentin missing. She'll wake up and realise you locked her door at some point." I hadn't been fond of the idea of locking her into the guest room, but it was that or let an as-yet-not-quite-trustworthy half-faerie run amok through the manor all night. After Quentin's betrayal, I'd take no chances.

Wanda's close call had shaken me, too. I was responsible

for Roseanne's well-being, but how far would I go to protect her when the enemy might have targeted my friends because of her presence here at the manor?

"I'll ask someone to watch her," Vance said. "And I'll let everyone at the manor know not to let her slip outside."

"Is it bad that I hope an estranged relative of Roseanne's shows up and takes her off our hands?"

"No." He laughed quietly. "I was just hoping the same thing."

"Unless you hired her to work as your new household staff."

His smile disappeared as swiftly as it had arrived.

"Sorry." I leaned over and rested my hand on his arm. "I never trusted Quentin, but I know *you* did, and that was more than enough for me."

He exhaled in a sigh. "Sarah adored him. I don't understand why he would have left us to the mercy of the Sidhe without trying to defend us."

"We haven't heard his side of the story yet." Though hell if I didn't want to wring his neck until the truth spilled out. Abandoning Vance's family to death made it pretty damn clear where his loyalties lay.

"No, we haven't." He ran a hand through his hair. "I'll worry about Quentin when we find him. I can't afford to spend all day chasing him around when he's already left the manor, in all likelihood."

"You think he's gone back to Faerie? I thought brownies were tied to the house they'd chosen to serve."

"In a manner of speaking. If the Colton family weren't his only masters…"

"Then he'll have gone to his other home." My nails bit into my palms. "Dick."

He shook his head. "I feel like I should have known. He was always too efficient. He did the jobs of a dozen people.

We've never had the need to hire other household staff since he came to serve my grandfather."

Vance's grandfather knew, but why not tell his children the truth? Okay, so Vance's family had suffered some major upheavals, but a *spy* in the house was a bloody major oversight.

"That implies he might not have had much time to go back to Faerie." Not that that let him off the hook. "I know it wouldn't make sense for him to put so much effort into keeping you alive when he was secretly working against you, but that doesn't mean he gave a single shit about the rest of us."

"No, it doesn't." Vance climbed out of bed. "I need to talk to the other mages and ask Drake to set up patrols for today. Then we'll go and see Larsen."

I yawned. "I want coffee and something to eat first."

"I'm afraid Quentin won't be able to make you those pancakes you like anymore."

"As long as I still have Isabel's cookies, I'm good."

Twenty minutes and a stack of toast and coffee later, we met Drake in the main room. Wanda no longer lay on the sofa and was resting in her room, but the memory of her near-miss was fresh enough in my mind to sharpen the claws of my anger and renewed my determination to find the person responsible.

"We need someone to keep an eye on Roseanne today," Vance told Drake. "Ivy and I have a potential lead on the people hunting her, but it means we'll have to leave the manor, and we can't have her getting into mischief while we're gone."

"Another mercenary was killed," I added in explanation. "We need to check if it's the same creature which attacked Wanda, but I'm not taking our half-faerie friend along with us."

"I'll keep her entertained," said Drake, conjuring a flame to his hand. "She won't get away while I'm here."

"And let me know if you see anything outside," Vance added. "Make sure the guards are on full alert in case the creatures that attacked Wanda come back."

"Nothing I can't handle."

He was probably right, but I didn't want anyone else getting hurt while we were gone. Whoever had sent that monster must know Roseanne was here. She'd been the target, and it had been pure luck that Wanda had survived. Luck, and the intervention of a double-crossing faerie who wouldn't be around to save us a second time.

"Watch for Quentin, too," I warned. "We haven't seen him since yesterday, but he might be lurking around, and there's no telling what he'll do now we've figured out his true loyalties."

"I'm on it, don't worry." Drake left the room, a flame dancing above his palm.

"Hope he doesn't set Roseanne on fire when she inevitably annoys him," I murmured to Vance.

"He's surprisingly patient sometimes," he said. "Good at bodyguard duty, too, even if he does get distracted easily. I can't count the number of times he's saved my neck."

"Yeah." I scanned the main room, seeing signs of the brownie's invisible presence everywhere from the spotless mantlepiece to the neat bookshelves. He'd touched everything in the manor and had relied on his inconspicuousness to get away with deceiving us in plain sight. "When we're finished with the mercs, we'll find Quentin and get the truth out of him."

"Yes, we will. I hope Roseanne doesn't make too much trouble while we're gone."

"I think she hates me after yesterday," I admitted. "She heard me muttering about Quentin and assumed I hated all faeries the same. Which I don't. I'm just having a hard time seeing the good side of any I've interacted with lately."

"I don't fault you for that," Vance said. "I was never raised to hate faeries, but that's largely down to my parents' trust of Quentin. I never questioned that loyalty, nor why he'd chosen to serve humans when most of his fellow brownies preferred to live with their fellow fae."

"Did he ever speak to you about the other faeries?" I asked, curious.

"Yes, but only when I asked. I remember he told me a little about the Summer Court, but I never had the impression he spent a great deal of time there."

"I get that faerie vows are binding, but he must understand he betrayed your trust. He's spent enough time around humans to know how we look at things like that."

Vance inclined his head. "He has, but he grew up in a realm vastly different than ours, and those beliefs are deeply entrenched. Even the half-bloods here have mostly been raised to believe this realm is their home, yet they still aspire to go back to Faerie."

"Yeah, good point." I sighed. "All right. Time to go and look at some more dead bodies."

Mercenary district was a warren of old houses and tower blocks near the canal, en route to what was left of Birmingham city centre. Once they might have been overpriced student housing or perhaps belonged to professionals who commuted into the city, but now the majority had been abandoned to disrepair or refurbished by unscrupulous landlords who then rented them out to people who'd choose neighbouring with man-eating monsters over living on the streets.

Though the canal was no longer dammed by a huge troll's nest, a foul smell lingered over the water like miasma.

"How's anyone meant to know if these mercs are the first

victims of this monster or if they're just the first who've been found?" I gestured towards a suspiciously human-like arm protruding from a stack of discarded old junk floating in the water. "Disappearances are common enough out here that nobody asks questions unless they have the clout to raise a fuss. There are goblin nests and all sorts. Plus on my last visit, I got thrown through the floorboards by a ghost. Can't forget that part."

We passed the tower block where Isabel and I had dealt with a misbehaving half-faerie spirit a few months ago, but luckily, our destination wasn't in the same block. When I tracked down the right building, I rang the buzzer and a middle-aged balding man answered the door.

"Come to see the bodies?" He grinned, showing gaps between crooked teeth. "Larsen said we weren't to bury them until they'd been identified, so I locked them in the utility room."

Lovely. We followed him down a corridor lit by strips of flickering light that did little to dispel the gloom. I lifted my blade, both so that I could stab anything that jumped me and so that I didn't trip over any obstacles in the dark.

The balding man watched me with interest. "Pretty sword, that. Where'd you get it?"

"You'd never believe me if I told you."

He laughed, the harsh sound echoing in the empty corridor. "I believe anything these days. Nasty business, these bodies. Can't think why Larsen wanted to keep them."

"We think there's an unidentified monster running around."

"I'll believe it. Might be one upstairs in this building, even." He laughed again when I tensed and lifted my sword higher.

"If that's the case," Vance said, irritation rolling off his voice, "you lead the way."

The old merc stopped laughing. "I mean no disrespect, Mage Lord. Your companion here's a little jumpy."

"Yeah, I've been known to accidentally stab people when I'm nervous."

We walked the rest of the way to the room in silence. Three bodies had been tossed into the cramped space, all having been ripped open by claws sharp enough to slice through skin and tear open their ribcages. I didn't need to look close to know their organs had been removed. Blood and other fluids leaked onto the floor, and I wondered what poor sod would have to clean up the mess. I doubted this dude would volunteer.

I swallowed bile and turned to the leering mercenary. "Did anyone witness the attack?"

"Some of us heard a weird noise outside," said the man. "Like a bird, a really loud one. Then there was a lot of screaming. By the time I came downstairs, they were lying dead outside."

"Where'd they live, anyway?"

"Ground floor. Right by the canal. Poor sods." He laughed. "All single, no kids. More loot for the rest of us."

"Unless the monster gets you next," I muttered.

"Ain't no shortage of monsters here," he said. "Don't get what's so special about these ones."

"The victims' organs have all been removed," I said. "Do you know any creatures that eat human organs and leave the rest?"

"No." He looked a little frightened now. "No, but what do you expect in a shithole like this? I'm moving next year, I am."

"You'd be lucky to live that long." I moved closer to the bodies. "I'm going to use a tracking spell."

Though I didn't hold out much hope after last time, I put on my professional face as I set up a tracking spell over one of the bodies, positioned carefully to avoid touching the man's cold, waxy-appearing face.

The green light of the spell enveloped me, but this time the vision showed nothing but the blurred front of the same building we stood inside. When it cut out, I tried a spell on the second body with the same result. The blood was fresh. They hadn't been dead for twelve hours yet. It usually took longer for a tracking spell to lose its effectiveness. Unless the bodies had been tampered with, magically, but what would be the point?

"The bodies were found outside the building?" I asked the balding man, who nodded. "Might be worth trying a tracker out there, too."

Malfunctioning spells aside, the pattern of attacks made no sense. Wanda had been right next to the manor when she'd been attacked, and Liam had lived a few miles from here in the opposite direction.

As I'd suspected, the tracking spells I used outside showed the same indistinct view of the building's front and nothing more. The balding man watched, wearing the same gap-toothed leer.

"Satisfied your curiosity?" he asked.

"Not really." Smears of blood marked the ground, indicating that nobody had intentionally wiped away the evidence, but the place might as well have been doused in cleansing spells for all the luck I had with the trackers. "Call Larsen and tell him to pick up the bodies. No human killed them, though, that's for sure."

We left. There seemed little point in lingering, and I'd need to employ a cleansing spell of my own to be rid of the lingering smell of effluence and decay. I might have asked the old merc how the inhabitants tolerated the stench, but my past experience had told me that humans could adapt to almost any environment. Unfortunately, so could the monsters that hunted them.

"What kind of monster knows how to meddle with a tracking spell, anyway?" I remarked. "Don't answer that, Vance. I know there's something I haven't thought of yet. Maybe the beast has some kind of ability that repels all other magic in a similar way to the ring."

"Not quite the same," said Vance. "The tracking spells still work, but their effects only avoid showing the murder."

"Yeah." I thought back. "Each tracking spell works perfectly fine until the creature—whatever it is—shows up. That's how it looked from my side, anyway."

"I think we should ask for more eyewitness accounts. He said the attacker sounded like a bird."

"Birds…" I trailed off. "Oh, *fuck*."

"What is it?"

"Furies." I pressed a hand to my forehead. "Remember them? They have big enough claws to do that kind of damage to a person, and we didn't let any of them live long enough to see how they devoured their prey."

Why hadn't I thought of the obvious sooner? We'd fought furies a few weeks ago when Fionn's lackeys had enacted a ritual to summon them from some hellish dimension, and for all we knew, some stragglers had been roaming around the city the whole time.

"That's true," he said. "The wounds match ones those creatures can inflict, but don't forget Liam's killer got into his flat without using the door or window."

"I don't know, maybe they can teleport, too." I shook my head. "Or use glamour. Death faeries like them must have tricks up their sleeves we haven't seen yet."

"Maybe," said Vance. "If we ask, perhaps the necromancers will be able to call up the victims' spirits to recount their deaths."

"After the last one, I'm not optimistic." I swivelled back to the building. "You're right about asking for eyewitness accounts, though."

The door was unlocked, so I walked down the dingy corridor, knocking on the first door I came to. Nobody responded, and I didn't get an answer until the fifth door.

"What?" grunted a male voice.

"Did you hear a bird outside yesterday?"

"Did I what?"

"We're investigating a—"

"I'll stick my knife in you if you don't go away."

I looked at Vance, who raised an eyebrow. I shrugged and moved onto the next one.

In the ground floor corridor, I got a grand total of three responses, all of which were about as polite as the first one.

"Hopeless," I muttered as we walked back to the door. "I can't believe I ever used to work with these people."

"Did you know the victims?" asked Vance.

"Nope. I didn't associate much with their type. Unlike Liam, they were the glory-hunting sort. Probably teamed up on a mission and got jumped on the way back."

We left the building—and stopped. A hellhound sat outside, tongue lolling, for all the world like a giant Labrador. Albeit one with deadly fangs. Given its comparative lack of height compared to the others I'd seen, it was the same one that had followed me out of Faerie.

"It's that hellhound again." I took a step closer. "It didn't attack me last time. I think it's… waiting for a new master."

Vance kept his weapon out, his eyes narrowed. "We already have a half-faerie running amok around the manor. I draw the line at hellhounds."

"I'm not actually going to adopt one of those monstrosities, Vance. I'm trying to figure out why they keep showing up when I killed their master."

"You have similar magic."

"Don't remind me." I approached the hellhound, one hand resting on my sword hilt. "Maybe I'll use a tracking spell and see if any of its buddies are here. You aren't cavorting with furies, are you?"

The hellhound whined. Probably didn't understand a word, but I had to be sure.

"Don't take this personally." I halted in front of the beast and pulled out a fresh tracking spell. "I just want to make sure you're not a villain."

I didn't need to cut the hellhound when it was drooling all over the place, so I carefully set up the spell over the puddle below its chin while angling myself so that none of the toxic stuff got on my hands.

The vision unfolded, showing the beast running through a wide field. Watching from all fours and in black and white was always mildly disorientating, but I glimpsed more dog-like shapes scattered across the hillside. From what I could see, there was nothing but fields and hedgerows in all directions. They weren't in the city. The hellhounds meandered or lay on the grass, for all the world like a pack of wild dogs.

When I locked eyes with one of them, a shiver ran through my body at the stark intelligence in its gaze. As if the beast could see *me* behind the other hellhound's eyes. *Impossible.*

I blinked and let the spell's effects fade away, rising to my feet. Vance rested a hand on my arm. "Are you okay?"

"Yeah. This hellhound didn't attack anyone. I saw others, too. Living wild. I think they were left behind after I killed Fionn." If Vance noticed me breathing too quickly, he didn't say. *Did I imagine that feeling? Like... like I was connected to them?*

"Where?" he asked.

"Way outside the city. I reckon they're like other wild faeries."

"They've attacked humans in the past."

"Only when commanded to," I said. "They're probably close to shifter territory than anywhere else, and those guys are more than a match for a hellhound. If they're spotted near humans, I'd say differently, but I don't think the hellhounds are the enemies we need to worry about now. It's definitely not them who attacked the mercenaries *or* Wanda. I didn't see any furies with them, either."

"No, but it makes sense that the furies are behind these attacks."

"Yeah, it does." Unfortunately, no other fae I could think of fit the description. "I guess it explains how they got the jump on the mercs. No regular monster can take out three seasoned fighters at once."

"The furies were difficult to kill," said Vance. "Certainly for anyone without magic. Though I can't think of a reason they would target Roseanne."

"Nor me." Unease slithered down my spine. "She and the furies are both Unseelie, though furies are in the same kind of weird grey area as hellhounds are. You know, not part of the Courts. They can also be summoned... and maybe commanded."

The hellhound made a whining noise and butted its head against my leg.

Vance glared, but the beast ignored him. "Ivy, if you want a puppy, I'll get you a puppy. Hellhounds aren't pets."

"I don't know why it came here rather than staying with its buddies." I crouched down beside the hellhound. "Go on. You're not coming with us."

The hellhound whined, a noise unsuited to a dog of that size. Then it turned around and sloped away, before breaking into a gallop and disappearing around the corner.

"Let's hope that creature came alone," said Vance.

"Yeah, I know. We don't need a dozen lining up on the doorstep." I thought back to my teetering list of problems to handle. "Should we tell everyone at the manor that we're probably dealing with furies? Or go and see the necromancers first? Or—shit, someone should probably let the Chief know, too. I ought to apologise on behalf of our unwanted visitor for insulting him."

He almost smiled at that. "Anyone would think you wanted to restore our diplomatic relations."

"Hardly." I shook my head. "Wonder if *he* knew about Quentin. They're both from Summer."

"I doubt it," said Vance. "The few half-bloods who lived here in my grandfather's time kept to themselves and hid amongst regular humans, from what I understand."

"Makes sense," I said. "I think we should warn him about the furies, though. They're death fae, so they'll naturally be drawn to his territory."

"Yes, and if they targeted Roseanne, they don't discriminate between human and fae when choosing their victims."

"Exactly." The Chief didn't deserve my warning, really, but I'd never asked him in depth about his knowledge of furies. He might be able to confirm if they ate human organs and remove any lingering doubts that they were the beasts that had attacked Wanda. "All right. I'll see the necromancers first, if you want to head back to the manor and tell the other mages what we've figured out. Then we'll drop in on the Chief."

"And the mercenaries?"

"Yeah, I need to talk to Larsen." I heaved a sigh. "And you know, I've absolutely no idea why the furies would target the mercs." Liam, I understood, due to his prior connection with Roseanne. The three victims today had been strangers.

"Should I drop you off at the mercenary guild?"

"Sure. I can walk to the necromancers' place from there. It's no big deal."

"I still worry about you, Ivy." He wrapped his arms around me and kissed me. "What happened to Wanda might easily have been you."

I leaned into his warm embrace. "I'm good. I'll see you in a bit."

A second later, I stood outside the mercenaries' door. Vance disappeared, while I went to find my former employer. To no surprise, he wasn't in the reception area, which was empty aside from a young woman hovering near the desk. Literally hovering. She was maybe nineteen or so with bright-green Summer eyes, glowing pale skin, and wings poking through holes cut into her leather jacket. Her waist-length raven-black hair swished over her shoulder as she fluttered gracefully towards me.

"There you are," she said. "I've been waiting long enough."

"For me?" I said blankly. "I don't work here anymore. I'm investigating an independent case for Larsen. Who are you?"

"I'm Lily. You've worked with other half-faeries before, right?"

"Once or twice. What is it?"

"I've lost my house," she said. "The new Chief divided up the territory and her trolls bulldozed my flat."

"The *new* Chief?" I echoed, my heart plummeting. "What happened to Chieftain Taive?"

"He was imprisoned for treason. We have a new Chief now, and she wants to divide our territory into Seelie and Unseelie."

My mouth dropped open. "What… when did this happen? Who is the new Chief?"

"It's easier to show you. Will you help me?"

"Possibly." Shit. Wherever Larsen was, finding out what in the living hell had gone down on half-blood territory was more important. "I can't make any promises until I find out who the new Chief actually is and what she did."

"But you're the faerie killer... I thought you killed bad faeries."

"I kill faeries who break the rules," I corrected. "How does it work? Can someone just step in as Chief whenever they feel like it?"

"No," said Lily. "No. She came in out of nowhere and said the territory needed to be divided in two. She's kicking anyone out of their homes who's on the wrong side."

"Sounds like someone needs a chat with my sword," I said. "She's not talking crap about immortality, too, is she?"

An awkward moment passed.

"Oh, no." Major fucking understatement. If a faerie was in power who believed the rumours Velkas and Calder had started, we'd have a mass exodus to the Grey Vale any day now. "What's she saying?"

"She said we can all gain immortality if we earn it," said Lily. "She's dividing us by Court and bloodline to start off with. I ran away before it got worse. I didn't know where else to go."

"Tell me more on the way." I left the building and half-walked, half-ran down the street, sending Vance a quick message as I did so. I'd been so wound up over Roseanne and the mysterious killer, it hadn't even occurred to me that half-blood territory was careening headfirst into a full-blown uprising. Deposing the Chief, though? I didn't like the guy, but if the alternative was another Calder, someone would have to put the guy back on his throne if we wanted any chance of restoring order. I didn't even know where to begin with the new Chief's threats and promises. While splitting Seelie and Unseelie made logical sense based on their conflicting magic, they'd lived together for a generation.

Vance responded to my message saying he'd join me as

soon as he'd finished conferring with the mages. It sounded like the council had wanted to grill him about the new security measures following the attack on Wanda, but this situation had the potential to turn into a major shitstorm, too.

Lily might be cagey about the new Chief's identity, but she chattered all the way to half-blood territory about the unfairness of the new laws and how everything had been upended.

"It's awful," she said. "My girlfriend is Unseelie, and she nearly got arrested when she protested over them knocking down our building."

"The new Chief must have had to arrest a lot of people."

"I think she's building a new jail."

"Of course she is." *Okay, focus, Ivy.* I'd assess how bad the damage was before going in with all guns blazing.

The exterior of half-blood territory remained unchanged, and the gates opened at our approach. An icy breeze crept inside my leather jacket and brought my arms out in goosebumps, while the rotten flowers and dying trees had vanished from the space in front of the gates, leaving an empty space of yellow grass. Half-bloods spread out, talking loudly. Most were Seelie and were more or less human in appearance, wearing human clothing, though there were a few hulking half-trolls and diminutive half-hobgoblins and half-gnomes. Piskies flitted about, their usual spark dulled. There was no sign of any of the armour-wearing Seelie knights who'd guarded the territory on the Chief's orders, though. *Have they all been jailed, too?* I thought of the hostile Unseelie knight to whom I'd spoken, the one dressed in spiky armour, and had the sudden suspicion that some of them had offered a helping hand in this coup.

"Where's Unseelie?" I asked Lily in an undertone.

"They're on the territory's other side. They outnumber us by nearly a third."

"Damn."

We attracted a few curious looks as she led me through the field, and I caught a handful of whispers along the lines of 'the faerie killer has come to save us' which I silenced with a pointed stare. I sure as hell hadn't volunteered for this shit. Past the field lay apartment buildings and other dwellings, but a huge swathe at the back had vanished, leaving a huge trench in their place.

"See?" Lily gestured to the open space, wings fluttering with distress. "She wanted a clear dividing line between Summer and Winter. My... my wings aren't strong enough to fly over."

I studied the gap. "I can jump it. Wait for me here."

I drew back a step, two, then leapt. Blue light trailed from my feet as I soared over empty air and touched down on the other side. Unseelie territory was mostly forest, by the looks of things, but the path leading to the Chief's clearing hadn't changed.

Two hulking half-trolls blocked my path, swinging clubs from their meaty hands.

"I'm here to speak to your Chief," I told them. "I'm Ivy Lane, here to see your new leader."

"Let her through," said a familiar voice.

Fuck. Please tell me it isn't her.

The trolls exchanged a conversation made mostly of grunts and then shuffled to either side, leaving a free path through into the clearing.

Alison the banshee sat on a throne made of what looked like bones, picked clean. Frost clung to the dark-branched trees and to her raven-black hair, and blue eyes shone in her pale face with the vibrancy of Winter magic.

The new Chief of the half-faeries smiled widely at me. "Hello, Ivy."

10

"You." Disbelief mingled with anger, partly at myself for not suspecting the banshee might have followed me out of the Vale upon Fionn's death. When she hadn't shown up during any of my visits to the other side, I'd assumed she didn't want to be found, or else something nasty had eaten her alive.

I'd never in a million years have guessed she'd have the audacity to steal the Chief's title. She'd never shown the slightest interest in ruling over the half-bloods' territory beforehand, despite the visible disdain she'd shown towards the former leader.

"Chieftain Taive has been removed from his position," said the banshee. "It was clear that my fellow half-faeries need a leader who better represents the needs of both Seelie and Unseelie faeries in this realm."

"What the hell are you playing at?" I hissed. "You can't depose the leader of the half-faeries. That's not how it works."

"You never learned our ways, human."

"You didn't live on their territory," I retaliated. "You didn't *want* to live here. Besides, being Chief doesn't mean you're allowed to split up Unseelie and Seelie faeries and bulldoze people's homes."

"My territory will be the stronger for it." Alison's foot tapped against the throne, jostling a protruding object that looked sickeningly like a human femur. "I'm Chief. I don't have to listen to humans."

"You live here," I said. "You could have gone anywhere else and started a new life after Fionn died. Why this?"

"After he died? You abandoned me in the Grey Vale, human, after I helped you."

"I was bleeding to death and had to destroy the ring before it swallowed up my realm," I pointed out. "I came back for you later, but you'd gone. Don't pin this one on me. It's all you, and I won't let you ruin others' lives because you feel like playing a game of make-believe."

"This isn't a game." Her eyes gleamed, vibrant blue. "The Chief was weak and wanted us to live like humans. Under my rule, we can be glorious once again."

"Where'd you pull that one from?" Fionn, probably. Fuck my life. "Might've escaped your attention, but your fellow half-faeries have this habit of being targeted by people who want to use them for their own gain. You're just one in a long line, Alison."

"I beg to differ," she said. "Summer and Winter have endured as separate territories for thousands of years. This is the correct way to live in our temporary residence before we go back to Faerie."

"Oh, for crying out loud," I burst out. "It's *not possible* for you to go back. Have any faeries come back to collect their abandoned offspring in your lifetime? It's cruel and unnecessary to keep lying to the others. As for immortality—"

In a gust of wind, Vance appeared in the clearing as though there weren't two club-wielding trolls right behind him. Both staggered in the breeze stirred up by his arrival and lifted their clubs, but at a single glance from him, they lowered their weapons again.

"This isn't your battle, Mage Lord," Alison warned.

"On the contrary," Vance said, "as the current leader of the mages, it's my duty to ensure the relationship between the half-faeries and the mages remains intact in the event of any changes in leadership."

"That doesn't mean you have permission to tell us what to do," she said. "My people have been down-trodden for too long, drained of our power, and forced into enclaves. We deserve to be allowed back to our true home, and the Chief was too weak and pathetic to chal-lenge the order and take the case to his full-blooded kin."

"And you think they'll listen to you instead?" I raised a brow. "You're a harbinger of death, Alison. Pretty sure both Seelie *and* Unseelie Courts hate your kind."

"I'm the harbinger of immortality," she said. "I'll *make* them listen."

"If Fionn told you that would work, he was lying," I said. "Just like Calder. You were the one who warned me of his plan. I thought you knew better than to trust someone who peddles the same lies and who isn't even still around to give you orders."

"Your human mind games won't work on me, Ivy," she said. "Most of the half-bloods wanted the Chief deposed."

"That may be, but demolishing people's homes is a dick move," I said. "What's your plan for him, anyway?"

"Execution." She grinned. "As a warning to other would-be traitors."

"Executing your leader is illegal," said Vance.

"We don't have to play by your rules, Mage Lord. We won't be in this realm for much longer."

"You'll be six feet under if you carry on like this," I said. "You're throwing away over ten years of peace for no cause."

"I beg to differ. My fellow faeries deserve true immortality, and passage back to our rightful home."

"Who are you working for this time?" Vance asked. "Fionn is dead."

"I serve nobody but myself," said the banshee. "I only allowed you to enter my territory so that I might inform you that our partnership with the mages is over. My people have no desire to cooperate with humans any longer."

"Did you *ask* anyone before you made decisions on their behalf?" I retorted. "I'm pretty sure the others don't want their houses knocked down or the old Chief executed either."

"He lied to us," she said. "It's thanks to you that we all found out the truth, Ivy. Did you know? If a mere *human* can speak to the Sidhe, so can we."

"That's not..." Oh, bollocks. She must have found out about the visit we'd had from Summer a few weeks ago. "The Sidhe came to interrogate me. They don't have any intention of bringing any of you into Faerie. The Chief, by contrast, helped save your lives." That was stretching the truth a little, but I was the one who'd persuaded him not to tell the others about Summer's emissaries showing up in Vance's garden. And with good reason.

"The Chief has done nothing but stand back and let us suffer the indignity of being trapped in a realm that doesn't want us," she hissed. "Every time our lives have been under threat, he's been incompetent and useless. He is not a fit leader."

"And you're any better?" I challenged. "Did anyone even choose you as leader? Or did you just take the throne without asking?"

She bared her teeth. "Nobody told me I couldn't."

Probably because she'd screamed in their faces. Bloody banshees.

"Regardless of who the leader is," Vance said, "splitting your territory into halves is a foolish move that will only lead to unnecessary discord."

"You've outstayed your welcome, Mage Lord." She jerked her head at me. "Both of you."

I didn't move. "I can guarantee this isn't the way to get the Sidhe's attention, if that's your aim. If it's not, and you're intending to take the other half-faeries into the Vale instead, you're condemning them to death."

"Isn't that a shame?" She laughed. "You have more in common with us than your fellow humans, Ivy. That's the only reason I'm letting you walk away from here today."

"Not if I take you out first." Blue light ignited along my blade.

"If you manage to kill me, you'll start the war you fear so much." She rose upright, hands shifting into talons. "Leave while you can. Both of you."

I hesitated for an instant, caught between the desire to spare the other half-faeries from her tyranny and the grim knowledge that anyone who'd fallen for her brainwashing tactics would believe me to be a villain. If I took her life, and the Chief was unable to regain control of his throne, the whole place might dissolve into anarchy.

She opened her mouth. A scream hit us like an avalanche, shaking the trees heavily enough to dislodge any remaining leaves. My eardrums burned, my teeth rattled in my skull, and my blade threatened to fall from my shaking hands.

Vance took my arm and the territory vanished along with the horrible noise. We landed outside, both staggering from the impact of her scream.

"*Ouch.*" My head pounded, and I felt damp blood trickle down my neck from both ears. "I think she burst my eardrums." Based on how fuzzy my voice sounded, she'd definitely caused some damage.

"Here." Vance handed me a healing spell and took one for himself.

"Nothing a healing spell can't take care of." I sighed in relief when the spell's cool breeze washed away the ache in my head, though my ears still felt a little tender. "I hope she didn't deafen anyone in there."

"No." His voice was quiet, angry. "We need to confer with the council on this turn of events. This is going to cause a great deal of turmoil among the other supernaturals."

"See what I mean?" Lily emerged from the gates, her wings fluttering nervously. "I don't know if what she's promising is true, but she's already demolished half our territory, and she said that's only the beginning. She wants to expand our borders, too."

"That's illegal, isn't it?" I looked to Vance for confirmation, and he nodded. "If it isn't safe for you in there, we can help, right, Vance?"

"Of course," Vance said. "Do you have somewhere to stay?"

"I have some human family, yes," said Lily. "But there are hundreds of people on the territory and not all of them can leave."

"I know." I rubbed my forehead, my ears still twinging. "How many do you reckon are on her side?"

"I don't know," she mumbled. "Nobody voted her in. She was just... there."

"Yeah." And she was too powerful for most—if not all—other half-faeries to stand up to. Worse, few would dare to oust her when she'd promised them what they'd always wanted.

Maybe the territory would survive being split. Summer and Winter *did* frequently get into arguments or all-out brawls. Winter fae were cranky all through spring and summer. Summer faeries were sullen all through autumn and winter. But more got along than not, united by a common cause. The slight issue was that that cause was a mutual desire to go back to their own realm. Nothing anyone else offered would ever compare.

"I will talk to the mage council and see what I can do," Vance said to Lily. "We should be able to help anyone who needs it."

"I... thank you, Mage Lord."

"And I can talk to my friend, the leader of the Laurel Coven," I offered. "Maybe the witches can offer shelter to people who are stuck and can't get back into their territory."

I hadn't intended to end up as an advocate for desperate half-faeries, but nobody deserved to be left out on the street because a banshee had decided to throw a tantrum. The house Isabel had inherited from Francine was unoccupied at the moment and I was positive that Isabel would agree that there was no reason not to offer some of the half-faeries temporary shelter there.

"Thanks." She blinked, her eyes watering. "I... I don't understand how this happened. I've never seen the new Chief before in my life. You know her, though, right?"

"She's a banshee," I said. "She used to work for the leader of the Wild Hunt. Long story short, she double crossed me so many times it was impossible to tell whose side she was on. Now we have our answer. Her own, apparently."

"The Hunt." Her eyes widened. "She said the leader of the Hunt was coming here soon and that he'd take us all back to Faerie with him and make us immortal."

"What?" He was *dead*. "She's lying. The only way to become immortal is to die and become a ghost. Calder thought he'd be an exception, but he was lying, too. And for the record, I *killed* the leader of the Hunt. He sure as hell wasn't immortal."

"What?" She stepped back, her mouth parting. "Why would anyone *want* that?"

Finally, I'd met a half-faerie with their head screwed on the right way. "Feel free to pass on what I said to the others, if you like. Whatever that banshee is planning will involve a one-way ticket to the afterlife for all of you. And the rest of us, too, probably."

She ducked her head. "I'll tell them. If they'll listen."

"Be careful the banshee doesn't overhear," I warned. "Come and see me tomorrow and I'll let you know if the witches can help."

Preferably without Alison guessing their plan. She was a nasty piece of work, and while I was pretty sure I could best her in a fight, the lack of any obvious alternatives made me reluctant to strike her down without someone ready to step into her place and restore order. And I hadn't even touched on her bizarre claims of Fionn's survival.

"I knew we couldn't trust that banshee," I growled under my breath. "I just have a weakness for outsiders and outcasts. Like Roseanne. I keep making the same mistake."

"It's not a weakness," said Vance. "I wish the Mage Lords had done more to aid the half-bloods stranded here after the invasion. When I was looking for information on those orphanages, it became clear to me that the half-faeries were given the impression they had no choice but to isolate themselves."

"Can you picture that banshee in a human orphanage?" I shuddered. "She's lost her mind. Or she's following someone else's orders."

She thinks Fionn survived.

"Whatever the case, the other mages will agree that we need to act swiftly to prevent bloodshed," he said. "Dividing the territory into Seelie and Unseelie will undo twenty years of peace agreements. Half-bloods have never experienced the conflicts affecting their kin in the faerie realm."

"I don't know, some of them will be all for it." I grimaced. "Besides, it's not exactly been peaceful over there in the past. Look how many half-bloods took part in the Trials. And if she's jailing anyone who disagrees with her or driving them off, any sensible people will find themselves outnumbered."

"Precisely why we need her removed from her position sooner rather than later," Vance said. "I'll tell Drake to call an emergency council meeting."

"And I'll call Isabel." I got out my phone and called her. "Hey, Isabel. Quick question: is Francine's house still empty?"

"Yes… why? Ivy, what did you do?"

"Not me. Our least favourite opera singer is back." I gave her the rundown, adding in my suggestion that she open Francine's house to displaced half-faeries for the time being.

"I know it's not ideal," I said, "but the one I've met so far isn't like our creepy little guest, and anyone who disagrees with the banshee is a potential ally. Plus, you know, she's massively screwing them over. But it's up to you."

"Of course," said Isabel. "I'll check with the others, but there's no reason we can't leave the doors open when nobody's using the house anyway. How *is* your creepy little guest?"

"Under watch at the manor. Drake hasn't called, so I assume she hasn't summoned a god or broken the furniture. Yeah, I know it isn't funny. I can't even handle this. I never got to see the necromancers at all."

Larsen and the murders had ended up dead last on my list of priorities, behind Roseanne, Quentin's betrayal, and the banshee's usurpation of the Chief's position. When the universe wanted to screw me over, it did so in style.

"What even happened to the Chief?" asked Isabel.

"He's in jail awaiting execution." I released a sigh. "The mages are going to set up an emergency meeting, but you know how long the council usually takes to come to an agreement, and I don't want any of the half-bloods to end up on the wrong end of the banshee's talons while they're waiting for someone to come and help."

"I'll call a coven meeting, too," Isabel said. "In case they make trouble for the witches, too."

"Good call," I said. "I need to be at the manor, but I'll try to drop by later, okay? Let me know what the coven says."

"Sure. You know, Ivy, maybe you should have stayed on holiday."

"I'm starting to think the same." I ended the call.

Vance did the same a moment later. "Drake said Roseanne is being suspiciously compliant."

I pocketed my phone. "Good. I can't take any more drama. What now?"

"Drake's called an emergency council meeting with the other Mage Lords," he said. "That said, some of them will want to focus on our own security after the attack on Wanda."

"Because this is exactly what we needed on top of the bloody furies rampaging around," I said. "Faerie doesn't fuck around."

"No," said Vance. "I would have to agree with you there, Ivy."

11

Vance took us back to the manor to grab an early lunch before the emergency council meeting. He also sent Roseanne into the back garden under the watch of a mage apprentice to stop her from interrupting, but I had to admit that would have added some excitement to the proceedings. The notion of sitting around explaining the banshee's coup to sceptical council members was irksome when I wanted to storm into the half-faeries' jail and get the Chief out myself. Or failing that, shove the banshee into the same cell for breaking over a decade of peace agreements into a hundred pieces.

Vance's new council consisted of two older members—Lord Ellsworth and Lady Sandford—and one younger, Lady Hewitt. Unfortunately, none of them had any experience defusing the live bomb that was half-blood territory, and since I hadn't attended any recent meetings, I had considerable trouble making myself heard.

"I propose we send in an envoy first," Vance said when he'd finished explaining the banshee's coup to the assembled mages. "This is a delicate situation made more complicated by the new division of the territory."

"Especially as she's shoved the Chief and all his supporters in jail," I added. "We're watching a dictatorship rise on our doorstep. Is there nothing we can do?"

"Can't the half-bloods living outside the territory vote on a leader?" asked Lord Ellsworth. "That was my understanding. All half-bloods are allowed a say, even the ones who don't live there."

"None of them got to vote," I pointed out. "She made herself leader and has decided she can change the laws on a whim. She's already evicted people from their homes to establish this new division between Seelie and Unseelie."

"Which is the Unseelie, again?" someone else asked.

"Winter. Seelie is Summer." Most of the mages had only superficial knowledge of the faeries, but if I had to keep explaining basic terminology, I'd be here all day. Every minute we wasted won the banshee more time to establish her rule, but the sticking point was that enough of the half-faeries would believe her stories that deposing her would be difficult if not outright impossible. Killing their dream of returning to Faerie would spark a riot or even a war—and if the banshee *did* manage to open a door to the Grey Vale, there might be an army waiting on the other side to claim our world as their own.

"The banshee is Unseelie," I told them. "She used to work for the self-proclaimed master of death, who was more powerful even than most of the Sidhe. Most half-bloods will be scared shitless of her, or else worship the ground she treads on. On top of that, she hates humans and thinks the half-faeries shouldn't be subject to our rules. It's a disaster waiting to happen."

"Then she ought to be deposed," said Lady Penrose, who'd been deposed from the Mage Lords herself for supporting

Lady Granville's attempt to oust Vance from leadership, though she'd unfortunately retained a seat on the council. "And any who support her should be punished, too."

"That's not feasible," I said. "I don't know how many real supporters she has, but anyone who takes her side has either been coerced or brainwashed into thinking she's their only hope to get home to Faerie. And I can guarantee that if we stand in their way, they'll take it as a declaration of war."

The trouble was, none of the mages had ever been in a position remotely close to anything the half-bloods had endured. Most of the half-faeries had either been raised by humans or grown up alone, with no one to help them assimilate into human society, and it was clear the mage council had filed half-bloods into the same category as regular faeries and had assumed they'd take care of their own. Though it wasn't fair to pin all the blame on the mages when this was at least partly the Chief's fault for being such a cowardly shit. If he'd had the guts to speak out against the Trials, whatever short-term unpleasantness might have resulted, we might not have come to this point. I reserved very little of my sympathy for him when the other half-faeries had more need of it.

"Return to Faerie?" echoed Lady Sandford. "Is…?"

"No, it's not possible," I said wearily, having explained the distinctions between the Courts and the Vale so many times that I'd been tempted to draw a map and stick it on the council room wall. "She's lying. This is one person's ambition, not a collective uprising."

"Then there's nothing to be done but to take swift and decisive action to remove this dangerous individual from power," Lady Penrose insisted, as if she had any intention of lifting a finger to do so herself.

. . .

"We're trying to avoid a war, not start one." They just plain didn't get it. "There needs to be someone ready to replace her, first, or at least the possibility of a fair election."

"For now, I'd suggest we offer safe passage out of the territory to every half-blood who may be in danger from the banshee's leadership," Vance said. "The witches have agreed to open a safe house to them, too."

"Why should we?" interjected one of the other mages. "If they don't want to live on the territory we gave them, they should move outside of the city and live wild like the shifters."

"Enough," Vance said sharply. Oh, boy. Insulting the shifters was a great way to land on his shit list. "These are people who believed they were making the best choice for themselves and their families by choosing to live amongst their own kind. Few had any say in the banshee's coup, and it's for that reason that I intend to offer our support to anyone who needs it."

"And the ones who want to stay?" Lady Penrose asked. "Are we to expect them to declare war on humans next?"

"No." God, I *hoped* not. "Like I said, we need someone to take her place. Oh, and it'd help if someone proved she's lying through her teeth when she claims she can take all the half-faeries with her to Faerie and make them immortal."

"They aren't immortal?" asked Lady Sanford. "I thought all faeries were."

"Pure faeries are," I said. "Half-bloods have the same life-span as regular humans. Like I said, she's lying, but they're absolutely convinced it's the truth, and nothing I say will persuade them otherwise."

"We need to protect our own first," Lady Penrose insisted. "There was an attack on our own property. Surely that should be the subject of this meeting, not the half-bloods."

"What happened to Wanda *will* be resolved," said Vance,

in his most dangerous voice. "However, the banshee's actions cannot be overlooked. I'll send a team to watch the territory and assist any half-bloods who want to escape. In the meantime, I can assure you I am doing everything I can to ensure our people are safe."

"Isn't there a half-blood downstairs?" Lady Hewitt said hesitantly. "How do we know she isn't working with this... banshee?"

"She isn't," I said. "Her human father was a mercenary, and he was the first victim of these attacks."

"She was the monster's target?" Lord Ellsworth looked aghast. "Then she cannot be allowed to stay in the mages' headquarters."

Murmurs of agreement followed. *Dammit.* I hadn't wanted to bring her up, knowing I had no hope of winning that argument. Not even when the alternative was condemning her to a gruesome death.

"The decision is mine," Vance said, "as the house belongs to me. For now, I will proceed with my intention to send an envoy to half-blood territory."

Lady Penrose's nostrils flared. "Is there any proof *they* aren't responsible for the attack on Wanda?"

Well, no. "If the banshee is, that gives us double the incentive to remove her from power, doesn't it?"

Nobody agreed with me. I didn't think it was true, personally, as I couldn't think why the banshee would order an attack on a bunch of mercenaries who were miles from the manor. Besides, what did she have to gain by murdering the estranged father of one of her fellow death fae? Or was Roseanne allied with her after all? I didn't dare allude to any of those possibilities while faced with a room full of mages looking for someone to blame without understanding the situation with any level of nuance, so I held my tongue.

Vance brought the meeting to a close shortly after. We'd

ended at a stalemate, but I assumed he didn't want to return to the thorny issue of Roseanne's presence at the manor when the decision was between us and her, not the council. Not that I knew how to tell *her* about the current shitshow on half-blood territory—or even if I should. For all I knew, she'd take it as a good sign and decide to move in with the other half-bloods after all, and I'd lose all hope of ever reasoning with her.

I left the room ahead of the others. As I reached the foot of the stairs, I stumbled and grabbed the handrail to keep from tripping head over heels over something… no, someone. "Quentin."

My hand shot out and grabbed the scruff of his neck. As I lifted him off the ground, the brownie made a furious noise of indignation. "Unhand me, human."

"Not if you're planning to disappear back into Faerie again." I carried him down the hallway, holding him at arm's length as he squirmed and kicked, and planted his feet on the floor of the main room. "Let me guess—you came to spy on the council meeting to find out what the mages planned to do on half-blood territory so you can warn them."

That was a stretch, I knew, but his reappearance immediately after that utter headache of a meeting had inevitably placed him in the firing line of my anger.

"What are you talking about?" The brownie backed across the room, wearing an aggrieved expression. "I am in no way affiliated with the half-faeries. I came here to explain to my master—"

"You'll have to go through me first. Vance is busy. Like I said, he has a shit-ton of problems without you adding to them. If you can't give me a damn good explanation for why you ratted us out to the Summer Court, I'll throw you into the new trench the banshee dug on half-blood territory."

"I told nothing of you to the Summer Court. Or the half-faeries either. I have not been to their territory."

"I don't believe you," I said. "You spied on my partner for his whole life. You deceived his family, betrayed their trust, and allowed them to be slaughtered in the invasion because you decided taking orders literally was more important than protecting Vance and his family. If Vance forgives you, you'll be lucky, because if I was in his place, I certainly wouldn't."

The brownie stayed silent through my entire outburst. When I paused to catch my breath, he spoke in his quiet gravelly voice. "None of us were in any way prepared for the invasion. We had no warning on either side. I obeyed my masters' orders because I thought it would keep my families safe."

"Well, it didn't." I tried to inject steeliness into my voice, but the sadness pooling in his eyes drove its way through my defences despite my best efforts.

"It is the greatest regret of my life," the brownie said softly. "The safe house was supposed to be more secure than the manor. My orders were clear: I was to stay here, while the Colton siblings remained safely away from the fighting. When I learned of what happened to Sarah, to their parents, you cannot fathom how I grieved them. They were my family."

"And yet you still decided not to tell him the truth. For years. He trusted you, Quentin."

"I had other lives to consider," he growled. "My orders were clear. If I told the mages of my allegiance to the Court, they would see me as a threat, and I would have to leave this realm without fulfilling my mission."

My brows shot up. "Mission?"

"I cannot share the details with you."

"You're under a vow? And you still expect me to trust your word?"

"I cannot force you to trust me, either. However, I am bound not to speak of those I serve. I can tell you honestly that I kept my master's secrets safe and never told the Summer Court anything that might have led to their interference in this realm. The Seelie and Unseelie Courts were not responsible for the invasion."

"Can you be sure?" I asked. "I mean, you've overheard every one of the mages' strategies, and even something mentioned offhand might have consequences."

The brownie looked outright insulted. "And has any of that information been used against you by the enemy? Have you ever had reason to believe the mages were compromised?"

Only when that spirit was possessing Lord Carlisle. Otherwise no, but Quentin had served three generations of mages since before Vance or I had even been born. "I'm not the person you should be asking that."

"You distrust my kin, perhaps for good reason, but I will gladly swear on whatever you prefer that I have never betrayed any of the mages, nor have I shared any secure information with those outside the manor. I retain allegiance to the family I serve in the Seelie Court because it is my duty to keep a foot in both realms for the sake of my mission."

"Which you can't talk about." I scowled. "Was it in any way connected to the invasion?"

The slight pause before his reply removed all doubts that I was right. He'd known something, if not the full details of what the exiled Sidhe were planning.

"I have very little magic of my own," he said. "The invasion couldn't have been prevented, least of all by me."

"I'm sure Vance will be thrilled to hear that."

"You report to Summer," said Vance's deep voice from behind me. "That means you can travel to the Summer Court, yes? Is that where you disappeared to?"

"Mage Lord." Quentin bowed sharply. "I must apologise for my disappearance yesterday."

I glared at him. "There's a hell of a lot of other things you need to apologise for, too."

"We're currently dealing with an uprising on half-blood territory," Vance said. "Someone intends to undo every peace agreement the mages have worked towards since the invasion. If you knew anything of this, you won't be welcome in this house any longer."

"I know nothing of the half-bloods. Part of my orders includes not speaking a word to any other faerie in this realm."

"Is that why you never spoke to Ralph?" His voice was sharp. "I respect that you might have different orders from your other family, but there isn't anything to stop me from releasing you from whatever vow you made to my grandfather."

"That won't be necessary," said Quentin. "I've broken no part of the bond, nor have I betrayed any of the mages' secrets to my other family."

"Maybe you never told our secrets to the enemy," I acknowledged, "but you must know there's a legitimate threat from the Grey Vale and we've been one mistake away from another invasion for a long time now. The half-bloods have ousted their leader in favour of a harbinger of death who's promising to take them back to Faerie—and believe me, you'd better hope they never find out you can do exactly that."

"If that is the case..." He offered a short bow to Vance. "With your permission, I shall pay my masters a visit and request for an envoy from the Summer Court to be sent here so that you can discuss the threat of the Vale directly with the Sidhe. However, I should warn you that my influence is minimal and even they have little sway over the Erlking."

That figures. "That might go some way to making up for decades of lies, but—hang on. You were told not to talk to any faeries. That includes Roseanne, right?"

The brownie stiffened. "Yes, including the harbinger. I told you not to bring her into the house."

"You can at least tell me what you know about the Morrigan," I said. "Like what makes her so dangerous."

Quentin paused for a moment, perhaps taken off guard by my demand. "The Morrigan is a powerful being who rules over Winter's outer territories. She is stronger than most Unseelie Sidhe and seen as a bad omen by most who know her name."

"The Morrigan had a daughter," I explained. "With a human man. She abandoned the child here. Her father was murdered a few days ago and his ghost asked me to protect her. The kid told me she can hear spirits, but the Morrigan can rip them from their bodies. Is that true?"

"Correct. However, the Morrigan would have little reason to come to this realm. Mortals have no interest for her."

"But why would someone want her daughter dead?" I pressed. "The same monster attacked Wanda... there's no reason to look at me like that, Quentin. The kid is innocent. Tell me the truth. Why would someone want her dead?"

"There are a great many reasons," he said. "Few trust the death fae, including their own kind."

"Too true," I muttered, thinking of the banshee. "But they killed her human father, too, and the two of them had never even spoken to one another, as far as I know."

"Regardless," the brownie said, "she is not to be trusted. You mentioned another harbinger has taken power among the half-bloods, too, correct? That is also cause for suspicion."

"What, you think the banshee sent someone to kill her

father?" How would the banshee even have learned she existed? "And tried to kill her, too?"

That was one possibility. The other was that someone had wanted Liam out of the way to ensure that Roseanne had nowhere else to go but into the arms of her fellow death fae.

"Mage Lord!" A young mage apprentice ran into the corridor. "It's your half-blood. She's gone."

"Of course she is," I growled. "That's it. Take another shot, universe. I'm done."

"Whoa." The apprentice backed away. "Sorry. I can't think how she slipped out. Unless she climbed over the fence."

"Dammit. Yeah, she probably did."

I ran into the conservatory and through the glass door onto the patio. Grey clouds gathered above the lawns, promising rain, and the wide lawns showed no traces of Roseanne. I crossed the garden to the back fence, but I didn't see any signs of her in the field on the other side either. Given how fast half-bloods could move, she might be miles away by now.

After I'd searched under every bush and behind every carved hedge, I returned to the conservatory, where Vance waited next to the piano.

"Any luck?" I kicked mud off my shoes, furious with myself. I should at least have attempted another apology for insulting her, but the banshee's coup had driven everything else from my head.

"No," said Vance. "She isn't around the front of the manor, either. She's obviously run somewhere else."

"Then we'll use a tracking spell. *She* isn't immune to them. I bet she left some hair lying around."

Faeries shed more than humans did, and I found a few strands of glossy black hair in the hallway. Tossing them onto the table in the main room, I grabbed a tracking spell from my pocket. Time to track down our little runaway.

In a flash of green light, I saw through Roseanne's eyes as she moved through the field behind the manor. At first, I thought she was running, much faster than I'd ever seen her walk. Then a glance down showed me she now had taloned claws in place of feet, similar to the ones I'd seen her shift her hands into. I hadn't realised she had a full shapeshifter form, but in the space of a few seconds, she glided over the fence and down the road, heading in a direction I was all too familiar with.

"Half-blood territory?" I cursed, letting the tracking spell fade out. "Why? Why does everyone insist on going out of their way to be as big a nuisance as possible?"

By now, Roseanne would already be behind the gates of half-blood territory and at the mercy of the would-be leader who'd made it clear that Vance and I would not be welcomed back there with open arms.

"She must have had a reason to go there," Vance said. "Don't forget she turned down the Chief."

"Yeah, but a death fae leader is far more up her street." I groaned. "If we go back there, the banshee won't go easy on us this time. Maybe we can talk to the guards and get our little problem back without resorting to violence, but that's about as likely as Alison shaking hands with the council and signing a truce."

For all I knew, my sharp words had been the last straw for Roseanne. Despite all the trouble she'd caused us, I owed

Liam, and I would not let Alison lure any more vulnerable half-faeries into doing her bidding.

"I'll go with you," said Vance. "The council will want to know, but I already made it clear that I will act alone if it means keeping our peace agreements secure."

"Not sure that'll be the outcome." I'd taken too many risks to keep Roseanne safe already, and now she'd gone into the one place my influence was almost zero. "The banshee won't let us in without a fight."

"Then we'll try to cause as little damage as possible." Vance lifted an iron blade. "While defending our own lives."

"Yeah." I gripped my sword's hilt tight, and tendrils of blue faerie magic swirled around the blade.

Vance took my arm. In a rush of air, we stood outside half-blood territory again. One look at the gate told me we wouldn't be getting back inside so easily. Flashes of blue and green light ignited the air like a daytime fireworks display. I'd thought the faerie magic in this realm was fading, but the energy pouring off the lawn set my own magic blaring. Blue light haloed the blade in my hand as I peered through the gate, trying to see what in hell was going on. A Summer-versus-Winter confrontation, by the looks of things. Green light clashed with blue, spiny plants sprouted and withered in the same instant, and the sound of clashing weapons assaulted my eardrums.

"Well, if she wanted to turn Winter and Summer faeries against one another, she succeeded." The racket swallowed my voice, and it took several seconds to realise someone else was calling my name.

"Ivy? Mage Lord?" Lily, the half-blood we'd spoken to earlier, peered around the corner. A nasty cut zigzagged across her cheek, her hair was in disarray, and her clothes were torn with briars. Behind her crouched a shorter Asian girl with Unseelie blue eyes and pointed horns poking from within her sleek dark hair.

"What's going on in there?" I asked.

"Riots." Lily bit her lip, moving closer to her companion. Her girlfriend, I guessed. "Some of the others don't want a new leader and they don't want their homes taken away. I didn't see who started the fight, but they won't stop."

"Shit." Had this been part of Alison's plan? Rile up the half-bloods until their combined magic ripped open the spirit lines without having to lift a finger? I'd expected her ultimate scheme to be of this nature, but not that she'd put it into action after our visit.

"I'm trying to help people get out." Lily gestured to a ragged hole torn into the side of the hedge. Similar holes were visible all along the road and half-bloods climbed out, bloodied and battered, some carrying armfuls of possessions.

Oh boy. I needed to see if Isabel had confirmed the coven's safe house was ready, but would they even have enough room for all these people in a single house? And what of the ones still trapped inside?

A gust of wind buffeted me in the back. Power crackled in the air, and the gate flew wide open as Vance stalked towards the entrance.

"Stop this at once!" he commanded.

The blasts of magic momentarily stilled when all eyes turned towards him. I held my breath and walked to his side, facing the sea of furious half-faeries.

A bolt of Winter magic shot over my head, icing the edges of my hair, and the fighting resumed anew. Weapons swung, while blasts of magic ignited the grass and froze the hedges. Both of us watched in disbelief as everyone ignored the Mage Lord's command. Last time he'd used the same tactic, the uproar had halted instantly, but back then, the Chief had been able to help him calm down the noise. The banshee had caused this riot herself, and Vance might as well have yelled into an empty room.

Angry lines marked Vance's face as he repeated his command. "Stop this at once!"

I doubted anyone had ever ignored an outright order from him before, but the half-faeries were in a frenzy, and I was willing to bet the banshee would be right at the heart of it.

"We need to find her."

Vance stepped forward, power crackling in the air, but the sheer volume of faerie magic was a force all on its own. Whenever someone was knocked down, they just picked themselves up and carried on fighting.

Let's see if this works instead. I lifted my blade and sent a blast of magic to the sky. It might not be as strong in this realm, but the turbulence of emotion fed into the blade and a vibrant stream of electric blue surged upward, above the frenetic bursts of blue and green light from the battle.

"Hey!" I shouted. "Cut that out!"

"Faerie killer!" someone screamed. "This is your fault."

A bolt of Winter magic flew at me. My shield deflected the oncoming attack into the crowd and knocked two half-faeries flying, but I hadn't dared turn my power up to max in case I seriously hurt someone. Some of them had noticed my arrival, but as others seemed content to continue beating the shit out of one another, anyone who stopped to listen was liable to have their head ripped off. Teeth snapped, claws swiped, and a cluster of half-redcaps ran amongst the battle with cries of delight at the crimson blood splattering the bright-green lawns.

"We need a better view," I said through clenched teeth. "Somewhere I won't accidentally kill anyone."

Vance transported us onto a balcony of one of the faeries'

apartment blocks. I blinked in a sudden flash of light when he activated a spell. "What was that?"

"It'll amplify your voice," he said. "See if they can hear you now."

"Hey!" Hearing my own voice at twice the volume was startling even to me, and a number of people looked up mid-fight. "Over here!"

I raised Helena into the air, willing my magic to draw upon the anger and pain rising from the brawling crowd. We were probably trespassing in someone's flat, but the odds were high that whoever lived in this building was among the rioters or fleeing for their lives. As the vibrant light spread, the fighting began to slow. Everyone, however distracted they might be, knew a Sidhe talisman when they saw one, and their eyes were invariably drawn towards me.

"Stop fighting and listen to us!" I shouted. "Where is your leader?"

From up here, I had a full view of the crowd, and I didn't see any sign of the banshee amid the uproar she'd created. Nor Roseanne, either. There were fewer brawlers than I'd first thought, maybe fifty at most, and more than a few of the fighters had crawled away for the gaps in the hedges or hid themselves behind trees.

"She's gone," yelled a blue-eyed Winter half-faerie who clutched a half-torn wing to her side. "She picked some lucky people to go with her and left the rest of us behind."

She's gone? "When was this?"

"Less than an hour ago." She beat her remaining wing, rising below the balcony we stood on. "She abandoned us just like the Chief did."

"No, she didn't!" said a golden-haired half-satyr with a smear of blood on one cheek. "She's coming back for us."

The Chief, I assumed, was still in jail or dead, but he hardly mattered at this point. The banshee had left the other half-faeries in chaos and skipped off to the Vale without a thought.

"Did anyone see where she went?" I asked.

"She went to Faerie, obviously," the half-satyr called. "And she's coming to take us with her."

"Bullshit!"

More angry voices chimed in, and when someone threw a punch, the fighting resumed as if it had never paused.

"We'll search for your leader," Vance called out, "but she has no intention of helping any of you."

Nobody paid him the slightest jot of attention. The riot was back in full swing, and even my amplification spell didn't matter when they refused to believe a word we said.

"Damn," I whispered. "What's the banshee's game now? She's turned everyone against one another, but if this is a Calder-style plot to stir up enough energy to break the veil, she hasn't succeeded."

"Yet." A grim edge entered his tone. "She might be waiting beside the Ley Line, or…"

"Not the forest. The Hemlock witches would never allow it." Without the ring eating away at their defences, they were back at full power, but they remained confined to the forest, unable to do anything to prevent the half-faeries from destroying one another. "She took people with her… why? To create her own personal army in the Grey Vale?"

Surely not. Whatever power she possessed in this realm, she'd never have a Sidhe Lord's magic, and the Vale would eat her alive. But aside from the forest—which didn't really belong to the half-faeries anyway—Faerie was the only possible option.

"I don't know." He scanned the chaotic scene below. "I doubt anyone here will talk."

"You're right there." I thought. "We can talk to Roseanne's

friends. See if any of them has seen her. She might've taken a detour on the way."

The tracking spell hadn't shown her arrival. If Roseanne had gone home instead of to half-blood territory, it'd take at least one weight off my mind.

Three seconds later, we stood in front of the block of flats. A couple of raindrops fell, and the bruised sky rumbled with thunder. I spotted the winged half-faerie we'd encountered during our last visit lurking near a swathe of bushes and made a beeline for her, calling out, "I need to talk to you."

"It's too late, ain't it? She's gone."

My heart sank quicker than the raindrops splashing against my jacket. "How do you know?"

"'Cause I saw her leave, duh."

"She came here." Dammit. "Did you see where she went?"

"No." A snort. "She's not the only one. People've been disappearing for weeks."

"What?" I asked, disarmed. "Who's disappeared?"

"People. You thick or something?"

Deep breath, Ivy. Don't punch her in the mouth. "If you saw her leave, you must've spoken to her. What did she say?"

"That she was going home."

"Fuck!" I threw up my hands, wisps of magic leaking out. The half-faerie shrank away into the bushes as I fumed, aiming a wayward kick at a fence post. "She's gone back to Faerie. With the banshee."

"Why did the banshee change her mind?" Vance asked. "Why go to the trouble of taking power over the half-bloods only to run away?"

"To cause anarchy? No fucking clue. This is the faeries we're talking about. Logic need not apply."

Expression tight, Vance pulled out his phone. "Drake's

patrolling the back garden. He said he saw a flash of green light in the field behind the manor."

"That's where I crossed over to Faerie the last time." It was also on a spirit line, but similar lines crisscrossed the entire city. Which reminded me: how had the banshee traversed the lines? Did she and I share the same ability to cross over the veil anywhere, without assistance? That was the only explanation for how she'd managed to return from the Grey Vale after I'd unintentionally left her stranded—and now she'd taken others with her, too.

"It wasn't you." Vance placed a steadying hand on my shoulder. "This is an attempt to get your attention."

"Strangely, that doesn't make me feel any better." I drew in a breath. "Right. Let's see what they want with me."

Vance and I landed in the field bordering the manor. A thin layer of mist hung over the grass, and a large number of black feathers were scattered over the area behind the manor's fence, as though a flock of a hundred crows had flown overhead.

"Are those crow feathers?" said Vance.

"It's a warning. Just in case we hadn't already figured out she has Roseanne." Dread stirred in my gut as I watched the mist swirl above the line where the spirit path overlapped with the field.

"I'll send a team of mages here at once," Vance said. "Ask them to watch in case anything comes out of the spirit line."

"The line goes through the whole city." I drove my heel into the rain-damp grass. "I'm the target, but if this is another attempt to break the veil, it'll be everyone's problem."

What was the banshee's game? She hadn't taken enough half-bloods for an army, but that didn't mean she didn't already have one waiting for her in the Vale. Would our word be enough to convince the council of that, though?

"I'll tell the mages," Vance said. "You call…"

"Isabel." *Focus, Ivy.* "I'll ask her to call Rick and ask if anything's up with the necromancers, too. Then I'm going in. You tell the mages to prepare for the worst and wait here. If I'm not back in an hour—"

"Absolutely not," said Vance. "I'm going with you."

"But you nearly *died* last time."

"So did you." His jaw set stubbornly. "We were unprepared when we went after the Lady of the Tree. This time we'll have iron, and you're more than a match for the banshee and any allies she might have gathered. You can alter the path through the Vale however you like now, can't you?"

"Yeah, in theory, but so can other faeries. The most powerful ones, anyway." I didn't know if the banshee qualified as such, but I'd already paid severely for underestimating her. "We'll need to be careful not to hurt any of the people the banshee captured, if they're with her, but what in hell does she need those kids for in the first place?"

Damn her. They were all changelings, transported from one world to another without true ties to either of them. Alison had taken advantage just like Calder, like every other faerie who saw people like Roseanne as nothing but pawns.

Fury ignited inside me and remained on a low simmer as we returned to the manor and made for the weapons room. I already had my twin iron daggers and my sword, but I added a spare knife to my coat pocket and a small container of iron filings to use in a pinch. I left all my spells behind except for healing charms, and those were more for Vance's benefit than mine. After the last time, I'd damn well be prepared for anything the Vale threw at us.

While Vance went into the meeting room to give the other mages instructions, I stayed in the hall and called Isabel.

"Damn, Ivy," she said, after I'd explained my overly eventful day. "You never catch a break, do you?"

"I was just thinking the same." I zipped my pocket one-handedly. "If Vance and I aren't back by nightfall, tell the coven to prepare for a potential attack from Faerie."

"Will do. I've spoken to Rick today already and he said the veil seems normal, but I'll ask him to watch out. Just—please be careful this time."

"I'll try." I'd make no promises. After my relentless slew of recent fuckups, it was on me to get us in and out of Faerie in one piece, Roseanne included. No pressure.

I ended the call and entered the back garden. Even from a distance, mist swirled above the field, pressing against the fences without crossing over the wards circling the mages' territory. It wasn't hard to imagine ghosts already material-ising within the misty haze as the veil split at the seams.

Vance strode to my side. "Ready?"

"Yeah. Hang onto me. I wouldn't put it past Faerie to try and separate us."

His hand squeezed mine. "I'm going nowhere."

I hugged him, because I didn't know when I'd next get the chance. Then we vanished, reappearing within the mist smothering the field.

Death was a step away. I felt the familiar tug as my body tried to stay behind and braced myself, aiming for the path that lay on the other side.

Then I held Vance tight and pulled us both into the Grey Vale.

13

Death's haze of grey mist was a familiar sight, but the horrible noise that ripped through my eardrums was a new feature. Screaming, not from the banshee but from the terrified faces that flashed before my eyes and disappeared before I could get a close enough look at them.

My back hit the ground, knocking the breath from my lungs. Vance groaned next to me and I quickly let go of his hand. I'd grabbed tight enough to draw blood.

"Sorry." I got to my feet, withdrawing Helena from its sheath. The blade hummed with a pleased resonance at being back in the realm of its creation, but my ears rang with echoes of the screams I'd heard. "Did you hear that?"

"No. I didn't hear anything." Vance stood, dusting silvery leaves off his coat, and pulled out his sword. I hoped he'd brought plenty of iron, because his mage powers were beyond reach here.

"We just passed through Death, and there was... screaming." I rubbed my ears. "Like the spirits were being tormented."

"No. I didn't hear anything."

"I'll pin that one on the banshee, too." She wasn't here, but I hadn't expected us to land directly on top of her location. Silver-leafed trees grew thick, forming a canopy of interlocking branches which allowed only the faintest trickle of light through. The silvery leaves on the path and the branches shone with an ethereal glow that only served to make the shadows between the trees look even more menacing.

"It always looks the same?" Vance observed.

"Yeah, this is the default setting." I gave the trees a cursory glance. "I can ask the Vale to take us to a certain place, if it exists, but I've never found anyone else unless they wanted me to."

"You've never used a tracking spell here before?"

"No, but if you can't use your mage abilities to get around, I doubt a spell would work. The only spell I've successfully used here is a healing spell." When I'd tried to save his life from the Lady of the Tree's thorns. Skin prickling, I shoved the unwelcome images away. "If I had to guess, we can use non-faerie magic on ourselves, but not on anything that belongs to Faerie. Including its inhabitants."

"That makes sense," Vance said. "That's why I was able to use my ability on both of us the last time."

"Don't remind me." My nails bit into my palms, recalling the sharp sting of thorns as Vance had displaced me out of a deadly trap and nearly died in my place. "I'll ask it to take us to Roseanne, for starters. She won't have any influence here."

I think. In truth, I didn't know the extent of her own capabilities, or whether she'd entered this realm of her own volition rather than being taken as a captive. If all death fae shared the same ability, maybe she'd only needed some instruction to do so herself.

Take me to Roseanne, I thought as we began to walk. *Take me to her.*

The Vale obliged. The path sloped upward beneath our feet, the trees growing further and further apart on each side until they vanished altogether. The path flattened, becoming a bridge stretching into the distance over a sea of clouds that bore a chilling resemblance to the place where I'd fought the Lady of the Tree.

"Okay… that's new."

The bridge didn't look at all sturdy, its edges as wispy and insubstantial as smoke. Vance hissed out a breath. Behind us, the route downhill had vanished beneath a similar haze, and I had little doubt that the path we'd walked here on no longer existed.

"This is all probably an illusion," I muttered to Vance. "Like that pond the Vale tried to dump us in the last time. If we do fall, I'll use my magic."

I trusted in my talisman's power a damn sight more than I trusted anything the Vale placed before us.

I led the way. Vance followed more slowly, a tight expression on his face. Worry for him scraped at my insides, but I reminded myself that we'd both come into this knowingly, and unlike the last time, we were prepared for the Vale's trickery.

The bridge narrowed until we had to walk single file, and the cloudy mass below might have concealed a giant shifter god for all I knew. I was so focused on watching for ambushes that I didn't see the castle until Vance pointed out the large shape silhouetted against the fog like a mountain dotted with turrets.

"Why is it always castles?" I gave an eye-roll. "Whose territory have we wandered onto this time, I wonder?"

We continued onward. The clouds surrounding the

bridge darkened to grey, and indistinct faces began to appear within.

"Really original," I muttered. "Don't look too closely at those. I bet they'll change to mimic people you know."

Vance gave a faint snarl and took my hand, his claw rough against my skin. "Is this the banshee's work?"

"Probably." Or the Vale itself had decided to screw with me. "The dead often hang about here, but I'm inclined to believe they're as much an illusion as the bridge."

An unmistakeable cry of terror ripped through the sky. Vance's grip on my hand tightened but neither of us quickened our pace in pursuit of the source of the noise. The cry turned to sobbing, but I ground my teeth together and walked on.

"Even if it's a real person, the odds of us saving everyone in here are low," Vance said. "I know you saved Roseanne before, but—"

"This isn't the place for heroism. I know. Learned the hard way in my first week here. There was this kid—" I cut myself off, shoving the memories away before Faerie used them against me. This was the absolute worst place to dwell on the past, especially when the faces appearing amid the smoke gained a veneer of familiarity.

Helena's face stared up from among the dead, and I shook my head violently. No... I *had* saved her. I'd helped her escape, helped her move through the afterlife into the next world.

"This is cheap trickery," I said loudly. "Including the screaming. Let's go."

We'd only taken a few steps when a dark cloud darted ahead of us, coalescing from wisps into a larger shape that entirely blocked the bridge.

"What is that?" Vance stilled, lifting his blade. "A ghost?"

"Close." The pillar of darkness warped into a more

human-like form. "It's a wraith. Think a super-powered ghost formed entirely of concentrated power left behind by the dead."

Vance swore under his breath. None of his weapons were any use against a ghost. My sword would more than suffice, but the never-ending drop on either side of the cloudy bridge did not inspire confidence.

I called my magic to form a shimmering shield as the wraith rushed forward to meet us. Every hair on my arms stood on end when a breath of icy wind slammed into the barrier I'd conjured. I raised Helena, stepping in front of Vance and stalking towards my enemy. The wraith's shape was humanoid, but there were long claws visible amid the grey. Whether that meant it had been a shapeshifter faerie in life or that the Vale was throwing another illusion at me was impossible to tell.

The wraith swept upward, claws raking at my face. I swung my blade at empty air as the creature dissipated into smoke then reformed itself behind us. Vance stiffened, knowing his iron weapons would leave no impact, and that now he was between me and the monster instead of the other way round.

You won't get us that easily. Treading lightly, I skirted around Vance, who held my waist to stop me from falling over the edge. I spared him a grateful glance and reached the monster on the other side. The light of my magic grew brighter as I focused on drawing upon the Vale's relentless store of misery and despair. The faces I saw might be illusions, but the dead lingered here in the Vale, and their rage knew no bounds.

The wraith swung a claw, eliciting a bone-deep chill where it touched my forehead. Helena's blade passed through its ghostly form, but I hadn't put enough power into the swing to take the beast out. As I readied myself to swipe again, Vance's clawed hand latched onto my arm.

"Ivy," he said through gritted teeth. "Watch where you tread."

I glanced down and saw the bridge had turned transparent. Rather than smoky cloud, the overlapping shapes of open-mouthed ghosts formed the ground beneath our feet.

The chill of the beast's touch deepened into a more primal terror, and my body's fight-or-flight reaction warred with the commonsense realisation that there was nowhere to run and that the Vale would dearly love for me to go plummeting straight over the edge.

In my moment's hesitation, the wraith dissolved once again, this time reappearing between Vance and me. Both of us took a step back, lifting our weapons.

"Bastard." I braced my feet, telling my unconvinced body that I was standing on solid ground. "Why do none of you know when to just *die*?"

I drove the blade through the wraith's smoky form. Knife-like teeth stretched in a mouth wide enough to devour me whole. I tapped into the screaming desperation of the dead, real or not, pouring their anger and terror and despair into the blade.

The wraith shattered into a pillar of light.

I staggered, but Vance's arm circled my waist, steadying me before I reached the edge. A glance told me the bridge had turned to cloud again, and no ghostly faces stared up at me.

"I knew it." My own curses flew back at me in a series of eerie howls, which I ignored as I marched ahead across the bridge.

Vance followed, without a word. A thin layer of sweat coated his forehead, and his mouth was pressed in a thin line.

Abruptly the bridge ran out and deposited us on a path

that looked identical to the one which we'd left. The same one, for all we knew. *The Vale strikes again.* And there was still no sign of the bloody banshee.

Vance didn't let go of my hand once until the clouds had disappeared. "The next time you feel like walking onto a bridge here, Ivy," he said, "don't."

"Don't worry, I'm striking this place off my list of ideal holiday destinations." I leaned against him, steadying myself against his warm, solid presence. Claws scraped my wrist, a reminder that he hadn't let down his guard. His expression was almost feral when I met his eyes, as if he knew this place brought the animal out in everyone, and if he couldn't use magic, he'd rely on his shifter side. Anything to keep me safe. Damn if it didn't warm my heart.

At least, until we saw the first bodies.

A few steps along the path, we came across a dark trail. Thick blood, not quite dried, splattered the silvery leaves. A teenage girl lay sprawled, her mouth stretched open in a scream, her torso split open to expose her innards. Nearby were two boys of the same age, both bearing wounds deep enough to split flesh and splinter bone.

"I... they're not fae." Their bodies were a mangled mess, with enough of their insides visible for me to see that their organs had been removed. Devoured, like Liam, like the others. I swallowed bile and looked away.

"Half-bloods," Vance said softly.

"Shit."

I forced my gaze back to the bodies, to look for Roseanne, but her face didn't leap out at me among the dead. There were at least a dozen half-bloods, a mixture of Summer and Winter, but the only magic visible were thick trails of blue Winter magic hovering around the bodies.

"Roseanne?" I called quietly. "Roseanne, are you here?"

"You shouldn't have come." She stumbled out from

behind a tree, covered in blood, and dropped to her knees, lifting her hands over her head. *She's alive.* Relief arose, tempered by wariness. I couldn't afford to trust my senses here.

"I came here to find you," I called to her. "Where's the banshee?"

"Gone." She lowered her hands—or claws. Blood stained them to the elbows. Her face was streaked crimson with tear tracks on both cheeks. "Go away."

"Come with us." I took a few steps closer, one eye on the corpses strewn across the leafy carpet. "While she's gone. Your father wanted me to keep you safe."

"So what?" she shot at me. "He's dead."

"So are these people." Every hair on my body stood on end as a chill swept through my nerves. "This realm is dead, too. Surely you can feel it."

"It's too late, Ivy." She took in a shuddering breath. "Why wouldn't you listen when I told you to leave me the hell alone?"

She lunged. On instinct, I brought up my sword in a wide arc and snagged her sharp claw on the edge. She screamed when the blade drew blood, but I'd held back, avoiding a fatal blow.

"I knew it." Vance's own clawed hands were wrapped around one of his iron blades. "You've been working against us all along, haven't you?"

Goddammit. Just for once, I'd like to believe the best of someone and actually turn out to be right. "Why do it? Why this?"

Cradling her injured talon to her chest, she scooted back a few steps. "You were too late, Ivy. She came to me weeks ago."

"You said you had a protective charm."

She lowered her gaze, her mouth pinching at the corners. "I lied."

A tittering laugh came from behind me. "I can't believe you actually followed me here, Ivy."

Magic blazed around me, forming a bright shield, as the banshee strode out behind the bodies of the people she'd slaughtered. No, the people she'd made *Roseanne* slaughter, I was sure. Not a single drop of blood covered her black silken dress or her porcelain skin, and her glossy hair shone almost as bright as her Unseelie-blue eyes.

"You," I snarled. "You were pulling her strings, weren't you?"

"You didn't have to make it so hard for her," she said. "She's pliant, but you made her doubt herself. I couldn't have that. I needed her. There aren't many harbingers left."

"I really wouldn't push me," I said in a low voice. "What the hell is your game? Fionn's dead. You were free to make your own life. You didn't have to use it up like this."

"None of us are free, human," said the banshee. "Our souls are bound to Faerie. To our home."

"Then why did you go to the trouble of deposing the Chief and starting a riot in the mortal realm," I informed her. "Why'd you even want half-blood territory if you just planned to ditch them and then slaughter anyone who came with you? Seems in poor taste when they offered themselves up to fight at your side."

"My people are more useful dead than alive." The banshee gave me a smile. "Did you truly think I aspired sit on the Chief's mockery of a throne? Why stay in the mortal realm when our home is there to be reclaimed? For centuries, we've suffered under the tyranny of the Courts, ostracised or forced into exile. No more."

"You aren't centuries old."

She let out a derisive laugh. "Didn't you know banshees

are reborn if they die? That means it doesn't matter if you kill me, Ivy. I'll come back."

Damn. If she was centuries old, it explained why she didn't talk like the average sixteen-year-old, at least, but made her manipulation of the other half-faeries even more repellent.

"I can kill your pet." I glanced sideways at Roseanne, who flinched.

"Be my guest." Her smile widened. "She's outlived her usefulness. She was willing to help me from the start—willing to turn on her mortal father and punish him for abandoning her, even—and it'll give me some satisfaction to see *you* take her life, Ivy, after all you've done to keep her safe."

"She killed Liam. It was her."

Roseanne studied her feet, blood dripping from her arm. Despite the talons, she looked vulnerable. Young.

"Cried while she did it, too. My furies had to do most of the work, in the end."

"I fucking knew it was the furies." Heat blazed under my skin as my magic awakened in blue fire.

"They're more reliable than hellhounds. More loyal. The hellhounds refused to listen to my call."

That's funny, because they were happy to befriend me. Maybe she didn't know, and I sure as hell wouldn't enlighten her. The furies were more than enough of a threat, and Roseanne's betrayal drove a knife into my chest. She'd even turned on her own father, but what choice had the banshee given her? I'd been willing to allow that Alison was as much a confused kid as Roseanne was, albeit a dangerous one, but knowing the truth of her longevity cemented the notion that she'd known exactly what she was doing when she'd set up the other half-faeries to die. She'd never believed them to be her equals.

Magic flared to life in my hands, and I aimed a killing blow—not at Roseanne, but at the banshee.

The ground gave way beneath my feet, and I fell. Air whipped past, tearing at my hair, and the banshee's maniacal laughter pursued me as I tumbled into the abyss. I stopped falling the instant my magic caught up with me, conjuring a shimmering blue shield that steadied me like a net.

My breath escaped in gasps, and I looked up to see Vance still on the path above, his claws at the banshee's throat. I shook my head frantically when he caught my eye, warning him not to waste his power on me when I could get out by myself.

I pushed upward from my shield and used it to propel myself upward, soaring out of the temporary pit.

I landed in front of the banshee and blasted her with magic. She flew back, head over heels, right into the path of Vance's claws. Blood spurted, red and vibrant blue, dripping onto the silvery leaves and mingling with that of the half-bloods she'd killed.

"Go on," she goaded. "Taking my life will only make me stronger."

"I wouldn't be so sure." I lifted my blade, keeping an eye on the path in case she threw me into another pit. "You *know* Fionn was a liar. He didn't care about you any more than his other slaves."

"You're still using the past tense." She laughed. "Fionn wants to thank you for disposing of the ring for him."

My heart missed a beat. *No. He's dead.* "Yeah, the ring's gone. You can't use it against me, or against my realm."

"Your realm would have been a small price to pay. You'd have stood at Fionn's side as an honoured queen."

I'd had enough. I nodded to Vance, and his claws drove forward, pinning the banshee to the tree. She screamed, high and loud, as blood streamed down her chest, but he'd held off on dealing a killing blow. Striding to his side, I gave him a nod and pressed the tip of my blade to her throat.

"Go ahead." She bared bloodied teeth at me. "It's pointless, you know."

"Not yet." Sure, she wouldn't stay dead for long, but she'd wrecked too many lives already, and her demise might win me the chance to get Roseanne away. "That's a risk I'm willing to take."

Movement behind me. I twisted the blade to the side as Roseanne flew at me in her full shapeshifter form, wings splayed, her talons glancing off the back of my jacket.

"Stay out of this," I warned. "I'll bet *you* won't be reborn when you die."

She reeled back from me, desperation shining in her eyes. "I—I can't let you kill her. He—"

"Is already here." The banshee laughed, the sound turning into a scream of delight. My ears burned, my hands trembling on the blade.

Vance snarled a warning, his claws no longer pinning the banshee to the tree. Beside the bodies of the fallen half-faeries, a column of smoke formed, thicker than the clouds, and solidified into a fearsome figure with glass-like bright-blue eyes.

Fionn was a wraith.

Apparently, my brain had reached peak "what the fuck?", because I just stared at him for a good ten seconds while the banshee lay in a bloodied heap and Roseanne shrank back into her human form and backed away from the new arrival.

"Ivy Lane," he said. "You'll come to regret taking my life."

14

M y tongue unstuck itself from the roof of my mouth. "No," I said. "I'm not interested in talking to you. Go haunt someone else."

Fionn laughed. His transparent form became more distinct, less like a smoky cloud and more like a spirit seen in Death—except infinitely more intimidating than any other ghost I'd set eyes on. His wraith form was as formidable as the body he'd worn in life—huge, at least six and a half feet tall, broad and dangerous. Inhuman, and not in an attractive way. Sure, he was objectively handsome, if you didn't mind the serial killer vibe. Which I did. His blue eyes gleamed with Winter magic even in death. "But Ivy, we had such a strong rapport. It seems a pity to cut our relationship short so soon."

"Don't fuck with me." I gave him a hard stare. "What the hell was the point in going to the trouble of recruiting all those half-faeries and then having your allies kill them?"

"Most of them were glad to offer their lives to a worthy cause."

"Does that include these two?" I indicated the banshee,

who half-leaned against the tree with blood streaming from the claw wounds to her chest, and Roseanne, crouched on the ground with her arms over her head as though she wished she could dissolve into smoke like a spirit.

"It's thanks to Alison here that I will live again."

"I've heard this shit before," I said. "You're dead. Existing as a wraith hardly counts as living. Even your hellhounds are coming to me, not you."

He laughed. "Hellhounds. And yet you insist we are nothing alike."

"For one thing, I'm alive, and you're not even a proper ghost." Bravado aside, I didn't know what he was capable of as a spirit. Who was to say how many of his abilities Fionn had brought with him into the afterlife? "If you want to make yourself useful, you can offer an apology to the Seelie Court for stealing their ring."

"You spoke to the Court."

"Yes, I did, and they're incredibly pissed off at you." Or they would be, when they realised the extent of the threat he presented. "What's the point in coming back? I doubt your army will listen to a wraith."

"That's where you're wrong." He gestured, and the trees parted on one side of the path, revealing a gap large enough to show the same castle I'd seen from the bridge.

"So many souls," he whispered. "So many changelings eager to join my army."

"You have half-bloods in the castle?" My heart contracted, and though the castle was far enough away for me not to be able to make out its features, its silhouette took on a sickening familiarity. "I thought you killed them all."

"Oh, these are the ones who were cowardly enough to try to run." He gave a careless gesture towards the bodies lying on the path. "The ones inside the castle will serve in my army."

You sick bastard. My hands clenched, but I hadn't a hope of running to the castle's doors before Fionn or one of his allies stopped me.

"You'll get to see my castle up close soon, Ivy, but we'll save that for later." He waved a hand and the trees closed in again, tighter.

Vance snarled, and I had no doubt that his claws would be at Fionn's throat if he'd been in corporeal form. Nobody could touch Fionn as he was now—except me. I gripped my sword's hilt, assessing the best way out with minimal damage. Taking out the banshee first would rid him of a temporary ally, but if he threw Roseanne into my path, it'd be an impediment. Maybe Vance could stall—

Fionn blew through me like a tempest, and pain racked my body from head to toe as though I'd plunged into an icy lake. My muscles seized up, my legs locking into place, no longer able to stand or fall but suspended in pain. I bit down on another scream, tightening my grip on the handle of my blade but unable to move.

Vance's roar of fury cut through the haze; as I watched, his blade passed through Fionn's transparent form. My scream of pain turned into a warning as his ghostly hand reached for Vance instead of me, and I seized the chance to call upon my own magic.

My sword glowed brighter, the blue glow enveloping my body. The talisman fed on the pain, but more than that, a spasm of disconnected rage arose, a reminder that my own magic hated Fionn with a deep loathing that went beyond description.

I broke through the chill and drove my blade into the gap where his heart had been. My blade left no impact, but blue light engulfed Fionn, bright enough to dazzle the eyes. Yet his shadowy outline remained intact.

Come on. I've killed a ghost before. More than once.

"Just fucking die already," I said through gritted teeth. Beads of icy sweat trickled down my back. The sword glowed bright enough to dazzle my eyes, but if anything, Fionn looked bored. "I told you before that your magic recognises me as an equal. We're on the same side, even if you don't know it yet, Ivy."

"I'll never stand with the dead over the living." My sword dropped a little. The echo of the pain rang through my bones. "And if you came back from the dead just to spout monologues at me, you're wasting your time."

Vance moved to my side, wielding an iron blade in both clawed hands.

"Don't bother to exert yourself, Mage Lord," he said. "Or is it shifter? The Mage Council has changed much since our last encounter. I remember their views on half-breeds well."

Vance made a low, angry noise. "Don't you dare speak of those you slaughtered in cold blood."

Fionn flashed him a smile. "So you did tell your lover, Ivy. I wondered if you would."

I ignored him. Yes, I'd told Vance that Fionn was most likely his parents' killer, because if I'd been him, I'd want to know the truth. Except if Fionn remembered he'd been the one who killed the Mage Lords, that meant...

Fionn's smile widened when he saw the realisation dawn on me. "I remember everything, Ivy. That's why I'll win this time."

Damn him. He had his memories back? How? "I'm pretty sure you *lost* the war, Fionn."

"Oh, I can see the curiosity is killing you, Ivy," he said softly. "You want to know how I regained access to my memories, and I'll be generous and answer for free. You see, I had to leave my physical body behind to be loosed from the tricky spells that bound me. You didn't truly think a god of death could ever truly die, did you?"

"I kinda hoped you would." My body locked to the spot again, this time not from his magic but from pure unadulterated horror at our predicament. To my knowledge, nobody—Sidhe or human—had full recollection of the events surrounding the invasion. Fionn had been left imprisoned, sleeping in a tomb, and when he'd awoken, only the fact that he'd had no memory of his previous existence had prevented him from unleashing a repeat performance.

Until death had removed him from the chains on his body locking his memories out.

Had this been his plan all along? His first goal had been to get rid of the ring, and while I'd managed to dispose of it without sacrificing the mortal realm as collateral damage, the fact remained that his one weakness was now off the playing field. If he'd willingly sacrificed his life knowing he'd be reborn, and knowing that he'd come back with full access to the memories he'd lost...

He wanted this. In his previous life, he'd ferried the Sidhe's souls to the afterlife. I'd known he had some special relationship to Death, known he'd considered himself a god, but I'd let myself believe that he held the same weaknesses as any Sidhe. That death was the end.

Fionn laughed. "I have to admit, it's refreshing to see you cowed into silence, Ivy Lane."

"You're hardly the first ghost I've killed." I lifted my blade again. "Want to finish this here, or in your castle?"

"What, without your mage?" Fionn laughed, louder. "I can't believe you brought a mortal here. You must know this realm is a poison."

"Must be why the only people who'll willingly ally with you are revolting clawed monsters from the abyss."

"Revolting clawed monsters." His voice resounded with delight. "Did you hear that, mage? Did she ever tell you she finds your shifter form repellent?"

"Shut the hell up," I snarled. "Shifters aren't fucking *furies*."

"Stop talking," Vance added. "You're less than the lowest spirit. Let the half-bloods go."

Unspoken words drifted between us. I knew he wanted to leave, to abandon what was bound to be a futile rescue attempt before we both met a grisly end. But he knew my desire to rescue Roseanne and the other surviving half-faeries would win out over self-preservation.

"You can't save them, you know." Behind Fionn, the trees briefly parted again, revealing the towering castle within which he kept his army. Or prisoners. "I'm a little surprised a Mage Lord would risk so much for the offspring of those who did so much damage to your own realm, but humans have always confused me. For instance, here you are, instead of at home protecting your own people."

"I'm here with Ivy," Vance said to him.

"And you're stalling," I added to Fionn. "Throw it at me. Give me all you've got."

"Very well." He nodded to Roseanne. "Kill them."

The words vibrated in the air, taut as a bowstring. *A vow. She's bound by a vow.*

"Run and hide!" I yelled at her. "Fight it!"

Roseanne screamed as the transformation took hold of her. Jagged black wings sprouted from her back and her taloned arms extended, though tears dripped down her still-human face.

I threw a shield in front of Vance and me and lifted my blade. Thrumming vibrations reminded me of my magic's instinctive murderous reaction to Fionn's presence, but killing Roseanne would be playing into his hands.

"Now who's stalling, Ivy?" said Fionn.

"Nah, I'm just deciding who to kill first."

My blade glowed brighter, feeding on the pain of the dead, the magic longing to burst free and obliterate Fionn. Instead, I lifted my blade and leapt at the banshee.

She screamed, high and loud, her own death knell ringing through the trees long after my strike severed her head from her neck. Her body half-transformed, talons flailing and turning into hands and then back again as she died.

Roseanne screamed, too. Wings beating, she threw her arms—one still bleeding—over her face. Was she fighting the vow? Nobody could escape such a command, and the effort would rip her apart. I'd have to watch her die.

God help me. She'd killed her father, slaughtered so many others, yet she'd been manipulated. Like every other half-faerie who'd been lured into this realm. I couldn't let her destroy herself.

"Don't!" I warned. "You'll die."

"Maybe I want to die. It'll only make me stronger."

Would she come back like the banshee? "Even if that's true, it's going to be very painful and unpleasant."

"I can't—" she snarled, her wings and talons back out. "You're lying. Fionn isn't, not like the others. He *can* help us be reborn."

"You don't mean anything to him." I fed more magic into my shield as she threw herself at me, fetching up against a barrier of shimmering magic. "He used you, same as he used the banshee. His only real allies are those monstrous furies. Even the hellhounds don't want to be associated with him any longer."

I didn't want to kill her, even now, but getting rid of Fionn seemed the only way to free her from the vow he'd forced on her. His ghostly form hovered on the side, watching eagerly as Roseanne beat her clawed fists against my shield.

I pushed my shield outward, feeding my rage into its glow and knocking Roseanne flat on her back. Then I threw myself at Fionn's ghost.

His hand closed around my wrist before my sword could pierce his ghostly chest. "Really, Ivy, I'm disappointed."

"Let go." I twisted, pain burning up my arm at his icy touch, and broke free of him.

Roseanne sprang to her feet. Her wings beat once, and Vance moved in and seized her from behind. His arms closed around her, pinning her wings to her back and stopping her from launching herself at me. He had plentiful experience with restraining mages whose power had escaped their control, and try as she might, Roseanne was unable to free herself.

Fionn sighed. "You're both wasting your time."

"So are you," I said. "What do you want, me to join you in the afterlife forever? Because trust me, I'd rather eat dirt."

"I will not be in this state for much longer." His eyes gleamed with a mixture of amusement and malice. "I have a thousand lives I haven't lived yet, and I hold the Huntsman's magic. As long as that remains the case, I will always endure, and I will always be reborn."

"And just when will this be?" If he believed he'd be reborn into a new body, that body had to come from somewhere, right? The same went for the banshee, but I didn't know nearly enough about the death fae to say anything with certainty.

"That's for me to know." He wore a wide grin. "It's too late for you to stop me. I remember every moment of the invasion, every mistake and misstep, and I will allow none of them to occur again."

"You're lying." Vance growled at my side. "You were imprisoned during the invasion, not after. You weren't awake to witness its end."

Thank you, Vance. He'd offered a welcome reminder that Fionn was a liar whether he had his memories or not. "You can't remember what you never witnessed in the first place, and I bet not all of your allies survived."

They couldn't have. At the very least, Vance had mentioned that Lady Harper had killed two Sidhe personally, and more would have been killed in the battle that had ended in the Mage Lords' deaths. The Sidhe might have taken out half of humanity in the process, but there'd been casualties on both sides.

"Oh, yes, Mage Lord." Fionn's mouth twisted into a cruel smile. "I remember it well. They did put up a valiant fight… they were all too willing to sacrifice their lives to a futile cause."

Vance didn't make a sound, but the colour had drained from his face, and the scales crept higher up his arms.

Fionn turned his smile to me. "You did me a favour, Ivy. Not just in enabling me to regain my memories, but in destroying the ring, you've given me a second chance to bring about the end of your fellow humans with my own hand. Watching your realm fall to the Devourer would have been amusing, I'll grant you, but there's something vicariously satisfying in the act of destruction, wouldn't you agree?"

"Yet here you are, taunting me instead of acting."

"I merely wanted to lay out my terms, Ivy," he said. "Your world will end. This is your last chance to decide. Stand with me or watch those you love perish."

"Get fucked," I said in answer.

Still laughing, Fionn's ghostly form dissolved, turning to smoke that swept over the ground. For the second time, the path fell out from underneath me—and Vance, too. Roseanne took flight from Vance's arms with a shriek as we both began to fall.

I reached for his hand, closing my eyes and trusting my magic to carry us home. We fell through grey, through nothingness, and emerged into a rain-drenched field below a grey sky thick with clouds.

"Well, that's it," I said. "We're utterly fucked."

15

"You aren't wrong." Next to me, Vance sat up. Rain trickled down his face in rivulets, and while the sky didn't appear any darker than earlier, the bruise-grey clouds made it impossible to tell how much time had elapsed since we'd left the mortal realm. "Fionn intends to be reborn… how, exactly?"

"Maybe possession, like Calder planned to." Calder had been more dangerous as a ghost than a human and Fionn might be the same, but Calder at least had been a known quantity. Fionn was another entity altogether.

"Of whom?" Vance enquired. "I doubt he'd lower himself to inhabiting the mortal body of a half-blood."

"Oh, shit. We left Roseanne." To top off our shit show of a mission, we'd left her behind in the Vale. It was too much to hope that she hadn't flown straight back to Fionn's side, out of the absence of any other options. "No, he'll want a pure faerie… a Sidhe. We have to warn Summer and Winter."

"Quentin," said Vance immediately. "He did promise to speak to the Summer Court."

"Yeah." I pushed to my knees, dampness soaking into my jeans from the grass. "Is anyone here… oh, it's Drake."

The fire mage ran towards us, his hood pulled up against the rain. "Is that you, Ivy?"

"What? Yeah, of course." I looked at Vance, then back at Drake. "What happened?"

Drake looked like he hadn't slept for a week. Stubble shadowed his face, and dark circles crouched under his eyes. "What happened is there are shapeshifter faeries all over the bloody city and you've been MIA."

"I did tell you we'd return within a day," said Vance.

"A day?" Drake exploded. "It's been three days. It's a good job you told me where you were going, because I've been fending off phone calls from other mages across the whole damn country. The head of the Mage Lords can't just vanish off the face of the earth."

"But… how?" I got to my feet. "Three days? We weren't there more than a couple of hours."

"What happened with half-blood territory?" Vance brushed wet grass off his coat as he rose upright. "Did the council make a decision?"

"Make a decision? They thought you were dead." Drake jabbed a finger at him. "Without you there, they're useless. *I* went to half-blood territory when I was looking around in case the veil spat you out in the wrong place, but all I found was a lot of injured half-faeries with no leadership."

"Yeah, that's why we went into the Grey Vale in the first place." My bruised and battered body seemed to think we'd been there longer, but the sky was the same shade of dismal grey as it had been before we'd left. "Wait, is the Chief—the last one—still in jail?"

"How the hell am I supposed to know? I've combed the whole damn city for the pair of you, in the pouring rain most of the time, and might I remind you *I* can't bloody teleport everywhere. Ivy Lane, this mess has your name written all over it."

"I don't get it. Time didn't pass that quickly the last time I was there."

"You're supposed to be an expert on the bloody faeries!" said Drake. "As for you, Vance Colton, approximately twenty-five major council members from across the country want to speak to you."

Vance began to walk, heading towards the manor's back garden. "That can wait. We need to put a security plan in place. We're facing numerous threats from the Grey Vale."

"Have you seen Quentin?" I asked Drake.

"No. Thought you fired him, Vance. Or you went off to Faerie together, for all I knew."

"He promised to bring help from the Summer Court," said Vance. "The Court certainly needs to know about this development, but even Quentin might not have known."

"Known what?" said Drake.

"Fionn's alive," I told him. "I mean, he's a ghost, but he's just as deadly in that state as he was when he had a body."

I told him the rest as we trudged back through the muddy field to the manor's rear entrance.

"And yes, I know I have to tell the council," I finished. "They'd better believe me this time. I'm not having a repeat of what happened with Calder."

"I'll tell them," Vance said. "You—"

"Should call Isabel, I know." I followed him through the back gate into the manor's garden. "It's lucky I told her we were going to Faerie."

"Call her," said Vance. "I'll update the council. They might ask to hear from you, but you should check with Isabel to see if the coven managed to help any of the half-faeries get away."

"Oh, they did," Drake said. "I checked in on her just in

case she knew where you were. I don't know everything that went down on half-blood territory, but some of them made it to the coven's old headquarters."

"Good." At least some had been spared, but it sounded like the rest of the half-faeries had fought themselves into exhaustion. "I'll ask her if the necromancers have had trouble, too. I wouldn't be surprised if this crap had knock-on effects on the veil."

"Figures." Drake walked ahead of us towards the manor, adding over his shoulder, "You know, I fucking *hate* the faeries."

"Welcome to the club." I hit the call button. "Hey, Isabel. Sorry, Faerie messed with time again. Vance and I just got back."

Isabel released a breath. "I hoped it was just Faerie's time delay. Did you find her?"

"Found her. Also found a shitload of problems. Among other things, she's doing Fionn's bidding. So was the banshee, before I stabbed her. Oh, and Fionn is alive, but I guess you inferred that from the first bit."

"Fionn…" she paused. "How? *Alive?*"

"Technically he's a wraith, so not strictly alive," I amended. "But he's alert enough to be a massive pain in the arse. And to have his memories of the invasion back."

A tense pause followed. "Oh, god, Ivy."

"Yeah, pretty much." I reached the patio behind the manor but didn't go inside. The rain sliding down my face cleared my head, made it easier to think. "I got Vance and me out, but Roseanne was left behind, and I didn't know we lost three days. I heard you convinced the coven to help the half-bloods?"

"Yeah, I've been dealing with that over the last few days," said Isabel. "We've put a few families up in Francine's old house. They're all absolutely terrified of what the banshee did. They're definitely not on her side."

"Good." My shoulders slumped with relief. "Oh, yeah, I should mention I killed her. The banshee, I mean."

"She really abandoned her throne? I should tell the half-bloods. They've been worried… but I don't know where the Chief is. According to them, he disappeared."

"From jail?" Better than being dead, but someone needed to restore order on half-blood territory who wasn't Vance or me. "He'll have to wait. Vance is going to update the council, and I expect they'll drag me in there, too. I'll have to go through the usual bullshit where I try to convince them the apocalypse is imminent and they tell me I'm mistaken."

"Is it?" Isabel's voice rose to a higher pitch. "But if Fionn's a ghost, that limits his ability to move around, doesn't it? He can't travel into this realm, can he?"

"He doesn't need to." I swallowed. "He has an army of half-bloods he coerced into joining his team. Roseanne wasn't the only one. And on top of that, she's the one who killed those mercenaries. On his orders. Her own father, too."

Isabel's breath caught. "That's sick."

"Yeah." The worst part was that Roseanne couldn't be my priority, not with Fionn directly threatening my loved ones. "He didn't tell me his plan, but he didn't expect me to show up, I don't think. He taunted me a bit, knowing I couldn't touch him as a ghost. Even my magic didn't leave a scratch on him. I don't know what else to do."

"Ivy, are you standing outside in the rain? Your teeth are chattering."

So they were. "Yeah. I don't want to go indoors and get waylaid by bullshit."

"Go in." Her voice took on a commanding edge. "Sit down. How long have you been on your feet? It's been more than a day for you, right?"

"God knows." I was running on adrenaline, but she was right. I'd crash soon, and then I wouldn't be of any use to anyone. "Fine, I'll go in."

"Do that," she said. "Powerful or not, Fionn *is* a ghost, and he's been defeated before."

"Sure would help to know how. Or who did it." Even Fionn himself might not remember, if he'd slept through that part. If only we'd had another eyewitness. One who wasn't a depraved megalomaniac. "See you in a bit?"

"No, you're going to eat something and go to sleep, and I'll see you tomorrow."

"All right, all right." I made for the back door. "See you soon."

"Ivy." Wanda met me inside the conservatory. I was glad she was back on her feet, though her face drained of colour when she saw me. "Er... do you want a cleansing spell or a drying spell?"

"Both. Neither." Now she'd made me aware of my own exhaustion, waves of tiredness lapped at me like an overly friendly dog. My clothes were soaked through. "Wanda, are you all right?"

"Yeah, *I'm* fine, but you..."

"Look like a drowned rat, I know." I released my sodden hair from its ponytail. "Did Vance already call the meeting?"

"Yes—he and Drake are upstairs with the rest of the council." Anxiousness pinched at her mouth. "I don't understand what's going on. I've been on bed rest for the last few days, but I heard some of it."

"Long story." I swayed on my feet. "I'll tell you, and then I think a need a nap."

———

My nap turned into a long one. I woke from dreams of Fionn riding around on a giant dragon when Vance pulled the necromancers' handbook I'd been using as a pillow out from under my head. I'd fallen asleep on the sofa in the back living room, and judging by the darkness shrouding the drawn curtains over the window, night had fallen.

I groaned. "Didn't mean to sleep all afternoon. Or evening. What time is it?"

"Late. I ordered dinner."

"You did?" Right. Quentin was—*don't go there, Ivy.* I sat up and let him pass me a tray of takeout Chinese food. "Where're the others?"

"Gone… mostly. Drake's taken the night watch. I made Wanda go and lie down. She's still recovering."

"You should take your own advice." I stretched my stiff neck and shivered. I'd thoroughly rinsed off the mud in the shower as well as employing a cleansing spell or two at Wanda's insistence, but I still felt the lingering touch of the veil on my skin.

"I know." He joined me, lifting the necromancer handbook in one hand. "What did you have this for?"

"Dunno. Must've left it lying around." I began shovelling chicken and rice into my mouth. "Did the meeting run overtime?"

"You might say that." Irritation underlaid his voice. "I also took a brief trip to half-blood territory."

"Ah." I half rose to my feet, but he rested a hand on my knee and pushed me back down. "Are they okay? I mean…"

"I didn't go inside, don't worry, but the fighting has stopped," he said. "We'll speak to them tomorrow. Same with the necromancers."

"I forgot to even ask Isabel how Rick was." I sat back down and resumed eating. "What else did the mages have to say?"

He paused, ate a few mouthfuls, then said, "Only that we're in no position to do anything about Fionn from this side."

"They did believe he's a threat, though."

"Of course. They also know what ghosts can be capable of, having witnessed it with their own eyes."

"It's a miracle." I gave an eye-roll. "It only took... what, four brushes with death for them to take our warnings seriously?"

"I have to admit I hoped the new council members would be a little more proactive than the previous ones," he said. "There are vanishingly few who qualify to hold Mage Lord status."

Even *that* was Fionn's fault, due to the massacre he'd perpetrated against the mages in the invasion. "Well, they need to get their shit together, asap. You should have woken me up so I could tell them so in person."

"You needed the rest."

"So do you," I retaliated. "They kept you for hours arguing, didn't they? And then they're going to call another meeting tomorrow morning and argue some more."

"They're also staying at the manor tonight, so I expect we'll get an early wakeup call."

"Yippee." I sighed. "I guess you gave me enough warning before I moved in here."

"You don't regret that choice?" His tone was light, but I detected a hint of uncharacteristic caution as though he wondered if I *did* have some regrets about embedding myself with the mages.

"Oh, no, I wouldn't miss out on the scheming and bickering for the world." I offered a smile to show I was joking, and I finished eating with a little more optimism despite the mire of shit we'd landed in. Vance was quieter than usual, but he was bound to be exhausted after returning from Faerie to a bunch of irate mages and no time for a power nap like I'd had. It didn't help that we kept running into signs of Quentin's absence from unwashed glasses to a pile of discarded papers someone had left in the upper corridor.

Vance picked up the papers, scanned them, and they vanished a moment later. "The other regions' mages aren't here yet, but they will be, if they deem this situation urgent enough. I'm not sure if it's worse than them staying away."

"Why?" I asked. "What's wrong with... oh, no. Lady Granville doesn't know what's going on, does she?"

"Unfortunately, it seems that Lady Penrose gave her a call," he said. "Lady Granville is still a Mage Lord, which gives her the authority to come back here if she sees fit, and I believe she's been telling the other regional Mage Lords that we're making rash choices without evidence."

"What does she want, us to drag Fionn's ghost through the Vale and shove him in her face to prove we're serious?" I followed him into the bedroom. "I doubt she'd trust *my* account, but she should have listened to you."

"She accused me of letting the situation slip out of my control due to the full moon and implied my shifter ancestry prevents me from making rational decisions."

I gasped. "Well, it's lucky for her that she wasn't here in person, else she wouldn't have walked away with her head still attached."

He didn't laugh.

I wrapped my arms around him, furious at the sheer indignity of her accusation. "That's total bullshit, Vance. Shifter blood doesn't mean anything."

"It does to some people. In some other regions, shifters don't have a voice on the supernatural council at all. To the mages, having shifter ancestry isn't looked on favourably. I suspect my father had to work hard to maintain his standing in the eyes of his fellow Mage Lords. Our nature is seen as a sign of instability. At the very least, it's unattractive."

"You, unattractive? Have you ever looked in a mirror?" I poked him in the shoulder. "Your mage ability probably freaks more people out than the claws do."

He lowered his gaze. "I did tell you I'm not entirely human, Ivy. That won't change no matter my position. In any case, some of the decisions I've made in my time on the mage council certainly come across as irrational to anyone who doesn't have the full picture. They think I'm stirring up unnecessary panic, and our last trip into Faerie didn't help matters at all."

"Please tell me you told her to go screw herself."

"I told her—and all the others—that Fionn started the invasion."

"Oh. They didn't know… right?" I'd told Vance, of course, but neither of us had felt that it was appropriate to share what amounted to a very educated guess with the council when the perpetrator was dead, or so we'd thought. There was no evidence but Fionn's own word.

"No. I made it clear the evidence suggests Fionn killed the Mage Lords in person, or Sidhe acting on his orders did. The others didn't dare challenge my claim."

"Damn." Very few of the current mages had witnessed the invasion in its entirety, because their entire front line had been all but wiped out. Even before he'd confirmed his involvement, I'd had little doubt that Fionn himself had been behind Vance's parents' deaths, as well as the massacre of which Vance had been the only survivor.

"Exactly." He leaned against the wall, his face drawn and exhausted. "They won't dare call me a liar for claiming that we saw his ghost, but we don't have a clear picture of his plan and there's no procedure for a hypothetical situation. The city is already set up to face more disruption to the veil, but we don't have an attack force to take into the Vale itself. Drake and I made that suggestion but were outvoted on the grounds that most mages' abilities will likely not work to their full effect in Faerie. And I have no authority over the other supernaturals."

"Sure, but they really ought to respect you more than that." Seeing his hands were half-hidden behind his back, I remembered Fionn's comment earlier about my supposed distaste for shapeshifting. "So you can shift your hands into claws. Big deal."

I ran a finger over the rough scales that extended to his elbows. Curved claws replaced his hands, the same dark grey shade as his scales. It didn't look like he was stuck halfway through a transformation. The scales blended seamlessly with his skin like a pair of gloves.

"See?" I said, as the claws flickered and turned back to skin. "That dragon shifter god is a scary bastard, but you're relatively harmless."

"Relatively harmless?" There was a mock-insulted note to his tone, and I was relieved to see a familiar gleam in his eyes. The claws that came out when he fought were a sight I'd grown as used to as his mage powers, and it hadn't occurred to me that he might still feel insecure about me seeing them in any other context. But shifters' abilities weren't just predatory, they were fixated on protecting the people closest to them, at any cost to themselves. What Vance thought of as an unattractive trait was one of the reasons I loved him.

"By the way, we aren't competing on screw-ups," I told him. "I let a half-blood under my watch get away and might have caused the apocalypse."

"Fionn planned it that way. It's not your fault."

"You think this is it? No second chances this time?"

"I think there's a strong possibility this is the last chance

I'll have to touch you for a while." He slid claw-free hands over my body and kissed me fiercely.

My hands wound into his hair as I kissed him back, and a breeze caressed my skin, stripping the clothes from me, layer by layer. A moan slipped from my mouth as the feather-light sensation brushed against my aching centre and then slid between my breasts.

"Oh—*Vance.*"

"I want to feel you," he said huskily. "I want to be inside you."

"You're making a damn good argument." I slid my hand underneath his shirt. "You're wearing too many clothes, though."

The breeze intensified, and between one breath and the next, we were on the bed, both unclothed, his body braced above mine. My hands explored his chest, moving south until I slid my hand up and down the length of him and heard his groan of pleasure.

His fingers settled between my legs and stroked my inner thighs until I rocked into him. Pleasure coiled tight inside me, threatening to unravel as we moved in time with one another, lost in sensation. Warm tingles spiralled down my spine in waves, and electricity ignited at my nerve endings. I moved faster, gripping his hips with my hands. My body clenched around him and I screamed, a hoarse cry of relief. His answering shudder came moments later.

We lay in a breathless tangle, my head resting on his chest.

"For the record," I said, "I like your claws. They're part of you, and I love you."

Vance made a faint noise of quiet contentment and pulled me close to him, and I fell asleep with my head buried in the crook of his neck.

16

"We're completely screwed," Drake said the following morning. "Sure, *we* know Fionn is a threat, but Lady Granville spent the whole night telling the other regional mages we're talking bollocks."

"You'd think being deposed from one council would disqualify her from influencing the others."

The three of us, plus Wanda, had gathered in the back of the main room over breakfast for a brief moment of calm before we went out to deal with whatever new shitstorm had erupted in the city overnight. The fact that Quentin being absent meant that Drake had nearly set the kitchen on fire trying to make toast did not help the general mood. He hadn't even needed to use his mage powers.

"You'd think." Drake half-heartedly bit into a piece of burnt toast. "Is there nothing to do but wait for him to show up here?"

"No, we need allies," Vance said. "Preferably ones on the same power level as Fionn."

"Which don't exist," Drake put in. "You forgot that small detail."

"Except the Hemlock Coven, maybe." Not that they were a viable option, given their confinement to the forest. "Or Quentin's Court."

Right. I need to get hold of the slippery little bastard. Nobody knew where he was, including Vance, but he inclined his head in agreement. "Yes, both are worth trying. We'll visit half-blood territory first."

"Assuming there's anyone around who hasn't given up hope." I took a last bite of toast and put my plate aside. "I don't know where Fionn got his army from, but the banshee can't have taken more than a dozen people with her, and most of them got killed."

"Maybe he was lying," Drake said hopefully. "Or... shit, the Sidhe can't lie, can they?"

"No, but who the hell knows with Fionn." I rose to my feet, brushing crumbs from my jeans. "Right. You have another council meeting later? I'm surprised they didn't drag you out of bed at the crack of dawn."

"I asked to schedule the meeting for later so we could both attend." Vance took my arm. "I suspected we'd have a few errands to run first. Drake, make sure the other mages are all accounted for."

"Got it, boss. If Lady Granville calls, I'll tell her where to shove her evidence."

"Don't," Vance said, though he sounded as if he very much wanted to say the same. "If she does call, tell her I'll be available later. She'll know we're dealing with an ongoing emergency."

"I can't believe she's still trying to interfere." Her demotion ought to have disqualified her from seeking power elsewhere, but she was as slippery as a bloody Sidhe and had wrangled her way onto a council with an open spot to fill and a need for someone with experience. Now, it seemed, she wanted to resume her attempts to undermine Vance and his new council. "She's not even here. She can't speak with any authority as to what we're dealing with."

Not that the council had seen Fionn with their own eyes like Vance and I had, and we had the added problem of not knowing where he'd strike first.

To start off with, Vance transported us both to half-blood territory. The gates were wide open, unguarded, and the territory itself appeared deserted at first glance. Hardly a trace remained of the bitter fight I'd left behind. The rain had washed the blood away from the yellowing grass, and the plants that had sprouted from the abundant magic flying around were drooping and dead. Normally, being on half-blood territory sent my senses into overdrive, but the only smell was a faint aroma of rot, and not a sound disturbed the silence. My skin prickled.

We walked further in. I held my sword high, its glow positioned to draw attention to me. The banshee's death left the surviving half-bloods living here without a leader, and while there was a slim chance the original Chief had survived the carnage, he might be their sole option to regain any sense of stability.

Several minutes had passed before I saw another person. When we neared the apartment blocks—the ones the banshee had left standing—a young girl peered out of the bushes, spotted us, and ducked back in with a whimper.

"I'm not here to hurt you," I told the girl. "I just wanted to know what happened here."

Hesitantly, she raised her head. A bushy squirrel tail poked out of the bush behind her. She was maybe twelve or thirteen, with blond spiky hair around her pointed face.

"They all vanished," she said. "And the woods… *moved*."

I blinked. "Moved?"

"Back there." She lifted a trembling hand. "Wait, you're Ivy, aren't you?"

"Yeah, I am." Where in hell was the Chief? "Is the prison still standing? Is the Chief still alive?"

"I don't know. I can't get through."

That did not sound promising. "I'll have a look."

Beyond the apartment blocks, the deep trench the banshee had dug when she'd demolished half the buildings had gone. Dense forest grew in its place, extending along our line of sight. Vance and I continued northward until we passed by the clearing where we usually met the Chief. His throne lay on its side, bare and forlorn. Nobody else was around.

Past the clearing we found the jail in an even worse state. The layer of trees behind the building appeared to have grown *into* it, their branches piercing through solid stone and their trunks merging with the collapsed roof. The entire back section looked to be inaccessible, but nobody stood guard at the front door. I held my blade aloft as I approached.

"Careful," Vance warned. "If anyone's in there, they won't be friendly."

"I doubt any prisoners are worse than what we've already seen." I pushed open the door, my sword's blue glow lighting the gloom on the other side. "Hello?"

No response. The blue glow of my magic made the broken bars and shattered cells even creepier. Dead bodies lay within, some crushed and others ripped by what looked like talons. Bile burned my throat. *That fucking banshee.*

Vance strode ahead of me, checking each cell. Halfway down, the collapsed roof prevented us from going any further. Nobody would be alive on that side, so we retraced our steps, scanning for any signs of the Chief. Vance and I counted at least twenty dead, but none were short, pale, staff-wielding Summer half-bloods. Either he'd been crushed somewhere near the back, or he'd escaped. None of the dead wore armour, either, which suggested his guards had escaped, too. If so, where had they gone? Into the forest? Or had they been taken to the Vale after all?

"Let's check in on the Hemlock Coven's forest now," I said to Vance. "We're close already."

In fact, the half-faeries' forest had entirely merged with the denser swathe of trees belonging to the Hemlock Coven, to the extent that I couldn't tell one from another. We continued north, past the sprawling trees that now extended right up to the jail's edge.

A wall of branches blocked our path. I veered away to find another route, with the same result. Scowling, I tapped into my magic and took aim at the branches.

Blue light arced… and fizzled out.

"What the hell?" The hairs on my arms stood on end. "Are the Hemlock witches *blocking* my magic?"

"I'll try." Vance frowned, concentrating. "Or not. Something is blocking my abilities. Like…"

"In the Vale?" Alarm bled into my voice. "It's not the faeries, is it?"

"No, it doesn't feel the same."

It couldn't be the faeries. Their forest had let us in, but every time we tried to walk deeper, we found our path thwarted by thick branches and roots. There didn't seem to be a way into the witches' part of the woods which didn't involve climbing a tree. The Hemlock Coven had turned their home into a veritable fortress.

"Screw this." I marched to a tree that looked easy enough to climb and fit my hands into the dents in the trunk that were deep enough to serve as handholds.

As I began pulling myself up, a shock of energy went through my palms like I'd jumped into an electric fence. I dropped to the ground, my hands tingling with static. *What the hell?*

"Ivy." Vance took my shoulder, steadying me. "Are you all right?"

"Why?" My voice shook. "Are they really going to leave us all to die?"

"I doubt they can do much from inside the forest." He raised his voice a fraction. "They weren't the ones to imprison Fionn."

"No, but we saved them from being destroyed by the ring." You'd think they'd have offered some guidance at the very least, but after their near miss, they likely didn't want to take any chances. "Fine. Back to the manor?"

In a blink, we landed in the main room. Drake, who was halfway out the door, startled at the sight of us. "That didn't take long."

"The forest threw us out," I told him. "Literally. The Chief has disappeared, and everyone else has given up, including the Hemlock Coven. I realise that they're stuck in the forest and can't leave, but they owe us."

"Yes, they bloody do." Movement in the corner of his eye prompted him to spin on his heel. "*Hey*, you little bastard, get back here."

I ran forward as Vance materialised in the doorway behind Quentin's retreating figure, preventing him from slipping out of the room again.

"I would advise you not to leave," Vance said in a low voice. "What are you doing here? Did you visit your other family?"

My hand twitched towards my sword. "Please tell me you brought help from the Summer Court."

"I was unable to persuade them to send an envoy," he said. "They did not see the situation as urgent enough to merit action."

"It will be when Fionn shows up in *their* Court." There went our last shot at gaining an ally on the same level as him. "Which he will. His plan involves finding a new body to possess, which will probably be a Sidhe."

"Fionn," he repeated. "He—"

"Is a wraith, yes, and he's also pissed off at us. Oh, and he remembers the invasion." I bit back more angry words, not wanting to give him any more delicate information that he might pass on to his other family. "In case it wasn't obvious, he's the one who killed Vance's parents, Quentin, and he called us into Faerie to gloat in person."

The colour drained from the brownie's face.

"Your position in the Summer Court won't protect you from his attempts to seize power again," Vance said. "I would suggest you choose a side, and quickly."

Quentin's eyes sharpened. "There's only one side on which I will stand, and that is against the exiles who wish to see us all driven to ruin."

"Then be honest with us," I told him. "I know you swore vows to keep your other family's secrets, but you don't look all that surprised that Fionn survived."

"The Huntsman has a certain reputation among my kin, as well you know," he said. "He is closer to Winter than to Summer, however, and our only connections to the Winter Court were severed during the invasion."

"Your... connections." Suspicion nudged at the back of my mind. "Were there others? You know, working for Faerie but living here in the mortal realm?"

"There were," Vance said. "You will tell us, Quentin. I assume that you requested permission from your other family to share certain details of your role, and of your purpose in coming to this realm?"

"Yes." The word ground between his teeth. "I shall, to the best of my ability. There are certain secrets that belong to the

Sidhe alone, but you should know that there was once a pact between the mages, the Hemlock Coven, and a number of other supernaturals. We were the Council of Twelve."

I snorted. "Who picked that name? Were they channelling Tolkien?"

He glared at me with beady eyes. "The council does not exist anymore. Most of its members were lost in the invasion, and the truth died with them."

I stared at him, no longer feeling like laughing. "Was one of them Vance's grandfather?"

"Originally," he replied. "Then after he passed, the role was given to your father and his wife. I was chosen as an emissary for Summer, and another fae was chosen to represent Winter. Two noble Sidhe were selected, too, one of Summer and one of Winter. Both were killed in the fight against their kin."

Two Sidhe, plus two lesser fae. Which left…

"Witches," I said. "The Hemlock Coven. Right?"

"Two of them, correct. Two others were—"

"Necromancers," Vance said, and Quentin dipped his head. "And two shifters, I'm guessing."

"Twelve," I counted. "To do… what? Keep the peace?"

"Essentially," the brownie replied. "I myself ferried messages between this realm and the Summer Court. The necromancers, witches, shifters and mages were concerned with the protection of this realm, while the Summer and Winter Courts sent messengers as needed to ensure our peace agreements went unbroken."

"What went wrong?" I backtracked. "Fionn. Obviously. He recruited other banished faerie lords from the Grey Vale and they broke open the Ley Line and invaded this realm. But you said nobody knew…?"

"Not until it was too late," he said. "Nobody on the

council could have predicted the sheer scale of his assault on this realm."

"Some of them were responsible for sealing away Fionn, right?" I surmised. "Before they died. You know, it'd have been nice if you'd told me some of this *before* Fionn came back. You knew about him all along, didn't you?"

"Not his location, nor that it was possible for anyone to revive him," he said. "I witnessed neither the events that led up to the invasion nor the council's collapse, as my orders from both sides were strictly to serve the human family I swore to protect."

"Except Summer initially told you to work for Vance's family in the first place, right?"

"I chose them," he said, with a nod to Vance. "Your grandfather was kind to me, on my initial visit to the mages, and I elected to serve the Colton family alongside my other masters. I am not disloyal. My vow compels me to serve both."

"Vow." The one kind of magic that could overthrow almost any other. "If the one way to save your family—to save Vance—was to take us with you to Faerie, would you be able to?"

"As a last resort? Perhaps, but I cannot guarantee that my other family would be able to help."

"I'd say this situation qualifies as one that needs a last-resort plan," I said. "We need the Sidhe if we're to have any hope of defeating Fionn. The Hemlock witches won't help. Nobody else in this realm is strong enough."

"Strength alone means little," said the brownie. "As you should be aware by now, Ivy."

Didn't I know it. I'd consistently beaten the fae with trickery, not brute force, but Fionn was nothing like any other opponent I'd faced. "Then what?"

"The remaining council members may be able to help you."

"I thought you said they were dead."

"Death is not always a barrier, Ivy," he growled. "As you know well."

"But the ghosts of those killed in the invasion were banished..." I trailed off when the truth hit me like an avalanche. "The necromancer. Frank."

17

Vance transported both of us to the front of the necromancers' headquarters, blasting the doors open without ceremony. Ignoring the shouts of alarm from inside, I stormed ahead of him and into the main room.

"Hey!" squeaked Colby, running in front of us. "Mage Lord—Ivy—you can't be in here."

"Ivy is here with my permission," Vance said to the room full of stupefied necromancers. "The situation is urgent. We're on the brink of a second invasion."

If his words didn't get through to the cloaked necromancers within the room, the sight of my sword would have even if they couldn't see its flaming blue glow. Most of my anger was directed at myself. How could I have forgotten Frank the bloody necromancer had been the one who'd told me why the Grey Vale had first been created? He'd even said he knew Vance's grandfather.

"What—what are you doing?" yelped Colby as I bent down to light the first candle by the giant summoning circle.

"Speaking to your mentor." I flicked the switch and then

moved to the next candle. "Are you acquainted with Lord Frank Sydney?"

"Lord Sydney? He used to be our leader, before Lord Evander."

"And now he's a Guardian." A flame leapt from the candle, and I continued on my path around the circle. Vance had moved to the other side, sending the remaining necromancers fleeing to the outskirts. All of them were young enough that they'd have been children in the invasion. The necromancers had lost their best fighters, same as the mages had, and the one person able to offer guidance—who'd made a pact with Quentin and the council—had decided to keep them in ignorance.

So much for the dead being more trustworthy than the living.

I lit the last candle and bellowed Frank's name at the circle. That did it for the remaining necromancers, who fled the room en masse. A column of swirling smoke appeared in the circle, announcing Frank's arrival.

"What is it?" he asked. "You'd better have good reason for drawing me away from the gates, Ivy. What have you done to the veil?"

"Not me," I snapped. "Fionn. When did you plan to tell me you knew about him all along? Unless you got caught in the memory-erasing spell yourself, you know everything about the invasion and how it unfolded."

Frank's jaw dropped. "You... who told...? The brownie."

"Got it in one, dickhead." I lifted my sword. "By the way, this talisman can kill ghosts, so don't even think about trying to make a run for it."

"That's not necessary," said Frank, his voice somewhat subdued. "What is it you want to know?"

"Why you felt the need to lie to everyone, for starters," I said. "Did you even tell me the truth about my own magic?"

"I haven't a clue what you're talking about. Your magic? I didn't lie to you. I've never seen magic like yours before you came along."

"Well, you worked with this secret council. You knew what really happened in the invasion, when everyone else has forgotten because all the witnesses either died or went back to Faerie, leaving us in the lurch."

"I'm dead, Ivy," he said. "I never lied when I said I'm restricted to certain parts of the afterlife, and moreover, I was deceased for a portion of my time on the council, too. I didn't witness the full extent of the invasion, and I knew little of the Huntsman before he came to this realm."

"But it's been twenty *years*. Besides, weren't you the one who locked out the dead after the invasion? You pushed them through the gates?"

His transparent body flickered, an expression of profound sadness crossing his face. "The other Guardians… many of the others didn't make it, including my fellow necromancer who served as a member of the council. The impact when the two worlds clashed took weeks to restore, and all we could do was drive everyone killed in the invasion past the gates to prevent further disruption. Asking questions of any of them wasn't an option."

"But you did know how Fionn was defeated, didn't you?" I pressed. "You knew they put a forgetfulness spell on his tomb."

"I knew something of that nature occurred, but I was too preoccupied with the veil to see the impact upon the realm of the living."

"Convenient," Vance growled, "but you haven't explained why you and Quentin deceived the rest of the supernatural community in the decades since, if just to preserve an old pact which was wrongly forgotten. Did you assume nobody would ever attack this realm again?"

The air in the room turned even colder than before, and though Frank didn't retreat from the Mage Lord's power, he didn't meet Vance's eyes.

"And even if you did," I added, "you knew when Fionn woke up, back in January. You've had months. No excuses."

"Perhaps I did stick too closely to my arrangement with the council. It was your grandfather's idea, Mage Lord. The council was set up to maintain peace both among supernaturals and between our realm and that of the fae. None of us thought we might ever be exposed to humans, much less forced to share our secrets widely."

"You didn't have to tell the whole planet, but I guess I can understand why you wouldn't want Lord Evander to know." Not that that let him off the hook. "For god's sake, Frank, you can't claim that you had no idea Fionn was going to try a second attempt at an invasion. Did you forget what happened with the ring?"

"No," he said. "I did not. However, I assumed you had successfully taken his life."

"Yeah, so did I, but I was operating on faulty information." A fresh wave of indignation took hold of me. "I did that without your help, too. This has gone too far. He's back, and he's claiming he can regain a physical body. Don't bother telling me it's impossible. That guy makes his own rules."

"Calm *down*, Ivy," he said. "You know I can't stay in this realm for long, and if I knew how to stop Fionn, I would endeavour to help you. However, nobody can fuse a soul with a body, not permanently."

"He claimed there's always a Huntsman. And banshees are reborn into new bodies when they die, so clearly something of that nature *is* possible."

"The secrets of the death fae are not for the likes of me, Ivy," Frank said. "Now, the people who *might* have some direction are among the surviving members of the Council."

"What, Quentin? He said the others were dead."

"The Hemlock witches," Vance said. "They're not alive, but not dead either."

"They also locked us out of their forest." I glared at Frank. "Even my magic couldn't breach the boundaries. Seems to me that you're all finding ways to wriggle out of helping."

He hesitated. "There might be a way for you to reach them. A risky one."

"Go on. Tell me."

"You can travel between realms, Ivy," he said. "If you can leave your body without using a summoning circle as an anchor, I would assume that you can also travel using the spirit lines, leaving your physical body behind."

My mouth parted. "I can travel on the lines?"

"I believe so," he said. "You can cross over into the spirit realm at any key point and move from one to another, using the spirit lines to guide you."

"What use is that?" My curiosity dimmed. "If I'm floating around without a body, I might get lost and lose all connection with my real body. How long can you disconnect without being stuck in Death for good?"

"For a necromancer? Indefinitely, as long as your body is kept alive, but the longer you stay severed from your physical form, the higher the risk you'll never return."

"Figures." When I'd gone to the liminal spaces and the Grey Vale before, I hadn't crossed without my body. It seemed a good way to land myself in an early grave.

Still. If I used my incorporeal form to slip into the forest and ask the Hemlock Coven for advice, it might just be worth the risk. Vance would understand. Right?

I met his grey eyes. *Maybe not.*

Anger lined his face, and my skin prickled as a breeze kicked up behind him. "If you're endangering Ivy, Lord

Sydney, no summoning circle will keep me from making you regret that decision."

"I'm not overly keen on the idea either," I said. "It doesn't seem that I have much choice. Unless there's something else you can suggest, Frank. You must know how risky it is to leave my body behind."

"Correct, but I'm fairly certain you have a necromancers' handbook in your possession that you never returned to the guild."

"Yeah, that Calder stole," I retorted. "And it sure as hell didn't mention travelling *along* the spirit lines."

Necromancers needed a tether, but I was no necromancer, and neither was Fionn.

"Is there a way to make Ivy's spirit reconnect with her body even if she's far away?" asked Vance. "If not, there's absolutely no chance this risk will be worth it. Fionn might attack us at any moment."

"There are several ways. Normally, a necromancer's body is contained in a summoning circle. If that isn't an option, there are spirit marks, certain glyphs…"

"Glyph marks," Vance said. "When Ivy was attacked while she was fighting Calder without a body, I used our shared mark to wake her up."

I blinked. "Wait, you did?"

"You might not have noticed, since you were injured." His mouth turned down at the corners. "I still don't like this."

"I can't stay any longer." Frank's voice faded, his ghostly form becoming much less distinct. "If you require my help again, Ivy, I'll be waiting."

"On the other side." Damn. Leaving my body to go spirit-line-hopping wasn't my idea of a good time, but it didn't have to be a repeat of my first disastrous encounter with Calder. Vance would be able to keep my body safe while I was gone, though with Fionn at large, the word 'safe' applied to depressingly few places, if any.

"This is dangerous," Vance said in a low voice.

"I know." I turned my back on the summoning circle, wishing I could put the universe on pause so that I had enough time to figure out what the hell to do. "I think it's the only way."

"And if Fionn finds out and attacks your body, like Calder did?"

"That's a risk no matter what I do," I said. "The Hemlock Coven is our only shot at getting answers. Frank wouldn't have told me how to travel on the spirit lines if he didn't think reaching them was an option."

"He didn't tell us the full truth."

"No, he didn't," I said, "but he doesn't *know* the truth. That's the whole point."

"Do the Hemlock witches?" He studied my face, his gaze serious. "Ivy, this might go wrong."

"Oh, it probably will," I acknowledged. "But like Frank said, you can bring me back with the glyph. I trust you."

He breathed out slowly. "I trust you, too, Ivy, but Fionn… he's been several steps ahead of us all along. He might be waiting on the other side."

"I don't think he knows about Frank," I said. "He also can't come out of the Vale, I don't think, not without entering the mortals' Death."

"Very well," he said in a resigned tone. "Where do you want to do this?"

"Any key point." I thought. "Maybe not near the manor, though. Just in case."

"All right." He took my hand and we vanished, landing in an empty field. "This place is uninhabited. I'll take you back to the manor while you're…"

"Not gone." I squeezed his hand. "Just on temporary leave."

"Ivy."

"Vance." God, I wanted to stay here instead. Stay with Vance. Stay human. My heart fluttered in my chest as though it suspected it might not have reason to beat much longer. My mind registered every sensation acutely: the cool breeze, the faint trace of rain in the air, the touch of Vance's hand on mine. Committing them to memory to take with me into the beyond.

I'll come back.

Vance's mouth closed over mine, stealing my words, leaving a mark that went deeper than any glyph.

"Love you," he said quietly.

"Same to you."

Closing my eyes, I reached outward. Rather than extending myself towards the place on the other side of the spirit line, I felt for the invisible currents running through the air, the unseen force waiting to propel me between realms. And instead of fighting the sensation, I let myself slide loose from my body, leaving myself behind for the grey void of Death.

18

Grey faces swirled in and out of view as my body turned transparent. The weightless sensation wasn't new to me, but I stiffened when an unseen force tugged at me, as though trying to drag me forward.

"Ivy."

I spun around. Frank floated across from me, and I lifted my hands, blue light springing to my palms. *Good. At least I brought my magic with me.*

"If you lied to me, I'll kick you into hell," I warned.

"That won't be necessary," he said. "You're in the first layer of the veil. You're being drawn to the gates, but your magic allows you to fight that instinct, as does your will to live."

"I've got plenty of that." I forced my feet to remain still, fighting the instinct to drift and let the currents carry me where they would. "And how do I get to another key point from here?"

"Follow the lights."

"What does that mean?" I lowered my gaze but saw nothing beneath us but fog. Above lay the same, and the scenery on each side was equally uninspiring. "Give me some direction here."

Frank reached out and pushed me. I yelped in surprise as my ghostly body flew forward in a straight line as though pulled by a magnet.

For a moment, I tried to slow myself, unsure if he'd pushed me towards the gates after all, but then I saw the silvery line beneath my feet, gleaming like a train track or tram line. As I hurtled along, a growing light caught my gaze somewhere ahead. *Follow the lights.*

When I reached the light, my pace slowed, allowing me to look around. Not that there was much to see. Magic circled me, providing enough light to see two more silvery lines heading in different directions, like a fork in the road. At a guess, the bigger lights must be key points and the lines marked the spirit paths, but losing my body had taken my sense of direction along with it and I hadn't the faintest idea how my location matched up with the world underneath. I needed to get to the spirit line on which the Wild Hunt had awakened to find my way into the Hemlock Coven's forest. That was west of my current position, but the two available paths only headed north and south.

I mentally flipped a coin and chose north, figuring I could easily retrace my steps if I ended up lost. As a ghost, I moved with surprising ease, following the path without having to consciously focus on the motion. That left my mind free to wonder how many people made a habit of travelling the spirit lines, and how on earth they navigated without being able to bring a map with them. The paths theoretically covered the entire country and beyond, and if I went too far in one direction, I might end up marooned in the middle of the ocean for all I knew.

Focus, Ivy. Based on my memory of where I'd left off, I was somewhere in witch territory, heading north. I needed to go southwest to reach the forest. I came to a halt at another crossroads that branched in two directions, east and west. This time I picked the leftmost path.

Partway down the line, I collided with a surprisingly solid force comprised of transparent figures forming a huddle on the spirit path. Most appeared human, some with wings or tails. *Half-faeries.* Were they the spirits of the half-bloods Fionn had killed in the Grey Vale?

"Who are you?" My voice carried an odd echo, as though I stood in an underground tunnel. "What are you doing?"

"Nobody passes through here," said a male half-faerie with the curved horns and cloven hooves of a satyr. The others caught his words and repeated them until the air rang with sinister echoes.

"This where Fionn's going?" I attempted to move along, but the spirits closed in, pushing me backwards. "Or is he already here?"

A winged half-blood girl with dark skin and curly black hair glided into my path. "No mortals can traverse the spirit lines."

"This mortal can. Get out of my way."

Magic rose to my palms in warning. None of them moved, but they didn't attack, either, though a brutish-looking half-troll with fists bigger than my head looked as though he might try.

"Why did Fionn send you here?" I asked. "Is he doing something on this spirit line?"

"We're supposed to stop anyone crossing between realms," said the winged half-faerie.

"What, going into Faerie?" Did he think I intended to return to the Vale with an army? "Good news. That isn't my plan."

Magic flared from my hands, drawing upon their own simmering emotions. Anger, grief, pain. They hadn't expected—or wanted—to die. They'd wanted immortality, yet they served Fionn even in death. Maybe they still thought he'd give them their chance, but these kids weren't the front-line attack forces. They were no threat to me.

"You can still move on," I told the spirits. "Head for the gates. It's the only way you'll have any peace."

I might have destroyed them, but it'd give me some measure of satisfaction if they chose to move on of their own volition. In any case, when I continued down the spirit path, nobody stopped me.

At the next key point, I drew to a halt. Given the ambush, I must be close to the right spirit line, but there had to be a more efficient way to navigate. I squinted through the shimmering light encasing me, glimpsing flickers of silver-leafed trees.

The Vale. If I could see the Vale, I ought to be able to see the real world, surely. Both realms overlapped with the line. I focused hard, recalling the weird double vision that occurred whenever I stood on top of the Ley Line during a surge of energy or when I tried to see through glamour.

My vision shifted. The silver-leafed trees became houses, albeit viewed from a skewed angle, as though I hovered several feet up in the air. Everything looked grey and washed-out. Did the necromancers see this all the time? No wonder they were so gloomy. I didn't recognise the street, but my only options were south and east. I picked south and continued onward.

The next key point revealed itself in a blaze of light, drawing me in like a beacon, brighter than the others. Now I knew where I was. The vibrant glow marked the intersection where the three spirit lines intersected, so all I had to do was keep going that way.

A large, doglike shape waited ahead of me. *Hellhound.* The beast sat in a wide-open area far bigger than the other key points, and which flickered between the silver-lit path of the Grey Vale and then the rain-drenched grass of the stretch of hillside we'd fought the first battle against Fionn. More hellhounds became visible, lounging on the grass or prowling alongside hedgerows. This was where they were hanging out? Like me, they could cross realms whenever they wanted, but they sat here at the crossroads as if… well, as if they were waiting for someone.

The first hellhound I'd seen approached me with its head bowed, its paws moving along the spirit line as though it were solid ground. I watched, wary but not afraid, until it reached my side.

"Don't suppose you'd like to help me take down Fionn before he unleashes whatever he's planning this time?" I hadn't the faintest clue if they understood human speech, but some of the others flicked their heads in my direction. None moved, though the one whose attention I'd drawn kept pace with me as I glided across the key point, searching for the stone building which once housed Fionn's body. I knew it lay somewhere here, in a crack between realms.

My vision kept flickering between the spirit line, the Vale, and the regular world beneath which would have made my head spin if I'd had a physical body to speak of. After a few seconds, I picked out the individual threads of the three spirit lines that intersected and then merged into a knot of pulsing energy. Within, I glimpsed the outline of Fionn's tomb.

I drifted that way, the hairs on my nonexistent head standing on end when I drew closer to the place where the three lines became one. The entrance to the place of Fionn's imprisonment stuck out like a loose stitch, a patch on the world that didn't quite fit.

The area was smaller than I remembered, formed of little more than a few trees crouched over a tomb of stone. I peered inside. Glyphs adorned the walls, but none glowed as they had before. Not a trace of the magic imprisoning Fionn remained, nor any signs of who had cast the spell. I wouldn't find answers here.

Enough dawdling, Ivy. I needed to find my way to the witches' forest and hope that leaving my body behind would remove whatever barriers they'd used to keep me out.

I left the hidden alcove and emerged in the tangle of spirit lines. A vibration thrummed along the line I chose to follow northward; hoping that wasn't a bad sign, I left the hell-hounds in the dust and angled back towards the city.

No more ghosts blocked my path. Perhaps they'd taken my advice and decided to move on, but a more cynical voice in my head wondered if they'd gone to report me to their master. I didn't have time to waste, so I kept moving, following the trail of key points to the Hemlock Coven's forest.

Even if I hadn't figured out how to see through the overlapping realms to the world beneath, the forest itself was easy to spot. A dark blot smothered the key point where two lines intersected, branches reaching upward from within and turning transparent where they met the line. A peculiar shiver passed over me when I looked down and realised I was floating *above* the forest. That ought to mean I should be able to get inside with no resistance, surely.

I floated downward to the thick canopy, and my transparent body passed right through the interlocking branches as though they didn't exist.

Yes. Triumph rushed through me as I drifted into the mass of trees that formed the Hemlock witches' home. The spirit line faded into the background, while I didn't see a single trace of the Grey Vale either. Just trees, dark and never-ending. I hoped the forest's trickery didn't work on ghosts, because I didn't have time for a detour through an illusory nightmare.

"Hey!" I called out. "Hemlock witches, I need to talk to you."

The forest lightened, revealing a familiar silver-lit path upon which stood none other than the Lady of the Tree. She stood draped in green silk, with the beauty and youth of her restored form, and with her gaze fixed somewhere over my shoulder.

"Part of the god is contained within the mortal realm." She spoke in a whisper, and I wasn't sure if she was addressing me or someone else.

"Oh, no." I held up my hands. "I'm not watching another vision."

The Lady continued as though I hadn't spoken. "The other part, in Death. But to access it, I need the power of Summer and Winter combined."

"Go away."

She did, mercifully, and the Vale's path faded into the forest once again.

I raised my voice to address the mass of dark trees crowding me. "Hemlock witches! I need to talk to you. It's urgent."

"Ivy Lane," growled the voice of Cordelia Hemlock. "I was trying to help you, you fool."

"What—holy shit." I jumped violently when the leader of the Hemlock Coven's face leered at me from within the bark of a large tree on my right-hand side. "You left your lair?"

Cordelia's dark eyes regarded me from below deep-set wrinkles. "I thought you came here to seek our advice on thwarting the Huntsman."

"Then what was the point of the..." I trailed off as the Lady of the Tree's words filtered back into my brain. *Part of the god is contained within the mortal realm... the other part in*

Death. A horrifying suspicion took hold of me. "Was Fionn sealed away like the other god? Partly in the mortal realm, and partly in—Death?"

"You already know the answer to that."

If only his physical body had been imprisoned in that tomb, Calder must have... "Calder didn't just free his body. He must have broken the seal on his spirit, too."

He'd wanted to possess Fionn's body, yes, but his ultimate goal had been to be reborn, and the living Huntsman had held the key to that.

"And," Cordelia said, with a touch of impatience, "to access it..."

"Requires the magic of Summer and Winter combined." The Lady of the Tree had woken the shifter god by gathering an influx of Summer and Winter energy in one place. Calder must have done the same. Not an impossible feat, considering he'd had direction from someone who'd done the same, but if Fionn's spirit hadn't been imprisoned in the same place as his body...

Dammit. How much more trouble could a dead man inflict on my life?

"Precisely," she said. "The Huntsman's spirit and his magic are one. They endure beyond his physical death."

"He can't die." Despair dug its claws into me again. "Not even if I dragged him into mortal Death?"

"That would result in the end of the veil as we know it, Ivy."

Shivers sprang to my phantom arms. "Yeah, we don't want that. Then... what? He still wants a body, doesn't he? Where does he plan to get it?"

"I assume he seeks out the lost cauldron of resurrection," she growled. "The cauldron contains the essence of life itself, and any who bathe in its waters are reborn."

"That's…" My throat went dry. "There's a cauldron that can bring someone back to life?"

I'd expected her to say he intended to seek out a Sidhe to possess. This was a thousand times worse. *The essence of life itself?*

"Yes, Ivy," said the witch. "Anyone whose spirit enters the cauldron is given a new body."

A strangled noise escaped me. "I—*what?* How did nobody warn me about this? Wait, you said it was lost?"

"The Huntsman's life once revolved around the cauldron, Ivy," Cordelia said. "It's said the cauldron is filled with the blood of the first Sidhe, or perhaps their gods. The stories vary. It is certain, however, that it is the cauldron that grants the Sidhe their immortality."

"Faerie blood." I gasped. "Is that where Velkas heard…?"

He'd been right, and so had Calder. Worse, the more I thought about it, the more sense it made. While everyone knew the Sidhe couldn't die, the fact that *I'd* killed one seemed an obvious hole in that theory. That they'd once been reborn fit with Fionn's claim that he'd ferried souls to the afterlife. To the cauldron.

His promises to the half-bloods had been true all along. Calder's, too. Didn't mean he intended to keep those promises, but if he could put *any* soul into the cauldron and create a new body, his callousness with his followers' lives no longer seemed like an impediment.

In fact, I'd bet my sword he'd done the same in the invasion. He hadn't just recruited allies from among the outcasts: he'd *made* them.

"Do you know where it is?" If Fionn was searching for the cauldron, it might be within the Vale itself, but surely the Sidhe wouldn't have put the means for his rebirth in the realm of the exiles. Right?

"The cauldron, I would assume, has not been moved since

the invasion," said Cordelia. "It has always rested upon the Ley Line."

"The most obvious place." Fionn's memory had been wiped. Why would anyone have bothered moving the cauldron if they thought he'd forgotten its existence? "*Where* on the Ley Line?"

"The cauldron's original resting place was at the line's end."

"It has an end?" That didn't even make sense, but if I didn't try to find the cauldron myself, Fionn would certainly get there first. "Why didn't you tell the rest of the council?" When Cordelia made no reply, I added, "Yes, I know you used to belong to this Council of Twelve, along with Quentin and Frank and whoever else died in the invasion. There's no need for secrecy."

"I thought the brownie would have told you much sooner."

"He and I never really saw eye to eye." I'd never trust him again, but Vance was the person whose forgiveness he'd have to earn. "He and Frank didn't mention the cauldron. Frank outright said he didn't know what Fionn was searching for, while Quentin is bound to keep the secrets of the Sidhe family he serves."

"There are very few individuals outside of the Sidhe who know of the cauldron," said Cordelia. "My coven's members are among that group, but we all assumed the knowledge of its whereabouts was forgotten, including by Fionn himself."

"Not anymore." Damn. I should have come back to the forest sooner, but would it have made a difference if I had? The Hemlock Coven couldn't leave, and nor could they survive another attack from Fionn. "So our immortal unkillable enemy has the means of creating himself an infinite army and knows how to use it. Do I have that right?"

The half-bloods would get their immortality after all. Our

realm would have to deal with another influx of Sidhe, all of whom would obey Fionn's orders without question, and either obliterate humanity or enslave them.

Two options remained: destroy the cauldron itself or kill Fionn, this time permanently. Given my lack of success with the latter, I'd have to hope the cauldron had a weakness of some kind. Taking the cauldron off the playing field wouldn't finish him off, but it would prevent him making a new army at the very least.

"He's already stronger than me," I said, half to myself. "Stronger than anyone in this realm. Quentin didn't manage to convince the Summer Court the situation was urgent enough to send anyone to help, and we don't *have* anyone in Winter we can contact. Who else can possibly challenge him?"

If Cordelia had a response, I didn't hear it. Pain burned through my shoulder, and I was wrenched out of the forest, out of the spirit line, and into my body once again.

19

The world spun in hazy circles. I lay on my back on the sofa in the manor's main room, Vance's hand resting on my shoulder above the glyph.

"Vance?" I lifted my head, with difficulty. My body felt numb, as if I'd taken a bath in an icy lake, but nothing hurt. "Vance—what happened?"

"Furies." Blood stained his arms and shirt, but it carried the blue sheen of faerie magic. "They attacked the manor. Similar reports are coming in from near the mercenary guild, too."

"Shit." I tried to rise upright, but my limbs refused to cooperate. "Is he here? Fionn?"

"Not that I've heard," he said. "We took care of the first wave of furies, but they must be crossing the Ley Line or the other spirit lines. If it *is* Fionn, he hasn't been sighted, and neither have the half-bloods."

"Probably because he killed them." With Vance's help, I shuffled back into a sitting position. "Are you hurt?"

"No, but I came back here to make sure it wasn't a diversion so they could get at you." Vance lifted a mug of the energy restorative he sometimes used. "This might help. Did you manage to reach the witches?"

"Yes, and I know what Fionn's after." He pressed the mug to my lips, and I took a sip of the disgusting, bitter liquid. "Cordelia told me he seeks a cauldron that can make anyone immortal. As Huntsman, it was his job to take the souls of dead faeries there to be reborn into new bodies. Now he has his memories back, he'll know how to use it, both on himself and on the spirits of the people he killed."

"A cauldron." He pushed the mug against my lips again, and I felt the slight tremor in his hands. "That's what he's looking for?"

"Yeah." I coughed, the potion burning my throat. "He didn't lie to the half-bloods. They'll get immortality as a prize for joining his army. All along, it's been possible to revive someone from death. In fact, I think it's how the Sidhe have stayed immortal. When they die, their spirits are ferried to the cauldron."

"By the Huntsman." Vance watched me, his grey eyes simmering with the warning heat before a tropical storm. "Whereabouts is this cauldron? Did the witches know?"

"Cordelia said the cauldron was on the Ley Line. Specifically, at the end of the line. Which makes no sense. I mean, the Line covers the whole globe, technically." Some of the sensation had come back into my hands, and I took the mug from Vance to drink the rest myself. "I know magic doesn't *have* to follow logic, mind. And Fionn certainly knows where it is, if he has his memories back. I don't know why he hasn't gone looking sooner."

A buzzing noise from my pocket told me someone was trying to call me. I drained the last of the bitter-tasting liquid and handed Vance the empty mug before fishing my phone out of my pocket with clumsy fingers. Isabel had tried to call twice, and a message stood out on the screen.

Ivy, the sky's gone all dark. I think it's the Ley Line.

My head snapped up. "Shit. There's been an attack—"

"On the Ley Line." Vance had his phone in his hand, too. "There's also been an incident at the mercenary guild, apparently. Furies."

"The Ley Line is Fionn's target." I managed to get to my feet, though my legs felt a little stiff. My trip into Death had slowed me down a bit, but the warm rejuvenation of the potion coursed through me, and I'd be back to full strength when I tapped into my faerie magic. I wouldn't disconnect with my body again until I knew Isabel was safe. Hell, even Larsen didn't deserve to be slaughtered by a mob of furies, though I wouldn't shed a tear if he was.

I grabbed my sword and checked that my spells and other weapons were in place. I could only assume Fionn wanted to distract me while he went after the cauldron, but for all he knew, I wasn't aware of its existence. He'd build his army while my eyes were elsewhere.

Vance took my arm. We landed on a road shadowed in darkness, which blotted out the sky like a layer of spilled ink.

"Holy shit," I breathed. "Those can't all be furies."

No, there were too many, and their distant cries sounded more like birds than the beasts Fionn commanded.

"I think they're crows." Vance tilted his head back. "Thousands of them."

He was right. "Wait. Isn't the Morrigan supposed to be accompanied everywhere by a swarm of crows?"

Roseanne. Damn. I should have guessed he'd find a new way to use her against me.

A blade appeared in Vance's hand. "Where are the furies?"

"Good question." I raised my voice over the clamour of a thousand bird cries that drowned out all other noise. "The mercenary guild?"

That was south of here, so I tore my gaze away and

crossed the road. Faces peered from windows and cars had stopped in the middle of the road as their drivers looked up at the sky.

"Get indoors," I told a group of youths who were goggling and taking photos of the mass of crows. "If you know what's good for you, I'd get the hell out of here before whatever's up there decides to come down."

I waved my sword for emphasis and continued onward. Somewhere over the rooftops, my ears picked up another noise beyond the racket the birds were making. Screaming. *Human* screaming.

I ran around another corner and saw a huge winged beast flying in pursuit of a group of fleeing humans. Two similar monsters hovered above the rooftops. Each was easily seven feet long from head to claws, their bodies cloaked in black feathers tipped in crimson and their pit-like eyes capable of generating a similar fear-effect to hellhounds to render their prey immobile. A few bodies already lay in the road, ripped open by the beast's vicious claws.

"Hey!" I yelled, brandishing my sword. Magic kicked in, flooding my body with energy that quickened my speed. As the first fury's claws reached for its human targets, I sent a bolt of vibrant blue from my palm that knocked it sideways into the path of Vance's blade. The fury fell, its throat cut.

Two more furies landed on the roof of a house, their claws ripping into the tiles, while another collided with a downstairs window in a shower of glass. I ran closer in case there were people in the house and glimpsed several people running over, waving swords and knives in the air. Mercenaries. An unexpectedly brave move on their part, but the furies flew too high and moved too fast for any human to catch them. One mercenary threw a dagger at the fury in the window that would have been a good shot if the knife hadn't bounced clean off the fury's feathery hide.

Vance waved a hand and the weapon reappeared in front of its owner.

The merc caught the dagger between his fingertips, looking around in confusion. "Whoa. Mage Lord?"

"Backup's on the way," he told the stupefied mercenaries, and then sent his own blade point-first through the fury's throat.

I fired a blast of energy at the furies on the roof. One screamed, a bloody hole torn in its chest, and toppled into the garden below. The second took flight in a shower of roof tiles, and the mercenary once again tried to throw a knife at the beast. He got closer this time, the blade skimming the fury's clawed foot, and I finished it off with a second blast of magic to the chest.

The merc goggled at me. "You're the faerie—"

"Killer," I finished. "Why're you out here and not at the guild?"

His face fell. "Those monsters dive-bombed us. Landed on the guild roof, and Larsen… he's missing."

Or hiding in the basement. "Well, I wouldn't try to fight these fuckers head-on. Find somewhere else to lie low."

As the merc ran off, a black car skidded to a halt at the roadside, knocking over a lamp post. Drake jumped out, shooting a fireball at the sky at another oncoming fury. Two more came screeching over the rooftops as the mages climbed out of the car.

"Good timing." I peered up at the sky, trying to see where the furies were coming from. Somewhere behind that mass of crows, perhaps, but the thick swathe of darkness pointed to a worse threat waiting in the wings. Literally. Were they a warning from Fionn or a sign pointing to the Morrigan herself? Roseanne's mother hadn't even come into the picture yet, but she was a death fae herself, and Fionn's involvement with both her and the banshee told me that he had a vested interest in anyone with the ability to meddle with the dead. And what had Roseanne told me? That the Morrigan could rip souls from their bodies with her claws.

Yeah, Fionn would definitely be interested in using that power. As if one death god wasn't enough to handle without adding a second.

I ran down the street and sheathed my blade in a fury's neck. Vance joined the other mages, using his ability to knock the furies out of the air so the others could reach them. The backup team was mostly comprised of fire, lightning and air mages, whose abilities were more easily able to aim at their targets from the ground than the others. Drake sent a wave of fire upward that knocked three furies out of the air. Vance's blade slashed through one, and I ran to his side, Helena's keen edge severing claws and biting into feathered flesh. Magic burned through my veins like wildfire, a reminder of the surge of death energy the beasts had brought into this realm through the Ley Line.

"Where are they even coming from?" Drake yelled at nobody in particular.

"Up there." I gestured at the low-hanging black smear across the sky. When I squinted, an odd flickering caught my eye. Like a glamour. "Damn. I think the birds are an illusion and there's some kind of opening to the Vale behind them."

"In the *sky?*" Drake said.

"Yeah." An idea hit me, and I sent a torrent of magic surging upward, aiming directly at the sky.

The sound of a hundred crows crying out hit my eardrums, yet the cloud cover of birds didn't budge. The flickering grew more intense, though, and an eerie silver glow filtered through. Definitely the Vale.

Vance knocked another fury out of the air with a well-timed attack and ran to my side. "What was that?"

"Look behind those crows." I pointed upward. "Fionn

opened the Vale in the sky. The birds aren't real, they're a glamour."

"Right." Face set, Vance lifted his hands.

A deafening crack split the sky as surely as a bolt of lightning; there came a shower of blood and feathers and the thud of the furies' heavy bodies hitting the tarmac.

Vance swayed on the spot, and I reached out a hand to steady him. "Whoa. You okay?"

"Yes." His mouth pinched, but he straightened upright and lifted his blade once again.

"Don't overextend yourself yet."

He'd hit most of the descending furies, but two had survived. I reached them first, decapitating one of them with a sweep of my blade. The mages took out the other, and in the ensuing lull in the fighting, I leaned on a garden wall to catch my breath.

Vance applied a healing spell to both of us. We hadn't suffered more than superficial wounds, but Fionn's intention might be for us to exhaust ourselves before we ever got into the Vale.

"There are too many of them. We need to take out the source."

"If it's possible." I shook my head. "The crows are supposed to be the Morrigan's signal, which suggests… well. Roseanne is here."

Or he wanted to remind me of the vow he'd forced her to swear. The next time we met, she'd kill me or die fighting his command.

Dammit, I won't let him beat us.

"I'm going to attack the birds again," I said. "See if I can break through."

Vance nodded, his eyes darkening, and I raised Helena. A stream of energy arced upward and split through the horde of crows in a current of blue light.

I braced myself for another wave of furies to arrive. Instead, a single bird descended, smaller than the other furies. More like a human-sized crow, her face beaked and feathered, but still dressed in the ragged clothes she'd worn in the Vale.

Roseanne.

"Wait!" I called to the mages, seeing them readying themselves to attack. "She's half-blood. Fionn's prisoner."

"Not the half-blood who brought them to our doorstep?" Drake shot me a look of disbelief as I ran past him.

When she saw me, Roseanne's flight path angled towards me. Her feathered wings beat, her taloned claws outstretched and her beak wide open in a cry of defiance.

"Hold on," I called to her. "You don't have to—"

"I have to kill you, Ivy." She swooped downward, and I shaped my magic into a shield and caught her mid-descent, holding her off the ground.

Roseanne fought, snarling, unable to break through my shield. "Let me go, Ivy."

"You know I don't want to kill you." Fionn knew, too. "Where is he? Is your master coming here?"

"Kill her!" yelled one of the mages, and a fireball shot over Roseanne's head. She cried out, the sound lost in the screeching of more furies descending over the rooftops.

At least the furies distracted the mages enough to keep their attention off Roseanne. One beast flew at me from behind; I slashed with my blade, sending it flying into the path of Vance's claws. Roseanne tried to strike me again, unable to break past my shield.

Vance moved to my side, his clawed hands slick with blood. "You can't make her see reason. Ivy. She's the enemy."

"Only because Fionn wants her to be. I won't give him the satisfaction of making me kill her."

Roseanne hissed and spat, clawing at the air. "Why aren't you fighting me?"

"Because you're a pawn in a faerie's game. You shouldn't die for it."

"I—have—to—kill you." She ended on a scream as her feathered body caught on fire. Her feathers blazed, and she fell to the road, rolling over and emitting guttural howls.

"Drake, stop that," I shouted at him. "Fight the furies instead. She's been sent to kill me. No one else."

"She nearly killed Wanda." Drake advanced on her, readying another attack.

"But—" One look at Vance's face told me he agreed with Drake, and I didn't blame him. I wanted to give her a good thwack on the head, but death was final, and I'd be playing into Fionn's hands no matter what I did.

Roseanne came upright unsteadily. Half her feathers were burned off, and her face shifted back into a human's, tears leaking from her eyes. When Drake took a threatening step towards her, she flinched and hid behind a car. Her sobs, wrenching and agonised, tore at my chest.

She hadn't asked for this. Her attack on Wanda, Liam's death—both had been the result of someone else pulling the strings. Our true enemy hid out of sight, but the wave of furies showed no sign of ceasing and the mages had begun to slow. Even with a steady supply of healing spells, the injuries and blood loss would take their toll, and it was only a matter of time before someone sustained a fatal wound.

A flash of green light shot past my head and collided with a fury. I gaped, looking around for the source. That was Summer magic. Had Faerie answered our call after all?

Another bolt of Summer magic knocked a fury out of the sky. Below, several armoured figures ran into view, led by none other than the Chief. I didn't know if I was more surprised that he'd escaped jail unscathed or that he'd actually come to join in the fight, but he'd brought at least a dozen others. I recognised Killian, the Chief's partner, who'd also dressed in armour and carried a trident-like weapon in one hand.

"Ivy Lane." The Chief veered towards me. "I should have known you'd be at the centre of this."

"And I hoped the Summer Court might have shown up to help."

"That's just the level of ingratitude I'd expect from a human."

"I killed your replacement. You're welcome." I watched the mages take out the last of the current wave of furies, but more would arrive soon enough. "I'm impressed you got out of that jail unscathed."

"*Some* of my people remained loyal enough to help," he growled. "Our territory was wrongfully taken from us, and I intend to take it back."

"That's…" I stopped myself before I said, 'hard to believe', though I was tempted to. The Chief had surrendered to every possible threat up until this point. Including the banshee.

"Some of us have built a home here in this realm," Killian said. "We don't want to see it torn to pieces."

"You and me both."

A fury dived towards the Chief. I shot a blast of magic at its chest, and the beast burst in midair, showering us with a mass of feathers and blood.

"I can defend myself," snapped the Chief, swiping blood out of his eyes with a hand.

"All right, I'll leave you in peace, then." *Seriously.*

Killian gave me an apologetic look and moved in to help, firing vibrant green magic at a descending fury.

Roseanne leapt out of her hiding place when its body crashed into the car she'd been crouching behind.

"What's *she* doing here?" the Chief said.

"She was forced to fight me against her will."

She was still limping, half her feathers scorched off, but when we locked eyes, she attempted to shift again. Even her claws were blackened and burned.

"Chief, I don't suppose you know of a way to break a faerie vow?"

"You can't. She has to fulfil the terms of the vow one way or another."

"Or twist them, I guess." I reformed my shield in case she tried to attack again. "Can an Invocation outdo a vow? Which is stronger?"

"I wouldn't use the language of the gods lightly, human."

"My sword came from a god. The magic inside it, anyway."

"What?" He stopped fighting and nearly got his head torn off by a fury's claw. I stabbed the fury in the neck, splattering us both with blood.

"You should know by now there's more to Faerie than your two Courts." I stepped around the monster's corpse, shaking blood from my talisman so I could better display the pattern of glyphs on the hilt. "The talisman the Lady of the Tree stole is the same. In fact, we both got pretty close to the god from which that talisman's power originally came. Remember the dragon shifter?"

His eyes bulged. "You did *not* tell me that."

"Didn't I?" I supposed I hadn't. He'd been pissed off enough at the notion of a human claiming two talismans that I'd never delved into where their power source actually came from. "It's the reason I can walk into Death and use magic in ways even the Sidhe can't."

The Chief made an incoherent strangled noise. "That's not possible."

I decapitated another fury, feeling almost sorry for him.

"So, if anyone can undo a vow, it's me, but you're the one with the expertise. Is there an Invocation that can break a faerie vow?"

"There isn't one." He recovered himself a little. "It's bad enough that you wield our magic, but the gods... no. It's not possible. You should be dead."

"Not the first time I've heard that." I kicked the dead fury aside. "Where—?"

The sky split with a sound like a thunderclap. The Ley Line itself reverberated, and bursts of magic shot upward, uncontrolled, as the faeries reacted to the sudden surge. My own magic flared brighter, and when I looked at Vance, his eyes had gone blank as his shifter side took full command.

"The Morrigan comes!" The Chief's shout snapped me out of my trance.

Above, the cloud cover had shrunk, the crows flying closer and closer together until they became an indistinct mass.

"How do you—?"

My words were lost in a screech loud enough to shatter glass and set car alarms blaring. The mass of crows descended in unison, plunging towards the earth.

"Run!" The Chief pelted across the road, and his fellow half-bloods followed suit, running as though the fires of hell were lapping at their heels.

"You cowardly little shits!" I shouted after them.

A billowing gust of wind hit me from above. I staggered, bracing my feet on the pavement. The crows had ceased their descent and instead converged into a whirlpool of feathers that gradually took on the form of another, larger bird.

My heart quivered. The bird was far bigger than a fury. The size of a house, at least, with thick feathered wings and cruel talons. The Morrigan's red-orange eyes burned like lasers.

"You." She spoke in a booming voice. For a moment I wondered if she was addressing me or Roseanne, who still crouched at the roadside, burned and bleeding. Her daughter was closer, but there was no hiding the talisman in my hand nor the vibrant blue glow around my body.

The Morrigan's eyes locked with mine, and a deep, visceral fear shot through my whole body. My legs locked to the spot. Cold sweat slid down my back. Primal terror took root in my soul, more potent than any hellhound's fear-effect. I saw my own death reflected in her eyes as her claw came down, cutting Roseanne off from the rest of us.

"She is mine."

The air stilled, like a held breath. I was willing to bet the mages were all frozen to the spot, too. Vance shouldn't be affected, but I couldn't move my head to check. Fear spread through me, thick and unyielding.

I forced words from my mouth. "You never claimed her before. Are you working for Fionn?"

In answer, the Morrigan raised her wings. A torrent of wind gusted towards the houses, ripping trees up by their roots, shattering glass, tearing off roof tiles. The air filled with screams and shattering glass.

For a second time, she lifted her wings, this time aiming at the mages.

I tried to scream Vance's name, but the wind caught me first. Not from the Morrigan, but from behind, a sudden gust that knocked the world askew. *Vance.*

When I lifted my head, the road had vanished, and we stood inside the manor's main room. All of us. The mages broke free of the fear-spell in the same instant I did. Except Vance, who stood rigidly in the centre of the room, his face ghostly pale.

Vance swayed on the spot, and I was just in time to catch him as he collapsed.

20

———

"This is a situation and a half," muttered Drake.

I just nodded. The Morrigan's hurricane-like attack would have killed every mage present if Vance hadn't transported them out of the way, but with their leader out of commission, the manor was in an uproar. Small mercy that the Morrigan had disappeared back into the Vale, taking her daughter with her. Whatever orders Fionn had given her didn't extend to this realm, if he'd given her orders at all.

She'd also seemingly taken the furies with her. While I didn't trust them to stay gone, I hadn't dared leave Vance's side since we'd returned to the manor. He lay on the sofa in the main room, and while he didn't look like he was in pain, a sheen of sweat covered his forehead and all the colour had drained from his face. His claws had disappeared, and I held onto his hand and squeezed it. No response.

"Will he wake up?" My voice came out as a croak. I'd resisted asking the question, knowing it wasn't the first time Vance had overexerted himself using his ability, but it slipped out anyway.

"Sure," said Drake. "He's pretty resilient."

"Has he ever transported this many people at once, though?"

"I don't think so." His forehead scrunched up. "And he's been shifting, too, right?"

"Yeah. Oh, god." I buried my head in my hands. "I should have just stayed in Death. Or caught Roseanne before he got to her." If I hadn't been foolish enough to pity her, to want to talk things over, we might have avoided this disaster.

"She wouldn't have listened to reason. But it's not your fault."

"Yeah, Vance would say the same. But if he *dies*—"

"Vance has had people try to kill him every other week since he was a kid. He'll be fine. Besides, we'll stop Fionn first."

"The Chief abandoned us, too." I scowled. "I hope he got pecked to death by the Morrigan's crows."

"So do I." Drake sighed. "Shit, as second in command, I should be the one giving orders, but I don't have a fucking clue what's going on and neither does anyone else."

"You know more than the others do." Not everything, though. "Like what Fionn's looking for. I only just found out. He's seeking something called the cauldron of resurrection."

"The what?"

"A faerie artefact that enables anyone to be reborn into a new body. He's planning to revive himself from death and then make himself an army out of those ghosts he's recruited. He might have already started."

Drake made a faint noise of incredulity. "What... shit, you're serious."

"Obviously."

"That sounds so fucking horrible it must be true." He shuddered. "So, what's the plan?"

"There isn't one." I let go of Vance's hand and stood. "I'm

not even certain where the cauldron *is*. The Hemlock witches told me it's on the Ley Line. At the end of the line."

"Scotland?"

"I don't think that's the end of the world, Drake."

"It might as well be. I grew up there, so I should know." He offered a shadow of his usual smile. "I did hear the Sidhe were first seen up there when the invasion was kicking off, actually. Hard to confirm the details, since they killed all witnesses, including my parents."

"Shit, Drake. I'm sorry."

"I'm in good company here." He shook his head. "So, this cauldron is Fionn's target. Why's it taken him this long to find it?"

"His memories were temporarily erased. Until I killed him." I paced behind the sofa, dread coiling in my gut. "Oh, and it's how he started the invasion. I should probably have mentioned that part."

Drake sank down onto the floor next to the sofa. "A cauldron capable of generating an infinite army of immortals. Are you going to tell the rest of the council?"

"I kinda hoped Vance would." I glanced at the sofa, biting my lip. "If it's on the Ley Line, I can travel up there faster than the average person if I leave my body behind, but..."

"We'll be fine," Drake said. "I'll hold the fort here. If anything happens, Vance said I can use that glyph to get you back into your body. That sound right?"

"Yeah." I didn't know if the same applied if someone else activated the glyph, but

I didn't see a lot of other options. If I left, and Fionn attacked the mages in my absence, it'd be my fault. If I left Fionn to seek out the cauldron without intervening, I'd share the blame for the consequences of that, too. In the end, it all depended on which mistake I could live with. And what Vance wanted me to do.

I took in a shuddering breath and then leaned to kiss Vance on the forehead. "Right. I need to get to the nearest key point on the Ley Line. I'll have to walk. Unless you don't mind me wrecking one of your cars."

"Wouldn't be the first time," said Drake. "Are you sure—"

The doorbell rang.

"Are you expecting anyone?"

"A lot of mages from other regions. Maybe it's them."

"They can fuck off." When they found out Vance was out of action, I was willing to bet Lady Granville would swoop in and reclaim the position she felt she'd been denied. "All right."

I grabbed Helena and ran for the door. A piskie flew into my face on the other side, and I swatted it aside. "Did you ring the doorbell?"

The piskie flew, zigzagging towards the gate. Someone waited outside. Half-faerie, judging by the faint blue glow that shone above his head. The boy couldn't be older than fifteen.

Crystal-blue eyes watched me below tousled blond curls. He wore jeans and a T-shirt and scuffed shoes and carried no weapons, but I kept a firm grip on my blade as I approached the front entrance.

"What?" I called through the gate. "Can't get past the iron?"

"Ivy Lane." He spoke in a bored drawl. "Fionn wishes to invite you to come and meet him. He would like me to remind you of the vow you swore to him."

"What? I didn't swear any vows." Oh, *shit.* I had, technically, when I'd had to convince him to heal Isabel—but that was before he'd died. Had the vow outlasted his death?

Avalin's did, when I got his magic, I reminded myself, and suddenly wished Lady Granville had shown up instead. At least she was a predictable threat.

"You did." The kid didn't sound all that enthused, more like he was reading from a script than anything else.

I studied him, the best I could from the other side of the gate. "Are you under a vow, too?"

He didn't answer. *Did Fionn force him to obey? Was he having trouble convincing the half-faeries to offer their willing loyalty?* He *had* killed a bunch of them, and presumably hadn't told them about the cauldron yet either. Maybe they were finally starting to see reason, but it was entirely too late for regrets.

Drake caught up to me. "What are you doing?"

"Fionn's blackmailing me into coming back. Sorry." I gave him a look that communicated *keep Vance safe for me* and then faced the half-faerie again. "I want a guarantee that he doesn't plan to attack my friends while my back is turned."

"That I cannot give you."

No. It didn't matter what I requested when Fionn had me by the throat. The one silver lining was that his request meant he hadn't gone after the cauldron yet, and if he intended for me to stand at his side as he did so, I might be able to figure out a way to stop him from using it. "You know Fionn won't give you immortality, right?"

"He will, and you, too, if you desire." He spoke in the same bored voice, as though he was selling second-hand furniture, not promising immortality. "Meet me in the field behind the manor."

He hadn't invited himself in. The iron had done its job, but that didn't mean I trusted Fionn to leave Vance the hell alone while I presented myself to him for whatever reason he'd concocted this time. Why pick now to invoke the vow I'd sworn to save Isabel's life? He hadn't so much as mentioned it during our brief altercation, but like always, he was waiting for the opportune moment. Vance was out of action. I was on my own.

Walking through the manor was faster, but leaving Vance tore at my heart, made me wish I could rip the vow clean out of me the way I'd once wished I could rid myself of Avalin's magic.

"Ivy." Drake hurried behind me. "Is there no other way?"

"Do you want to test if the manor's wards can keep out a death god while the Mage Lord is out for the count?" My hands clenched helplessly. "I swore the vow because Fionn had Isabel shot by an instant-kill bullet and she'd be dead if he hadn't healed her. I don't want to see what he'll do if I break it."

Drake sucked in a breath. "He's not going to spare us because you go with him."

"At least he'll be under my watch." I lifted a hand and indicated my pockets where I kept my daggers. "I have iron. I can survive Faerie. You should keep an eye on things here. Stay in touch with Isabel, too. And when Vance wakes up…"

I choked off, unable to say more. *I'm sorry. Vance, I'm so sorry.*

Outside, the dark sky churned with clouds. Fog pressed against the fences, and the air held an odd, hazy quality. *The veil is damaged.* No surprise after the sheer number of furies Fionn had unleashed on the city, on top of the Morrigan's brief appearance. I hadn't spoken to Frank since my trip into the Hemlock Coven's forest, but I suspected he'd be lying low. Waiting for the storm to blow over, or to be swept away in its wake.

What outcome was most likely? If Fionn's plan failed, he'd remain a wraith, an eternal thorn in my side. If he succeeded, if he was reborn again in the cauldron's waters, he'd be back to full strength. And if I then used some means of trickery to dodge the vow and took his life as I had before, he'd proven that death was no obstacle to his ambitions. He'd keep coming back, keep trying again, until my life and my realm had been extinguished.

The half-faerie waited for me in the field. Beside him stood Fionn, his ghostly hand beckoning me into Faerie. A smile tilted his mouth.

He hadn't spoken the vow yet.

I broke into a run, putting every ounce of faerie-magic-enhanced energy into my speed and leaping over the threshold into the Vale. The second I landed, I threw myself out of my body and crashed into Fionn's wraith-form.

My spirit collided with his, punching, kicking, blasting magic with every hit despite the lack of any impact on his transparent body. I'd taken him by surprise, and I got in a few hits before he tried to grab me.

I flew out of range, magic coalescing around my hands. Once, when I'd fought Calder's spirit, I'd conjured the likeness of a sword. Now, too, I imagined the blue energy streaming from my hands forming a mirror of my talisman. The threads entwined into the distinct outline of a sword, pointed directly at Fionn.

He didn't even blink. "What did I tell you, Ivy? Your magic and mine are too similar for you to leave an impact on me. I might also remind you that you swore a vow to do my bidding."

"I don't owe you a thing. You died. Our vow is null and void."

"I think we both know that even death itself cannot unravel a vow." He extended a hand through my chest.

A torrent of ice slid over me, locking my grip around the blade. I gritted my teeth, telling myself it wasn't real, but the frigid pain was as solid as the sword I'd conjured and my body refused to move. My *actual* body lay several feet away, prone and pale on the Vale's path.

"I didn't know you'd already worked out how to spirit

travel, Ivy," he said. "I wanted to establish more trust between us before I taught you that side of your power."

"I wouldn't take lessons from you if you were the last person in existence."

"Wouldn't you?" He moved closer, a smile curling his lip. "Who *has* been teaching you, I wonder?"

Frank. A bizarre sense of protectiveness seized me. I might be pissed off at the old necromancer for omitting the truth, but I refused to let Fionn get his ghostly hands on him. "Maybe I taught myself."

"Maybe you did." He smiled at me in his creepy serial-killer way. "But someone told you that I seek the cauldron of resurrection. Was it the Hemlock witches, by any chance?"

I tried to hide my reaction, but he laughed. Baring my teeth, I said, "Did it piss you off when you couldn't get into the forest?"

"Oh, the forest is a low priority," he said. "The cauldron, as you rightly guessed, is paramount. Death is not natural to our kind."

"Oh, cry me a fucking river," I spat. "You have your magic, you have an army—an unwilling one, mind, but that's your own damn fault. The only thing you don't have is a body, and that's more than a fair enough punishment for trying to destroy my realm."

"Your people seem to have misplaced something else. Caelan?" Fionn smiled at the blond-haired half-Sidhe who'd brought me here. He strode into view, staggering under the weight of a sword which looked too heavy for him to carry. *The life-drinker.*

"You can't use that." Despite lacking a body, my heart did a pretty convincing imitation of sinking in my chest. "It's mine, for a start. Also, you're dead."

"Both of those matters are temporary inconveniences."

I'd had enough. I let the illusory sword dissolve and fell

back into my body, lifting my head. My limbs were a little stiff, but I hadn't broken the connection for long enough to lose all sensation. Lifting my real blade, I faced the blond half-faerie. "Give that to me. If you hold it for too long, it'll burn off your hands."

"Play nice, Ivy," said Fionn. "I'll make this fair for both of us. We shall fight a single bout. You win, and you get the cauldron. You lose, and I get this talisman."

I swivelled to his ghost, fighting a wave of exhaustion pushing at me despite the magic bolstering my strength. Fionn was *dead.* My magic had little effect on him, and neither did my sword. If I conceded, I'd lose so much more than the talisman. What else had he stolen from the mages' storerooms? How had his servant got in there to begin with?

He laughed at the horror on my face. "Oh, Ivy, you didn't really think those fragile wards on the mages' depository could keep me out, did you? The harder part was getting someone else in. I still have some difficulty handling physical objects, but that won't be a problem for much longer."

He flew forwards, straight through my body and spirit both. I sank to my knees, an icy chill spreading through my bones. He hadn't stabbed me with a weapon, but as a wraith, he *was* a weapon, with a thousand times the power of a regular ghost. His touch was cold enough to burn down to my core.

I couldn't move as he reached downward, into my chest. His ghostly hand clenched. I screamed, pain radiating through my very being. My spirit came loose from my body, locked in his grip, unable to escape.

"Ivy Lane," he snarled. "You don't know who I really am, and I suppose I can't fault you for your ignorance. At one time, my entire existence revolved around removing and reuniting spirits and bodies. I can snuff your spirit out like a candle, or I can crush your physical body with one blow. Or you can concede to me. Those are your options."

What choices? If I died, he'd have a free shot at the mortal realm, and everyone I loved would pay the price.

"If I concede to you, you'll get the talisman," I choked. "That's all. Right?"

"Right you are, Ivy," he breathed in my ear. "Well?"

"I concede."

21

Fionn released me. I fell back into my body, gasping for breath.

Oh, god. On top of everything else he had in his favour, Fionn now wielded the life-drinker sword. Or he would, once he'd regained a new body. Underhanded though his methods might be, the talisman belonged to him, and unlike the Lady of the Tree, he was strong enough to use it.

I rose upward on shaky legs and glared at Caelan. "What else did he have you steal from the mages?"

"You're scared I took your Invocations?" Fionn laughed, his carefree mask back in place again. "I know them all by heart, Ivy."

Okay. He didn't take them. But he can. He could walk anywhere he liked. Everything, the fates of everyone I knew, depended on me not pissing him off any more than I already had.

I faced him, readjusting my grip on Helena, and wished my body would stop shaking. "Why did you even need the sword? Why take it?"

"Because I can." He beckoned. "Come with me, Ivy."

The vow rang through my body, through my spirit, compelling me to walk. My feet walked without me consciously guiding them, and Fionn didn't look back to make sure I was behind him. He didn't need to, not when he had me by the neck whether he used the vow or not. My only consolation was that as long as I was with him, his attention was on me and not on my allies.

My heart twisted. I'd left Vance in the worst state possible. If Fionn sent his allies to attack mine, I would end him, vow or none. And if he managed to get himself a new body first, at least I'd have the satisfaction of ripping out his heart with my bare hands.

Magic seethed around me, curling from my sword towards the back of Fionn's neck. He halted his walk as the blue tendrils wrapped around his ghostly throat as though to strangle him.

"Now, Ivy," he said. "None of that."

"I'm not doing anything," I said. "My magic wants to choke you to death. What exactly did you do to Avalin to make him hate you so much?"

"That's for me to know." He resumed walking—well, floating—and though the tendrils of my magic kept trying to reach for him, they made no impact.

Dammit, he does know. He remembers that, too.

The time when the castle appeared amid the silver-leafed trees. Fionn walked straight towards it. I followed, a sick taste in my mouth. He'd replicated Avalin's castle almost exactly, down to every turreted tower and arrow-slit window.

"How pretentious."

He laughed. "I thought you'd say that, Ivy."

"You don't know me." Whatever vow he'd made me swear, whatever memories he'd gained, I was still an unknown to him. I hadn't been a factor in the invasion. Neither had the talisman I'd claimed from Avalin. Fionn might have stolen the life-drinker, but I had a hard time believing he'd be able to claim my other talisman when Avalin's power despised him so greatly. Maybe I could work with that.

"I know you, Ivy," said Fionn. "I know you care for that half-blood."

"Roseanne?" My heart twinged. "She's thirteen years old. I realise you don't have a shred of compassion, but your half-bloods do, and they won't all obey you forever."

"That's where you're wrong."

When Fionn reached the castle's entrance, the spell on my legs brought me to a halt at his side.

"My army," he said softly. "I offer them their greatest dreams, and who in their right mind would ever refuse?"

The doors swung inward. Half-faeries filled the space inside the entrance hall, hundreds of them, pressed together in a sea of ghostly forms haloed in blue-green light. Where had he found so many?

"Are you really planning to revive them in the cauldron, like you promised?" My heart dove sickeningly. They were dead. All of them. "Or is this a ruse?"

His teeth flashed white in a grin. "I will keep my promise, after they bear witness to my rebirth."

"That's the plan. You want an audience." None of them seemed to have noticed my presence at all. Fionn had every one of them enthralled. "And you want *me* to be a witness so you can gloat at me some more?"

"No." His smile turned feral. "No, you're going to stay here, Ivy, while I use the cauldron to forge a new army."

My knees buckled under the force of the vow's strength. *Dammit.* I could no more shake off his command than I could cut off my own hand. My feet carried me into the castle, past the sea of ghostly half-faeries and through a door off the main hall. Despite the number of people inside, an eerie silence filled the entire castle, as though everyone was holding their breath. I knew where my legs were taking me before I reached the room identical to the cupboard-sized space I'd slept in as a prisoner in Avalin's castle.

"It could be worse, Ivy." Fionn hovered in the doorway, trapping me in the room I'd been willing to tear the world down to escape. "I'll even let you keep your sword. You can't lay a hand on me, after all."

Sure about that? Even now, my magic yearned to rip his ghostly head in two like scrap paper. Cold sweat ran down my neck, and my hands trembled with the effort of fighting the vow. I had my sword in both hands. If I could just *move*—

"Don't exert yourself," he said. "It'll only be more uncomfortable for you if you struggle."

"I'll teach you what uncomfortable means," I said through gritted teeth. "You know, forcing me to stand at your side isn't going to make me like or respect you, Fionn. Everyone knows you're a liar."

"Those half-bloods downstairs say differently."

"That's because you brainwashed them." I injected as much disdain as I could muster into my voice. "I'm not afraid of you. You can conjure up all the illusions you like, but this place gave me its worst while I was a child without any magic. I still walked out."

"Yet you bent to me so easily."

"You bound me to your word. I'll learn how to break it." There must be a way. My magic despised him. We were polar opposites, not allies.

"I doubt so, Ivy." He gave a sigh. "This isn't what I wanted. The first invasion should have been the end of the Courts, but the Sidhe were more devious than I expected of them."

"I'm really not interested in your monologues." A lie. I *did* want the full story of how the invasion had failed, how he'd ended up trapped in that tomb, but he'd only offer the truth to me if it no longer mattered that I knew.

"Now, you can't fool me, Ivy Lynn. I know you want to hear me out."

"Lane. You can at least get my name right if you're going to lock me in a castle and force me to listen to your whining."

He offered a wolfish grin. "A long time ago, whenever a Sidhe betrayed their Courts, they were cast out into the wilderness that exists outside of Summer and Winter. The trouble with that arrangement was that those exiles frequently came back and enacted mischief upon the Courts. Thievery, murder, and other such inconveniences."

"Sounds like you'd get along well with them, Fionn."

"Yes, and it was something of a nuisance for the Sidhe to repeatedly have to cast out the same criminals," he said. "Eventually, someone proposed a solution. You see, there was a path that led from the Courts into the place known as the Death Kingdom. Few spoke of that place, though all Sidhe knew it existed. The Death Kingdom had a somewhat unpleasant reputation, and two beings alone claimed dominion in that region. The Morrigan and the Huntsman."

"Is there a point to this story?"

"Yes," he said. "Beyond even the Death Kingdom lay a corner of Faerie that was all but uninhabited, and that interestingly held no magic at all. The ancient Sidhe had created the place as a prison of sorts to contain the gods that once ruled their territories. When someone suggested sending the exiles there, it seemed an obvious solution."

Who made that suggestion? Surely not Fionn himself, though his role as Huntsman had likely taken him close to the land of the exiles.

"What do you want, a round of applause?" I asked. "For creating an army out of a bunch of criminals and killing millions of innocent humans in your failed attempt to take down the Courts?"

"The damage was unfortunate." His smile suggested otherwise. "A mortal like you can never comprehend the eternal nature of those who dwell in these lands. The Sidhe exist in an endless present in which nothing ever changes and things simply *are*. I showed them that they can be otherwise. I wrote history."

"And got yourself shut inside a tomb for a few decades as a result."

"Oh, I won't make it easy for you by telling you how that unfortunate mishap came about," he said. "I thought you should know the truth of your position, though, Ivy. I am stronger than any Sidhe of the Courts. Stronger than any talisman. The ring might have been my undoing, but it is gone now. Thanks to you, Ivy. You disposed of my last weakness."

My breath lodged in my chest. *I had to.* He might want me to spend my last hours wracked with self-loathing, but in the end, my emotions and thoughts remained my own.

Noting that I had no intention of replying, he said, "I'll see you again, Ivy, in the flesh this time… very soon."

No. I moved after him. Pain wrenched through my body, tearing through my skin like live currents in my blood. I blacked out for a moment, and when I blinked back to my senses, he was gone, and the door had closed behind him.

"Shit!" I pounded against the door with both fists. Locked. The window was a narrow sliver barely wide enough to accommodate an imp or piskie. No doubt he'd taken measures so I didn't use my magic to break through the door or shatter the walls, too.

I took in a shuddering breath, trying to calm my thoughts. He hadn't taken away my weapons. Perhaps he'd forgotten I carried my daggers as well as my talisman, though iron was no threat to him as a ghost. When he was reborn, though? His new body would be just as vulnerable to iron as the old one. There was the pesky matter of the vow I'd sworn, but I'd wriggled around that one before. I'd take him down. I could be patient until then.

Or not. The creak of a door opening outside drew me to the window. Through the narrow gap, I watched the army leave, a steady flow of smaller figures following Fionn out of the castle. He couldn't possibly have found all those half-bloods in a single city. There were thousands across England alone and doubtless even more worldwide, and it was no wonder I hadn't seen Fionn or any of his minions on half-blood territory recently. They'd been working on globe-spanning recruitment tactics the whole time, ferrying souls across Death to the Grey Vale, ready to be sacrificed.

And now he was about to take them on their final journey.

My nails bit into my palms. Magic burst from my skin but fizzled out on connection with the window. Fionn, visible as a glowing column at the front of the group, lifted his head towards the castle. I didn't need to be able to see him up close to know he was offering me a last knowing smile before he led his army out of sight.

Dammit. I swore loudly, wrenching my attention away from the window. *Think, Ivy.* Every vow had a loophole. The Sidhe were experts at unravelling them, at twisting words, but his command to *stay here* had no obvious double meaning.

Wait. My physical body was bound, but he hadn't speci-fied that I had to stay *in* my body. I didn't know if that would be enough to skirt the terms of the vow, but it'd also get me around the pesky lock on the door, too.

I lowered myself to the floor, my back to the wall. Took in a steadying breath. Then I shifted out of my body. As a ghost,

I rotated towards the window and glided straight through the castle wall.

It worked. I hovered high up in the air, the castle grounds stretching beneath to the endless forest beyond. Fionn's army had long gone, but if I moved fast, I might be able to catch up to them before his rebirth.

Except confronting him without a body was a good way to end up worse than dead. I'd left my allies in the mortal realm, too. I only had my magic, a constant presence, glowing brightly as it drew in the pain the half-bloods had left behind. Despite its inherent loathing of Fionn, it wouldn't be enough to take him down. I needed more.

I needed an army.

Not many of those lying around. Nobody would be left in the castle, and the Vale itself was full of hostile forces, some of which would be a threat to me even as a ghost. While there was a chance I might be able to travel through Death and back to the mortal realm without bringing my body along for the ride, how could I guarantee that wouldn't permanently sever the connection and leave me to drift around as a ghost while my body expired in the Vale?

I had to start somewhere. I scanned the forest and saw movement stirring among the trees below as a large, furred shape detached itself from the forest and padded towards the castle. *Hellhound.* Its huge paws padded against the leaf-strewn ground, and it lifted its head to watch me, its tongue lolling.

As I glided down the castle's sheer wall, two more hell-hounds followed. Then another three. Had they been waiting in the forest all along? When my transparent feet touched down on the ground, a good twenty or so hellhounds were gathered in front of me and still more fanned out of the forest, each one equally huge and fearsome.

"Were you waiting for me?" I addressed the frontmost

hellhound, the smaller one with which I'd interacted back in the mortal realm. "Are you going to help me?"

The beast let out a growl that I assumed meant yes. By now, the hellhounds filled the entire space outside the castle, easily a hundred of them.

I asked for an army... "Will you follow me?"

Another growl of affirmation. They understood, at least a little, but why had they picked me over Fionn? Because they recognised my talisman as the same power that Avalin had commanded? Fionn had been their original leader, though it had been Calder who'd initially summoned them to the mortal realm, but for some reason or other, they'd chosen to follow me instead of the Huntsman.

"You want to fight on my side?" Not the army I'd been expecting, but they shared my ability to travel between realms, to traverse the spirit lines, as they didn't belong to this realm or to any other.

Together, we might have a chance of ambushing Fionn before he reached the cauldron.

"My body is bound by a vow," I told the hellhounds, not sure if they understood more than basic commands. "Can one of you keep an eye on it?" I pointed up the sheer castle wall. "If I'm attacked, touch the mark on my shoulder." I gestured to my upper right arm, though my ghostly body didn't show any of the blemishes of my mortal form. "Or, I don't know. Shake me or something. Wake me up."

The smaller hellhound growled and then bounded through the castle's open front door. A second hellhound peeled away from the group and followed. Whether they'd understand my instructions was debateable, but I'd have to assume that they'd wake me up if my physical body got attacked, or at least jump to my defence.

I'd covered all my bases. It was time to go. The rest of the army crowded around me. Waiting for my command.

I took in a breath. "We'll need to move quickly to catch up to him. Can you run fast?"

The hellhounds growled. One large beast bowed its head before me, resting its front paws on the ground. *It wants me to ride?* Tentatively I approached at a glide and positioned myself so that I settled on its back. It was a peculiar sensation, partly like sitting on real animal and partly like floating in nothingness. I didn't have a clue how to stay in place, but though my head spun with vertigo when the beast rose upright, I didn't fall. When I looked down, both my legs and the hellhound's body appeared more present, somehow, as if sitting on the beast had solidified my ghostly form, at least temporarily.

"Come on." I raised my voice and called to my army. "Let's give him hell."

22

Leading an army of hellhounds through Death sat right at the top of my list of weirdest experiences, and considering all the time I'd spent around the faeries, that was saying a lot. I hadn't thought it was possible to ride on a hellhound as a ghost, but that strange sense of being half corporeal and half not persisted as we followed the steep path through the forest. I'd never ridden on a horse in my life, but I had some idea of what to do, and the hellhound moved without my needing to give any instructions.

"We need to cross through the realms and follow the Ley Line," I told the hellhounds. "Keep going until we catch him up."

He might try to twist the vow against me again when we did, but the presence of an army of hellhounds ought to be enough of a distraction, or so I hoped.

Grey smoke distorted the world, a sign that we'd passed from the Vale to the other side. For a few seconds, I feared I'd fall, and I closed my eyes and took in a few breaths. Then I remembered I didn't even have lungs.

You can spirit travel, for god's sake. Get a grip.

I opened my eyes and focused on the solidity of the hellhound's steps as it bounded along the murky path. The Grey Vale's trees had disappeared entirely beneath the greyness of Death, but I reminded myself that the hellhounds had followed Fionn down this path for countless years. They knew where they were going.

The host of hellhounds bounded through smoke and eerie silence. Time fell away, and when a sudden chill wind buffeted me, I nearly fell off my mount. The air vibrated, tension thrumming like a plucked string. Not the vow, but a restlessness in the very atmosphere that I could only assume came from the Ley Line itself. A reaction. Fionn hadn't reached the cauldron already, had he?

My hellhound steed growled a warning. A blot appeared on the path ahead, vaguely human-shaped. *A wraith.* Fionn? No, it wasn't him. His army was nowhere in sight, and the wraith stood alone, planted in the middle of the path like a giant tree.

"Don't stop," I told the hellhound. "We'll crush it."

Magic hummed to life inside me. I raised my hands, imagining I held a sword. The magic flowed into shape, forming the outline of Helena, complete with the runes glowing on the hilt. The symbols even shimmered like real glyphs. *That's new.* I didn't have time to stop and see if I could read them; we were rapidly gaining on the wraith. While its form remained indistinct, it really did look like more a tree spreading its roots across the path than a person.

I raised my sword. "Get out of the way or I'll mow you down."

The wraith's root-like appendages lifted upward, jabbing at me. The hellhound veered to the side, and I swiped my sword, repelling the ghostly branches. *Branches?* This enemy was undeniably a ghost, but its root-like appendages reminded me of another battle I'd fought.

Of course. Who had helped free Fionn? Who'd wanted a new body badly enough to make a deal with Calder, to hand him the knowledge he'd used to unleash terror upon our realm?

I leapt clear of the hellhound's back and landed in front of the face leering at me from amid the fog, warped and inhuman yet chillingly recognisable as the Lady of the Tree. She'd left part of herself behind when she'd died after all.

"You." I deflected another strike from her ghostly roots, easily dodging around them in my incorporeal form. The hellhounds snapped at her, too, but their sharp teeth were unable to leave an impact on her transparent body.

"Ivy Lane," she crooned. "Up to more trickery, are you?"

"Why didn't you go with Fionn?" My sword's light grew brighter, illuminating her ghostly face, her pit-like eyes glowing within the fog. "You'd really give up your shot at a new body for the sake of revenge on me?"

Magic surged from my blade and crashed into her. Branches splayed out, roots whipped back, but her tree form was sturdy even as a ghost.

"You're too weak, Ivy," she said, accompanied by a flurry of stabs from her roots. "You're no match for him. You'll lose."

"Or did he abandon you?" I ignored the jab—both verbal and literal. "He didn't even give you the life-drinker back. Now he's sent you to hang around here while he and his friends get shiny new bodies?"

"He *will* reward me for my loyalty." Her voice broke into an incoherent scream, her face twisting and warping like a ghostly version of the aged face she'd worn when we'd first met.

Unexpected pity filled me. Being exiled into the mortal realm had stripped away whoever she'd been in Faerie, and without the life-drinker, she was nothing more than a husk waiting to expire, pain and power concentrated into a single form.

I let her pain feed into my magic, into the shimmering blade, and drove it through the heart of her tree.

"I *will not expire!*" Her voice cracked like a whip, her rage building, refusing to be extinguished.

Dammit. I don't have time for this. I whipped the blade free, the glyphs catching my vision. Invocations. I'd used one on Calder, to erase his memory. Ghosts weren't immune.

One of the glyphs brightened, travelling upward along the length of the blade, its meaning filtering through my mind. One I'd seen during my last visit to the mages' storeroom.

Break.

The word exploded from my mouth, leaving a coppery taste as though I'd bitten my tongue in my real body. I staggered back, the word hanging in the air.

The Lady broke. Her tree-like form shattered in a dazzling flash of blue-green, roots and branches reduced to shards. Her final scream lingered for a moment before fading to silence.

Okay. I'm gonna use that one on Fionn.

Sending a silent thanks to whatever universal translator in my magic had led me to that word, I returned to the hellhound waiting for me to climb onto its back. "Let's go."

Back on my steed, I led the way along a path that grew more distinct the further we moved. Ground trampled flat by hoofbeats formed a curving line northward, undisturbed by any landmarks. No further ghosts barred our way, but I glimpsed the first bodies shortly after. At least two dozen dead lay strewn on the path as though carelessly tossed aside. I raised a hand to stop the hellhounds, not wanting them to tread on anyone who was still alive, but not a soul stirred. Beyond, more bodies lay, too many to count. Hundreds.

My stomach churned. They were half-bloods, the same

ones whose ghosts had been trapped in the castle. Fionn had killed them *here,* close enough to the cauldron to almost be within breathing distance of their lifelong dream. They hadn't been able to pass through the veil with their physical bodies, so he'd taken care of that limitation in his own way.

Rage burned inside me. There was no sign of a struggle. They'd gone willingly. Every single one of them, trampled by the Hunt. I didn't see Roseanne among the dead, but there were so many that I hadn't a hope of identifying a single person.

She might not be here. She'd still been alive when I'd met Fionn in the Vale the first time, and then the Morrigan had taken her. Would she have bothered to seek out her child only to sacrifice her life for Fionn's cause? I hoped not, though the Morrigan doubtless possessed an agenda of her own.

"Let's go." I addressed the hellhounds, pointing a shaky hand northward. "We need to kill the person who did this."

I'm coming after you, Fionn, you bastard.

As we continued onward, a sound like the hum of a thousand voices reverberated through the air. Was that the cauldron? My ears burned, my teeth rattling in my skull, but I ignored the mimicry of physical sensations and continued until the hellhound's feet touched down on grass.

The vast black cauldron sat in the centre of a field easily the size of a football pitch, more than large enough to accommodate every one of the hundreds of half-bloods gathering around its base. Admittedly, as ghosts, they didn't take up much space, but the hum of hundreds of voices mingled with the vibration in the air and made me certain that the presence of so many ghosts on the Ley Line at once was bound to have caused some major issues over on the other side.

As for the cauldron? Aside from its sheer size, the only

striking factor was the blue sheen roiling off the surface. Faerie blood. The Lady of the Tree had been right all along.

Who did the blood belong to? Nobody who was alive today, in all likelihood. This artefact, this relic, had been around for millennia. And one person alone knew how to use it.

The cauldron's contents swirled, and a voice rose upward from within. "Sorry to disappoint you, Ivy. You're too late."

Fionn appeared within the swirling blue haze, indistinct at first, but already more solid than the ghost he'd been beforehand. He flashed me a knowing smile as he stepped out of the cauldron, smoke coalescing around his body and forming armour identical to that which he'd worn in life. A shimmering blade completed the ensemble, again identical to his previous one. Had the cauldron conjured up a *talisman*? Or was it simply a glamour? It didn't matter. Fionn didn't need to wield a talisman to make effective use of his magic, and now its sole weakness had been obliterated.

"I should have guessed you'd defy me," he added. "I'm disappointed in my hellhounds, I admit."

"They aren't yours." I looked for my army, but they'd retreated to the clearing's edges beyond the sea of eager-eyed half-bloods. All of them watched the cauldron with expressions of raw hunger and desperation. "The hellhounds are smarter than you are. They know who's on the winning team."

"They can't come near the cauldron," he told me. "It repels them. They are death, and it is life."

"Ironic for a god of death." *Ah, shit.* My sword looked even more insubstantial when faced with his solid blade, and my magic couldn't touch him regardless of whatever form it took. Even my army had its limits.

"I didn't want to have to do this, Ivy." He beckoned to a group of half-faeries, all of whom wore transparent armour that resembled the sort worn by those who'd lived on half-blood territory. Some might have been among those who'd defied the Chief, though I didn't recognise any of their transparent faces. Their ghostly hands made no impact on me, but the collective press of bodies pushed me away from the cauldron.

I opened my mouth to speak, tasting the Invocation on the back of my tongue. Fionn gave a casual gesture and my mouth locked shut on the word, the tongue-tying spell pushing the command back down my throat. I shot him a look of venomous fury.

Fuck. It can't end like this.

The sound of hoof-steps echoed. The half-faerie ghosts parted to let a group of knights ride up to the cauldron on their black steeds. Fionn's entourage. The horsemen were already immortal, as far as I knew, and probably had no need for the cauldron.

I fought against the spell binding my tongue. Anger rolled through me, and the fury of the other half-bloods lapped at me, too. While a fair bit of their rage was directed at me because they thought I was here to stop them getting their shot at immortality, there was pain there, too. Fionn had brutally killed them all, and now the cauldron was their only hope to regain their lives.

The warriors closed in around me. Each drew a sword or staff, a talisman wreathed in light. A single flash of green stood out amid the sea of blue. The life-drinker? Had Fionn ceded it to one of his minions? If so, he'd doubtless bound them with a vow to stop them claiming it for themselves, and to stop me from stealing it from his grasp.

Fionn's gaze followed mine, and he laughed. "You're wondering why I handed the life-drinker over to another of my Sidhe warriors? I have a plan, don't worry... especially for your friends."

The dam broke in a flood of magic that shattered the spell holding my mouth shut. I spat at him, and while my magic left no impact on him, my spittle hit him on the cheekbone. He lifted his arm to wipe it away, the slightest hint of annoyance entering his expression.

"Really, Ivy," he said. "You can't summon up an ounce of respect, can you?"

"Respect?" I forced a disbelieving laugh. "After everything you've done to hurt me and my friends, you're lucky I only spat at you. You're the one who owes *me* an apology, a hundred times over."

"I can do better," said Fionn. "I'm willing to offer you a new body of your own."

"No." I made to spit at him again but stopped myself at the dangerous blue glint in his eyes. "Absolutely not. What makes you think a lifetime of enslavement to you is preferable to a regular human lifespan?"

"Some would make that choice." His smile was back in place. "Wouldn't you like a stronger body to match your magic? You must be sick of being so utterly *breakable*."

"You people break as easily as we do, given the right push," I retaliated. "And immortality is overrated."

"You may yet change your mind, Ivy," he said. "I have lived a thousand of your lifetimes. I was born before your distant ancestors crawled out of their caves, and I still remember how your people happily knelt before me."

"You skipped a few centuries," I told him. "Modern humans don't care for destructive psychopaths rampaging through our realm and destroying everything in their path. We don't want you."

"Would you say the same if you'd remained in the Grey Vale and hadn't adapted to living with mortals again? If your mage hadn't claimed you as his?"

"Claimed me." I laughed. "See, that's where we share a

fundamental difference, Fionn. You can't fathom choosing someone as a partner without ownership being involved. Vance and I are equals. I'm not his property."

"You won't be seeing him again, Ivy," he said. "I know you've been anxious to know if it's possible for you to use an Invocation to cage me again. Allow me to dispel that notion. As the Huntsman, I am immune to all commands except my duty, and I've already escaped those chains. Without the ring, my magic cannot be undone."

He can't be affected by Invocations?

"That's right," he went on. "The Courts needed a Huntsman who was impartial, who did not favour one side over the other. The only way to ensure that was to make him immune to any order. Even vows."

Even vows. Every word he spoke stole a shred of my rapidly shrinking supply of hope that I had a chance in hell of beating him. The Sidhe had created someone who couldn't be controlled. They'd thought they were ensuring he wouldn't take one side over the other, but in the end, he'd chosen his own side above all else. And in the process, he'd doomed everyone.

"Did you want a round of applause?" I asked. "Because you're going to be disappointed."

"I can order you to."

"No." I felt the phantom echo of his command tug at my spirit, but I resisted. "You told me to come with you to the castle and stay there while you forged your new army. My body did exactly that, and you can't give another command. I already held up my end of the bargain."

"Word play." A smile ghosted his mouth. "No matter. When you're reborn into a new body, I can put you under all the commands I like."

"Not on your life." I surveyed the spirits pressing against the cauldron, eyeing the blue sheen on its surface as though hypnotised. "Aren't you going to let anyone else share? They've given up so much for you. Seems a shame to let them down."

"You're quite correct, Ivy. You—" He pointed to a pale teenage half-blood ghost. "Go to the cauldron."

The spirit obeyed, drifting away from the others. His fellow half-bloods looked on enviously as he glided over the cauldron's edge, including the group of warriors who stood between me and Fionn. He, too, had turned his head slightly. Now was my chance.

As I made to lunge at him, a shadow fell over the clearing. Above, a flock of crows passed overhead in a black flood like ink spilling across the sky.

The Morrigan had arrived.

23

The huge bird burst out of the cloud of crows and landed in front of Fionn with an earth-shaking crash. Her fear-effect caught me full in the face. Even as a spirit, raw terror lanced through me, and the other half-faeries gasped and quaked.

"We had a deal," the Morrigan told Fionn in her gravelly voice. "Half the souls. I want them now."

Fionn's mouth twisted in annoyance. "You'll get your wish."

"What?" One of the half-bloods spoke up. "What does that mean—?" He cut off in a strangled cry as the Morrigan's claw extended through the ghost like a fishing hook, reeling him over to her.

As the half-faeries stared, transfixed, she swept the ghost behind her and reached for another. The spirits whimpered, unable to move or hide. Their fear lapped against me like the waves of a vast ocean.

I managed to force open my mouth, addressing Fionn. "Half the souls? You're handing them over to her?"

Evidently, yes. He made no move to defend the other half-bloods as the Morrigan continued to reach out her taloned hands to claim one spirit after another. I'd known he couldn't possibly be generous enough to offer them all immortality, but offering half his allies to the Morrigan as payment for her help was a major dick move.

"Eat *his* soul," I called to her. "He'll screw you over too in the end, I can guarantee it."

The Morrigan ignored me, intent on herding the struggling ghosts into a terrified mass. Whispers rose among the others as they began to shake off the immobilising effect of her power, but Fionn's horsemen had moved to surround the clearing and leave no means of escape.

The collective shock and disbelief of the half-bloods added to the pain and rage fuelling my magic. The blue glow brightened as I stood locked in indecision over who to strike down first.

An anguished scream came from behind the Morrigan. Roseanne.

"Stop!" she cried out.

"You brought your daughter?" Incredulity leaked from my voice. "What do you want with her?"

The Morrigan paused midway through hooking her talon through a struggling spirit. "She followed me."

Roseanne let out a quiet sob. I shook off the chains of the fear-spell, drawing in all the magic I could reach. The half-bloods' agony manifested in the bright-blue glow wreathing the sword in my hands as I pointed it at the Morrigan's throat.

"I wouldn't do that, Ivy," Fionn called to me. "She's immortal. Like me."

"The hell you are. I'm not letting her take Roseanne *or* the other spirits."

"I've had enough of your insubordination, Ivy," Fionn said. "Throw her into the cauldron."

The Morrigan didn't need any encouragement. Her claw hooked through my chest, yanking me into the air. I scarcely had time to scream before she threw me into the churning abyss of blue-tinged blood.

A shimming blue barrier blocked my path as my sword dissolved into currents of magic, forming a net across the cauldron's surface. I lay sprawled, breathless, above the swirling currents. Lifting my head, I spied a flurry of movement across from the cauldron. Evidently some of the half-bloods had broken free from her fear-spell and tried to make a run for it, and while every escape route was barred, the clamour was enough to keep their attention off me.

It wouldn't last. I had to act quickly, before my shield collapsed and sent me plunging into the cauldron. I didn't want a new body, immortal or otherwise. I *especially* didn't want to be enslaved to Fionn for an eternity. How many spirits had passed through here, willing or unwilling? How many dead lingered, abandoned, stuck in emptiness thanks to the Huntsman abandoning his post in pursuit of grander schemes?

"No more trickery from you, Ivy." Fionn extended a hand across my shield, which began to dissolve.

As I fell, I spoke the Invocation. *Break.*

The command wrenched loose from me, shaking the world. The cauldron tilted sideways as a deep crack spread across its surface. More cracks followed, splintering outward until a thousand lines leaked blue-tinged blood onto the ground below.

Fionn uttered an incoherent scream. Thick blood drenched the ground, already dissolving, its potency drained away. I hovered above a shield I no longer needed, watching the Morrigan's winged form disappear into the sky. Doubtless she had Roseanne with her, but the other half-bloods had scattered, and even Fionn's soldiers were unable to catch all of them.

Fionn himself stomped a foot, sending another, smaller quake through the earth. Even his horsemen flinched away as his body began to change.

Talons took the place of hands. Wings burst from his shoulder blades, and his armour melded with his skin, becoming scales as he continued to grow into a beast easily the size of the Morrigan. Malevolent black eyes burned into mine. Even my magic's roiling anger quietened in the wake of Fionn's wrath.

He flew at me, raising a clawed hand.

Before his blow connected, pain tore through my shoulder. A sharp burning sensation pulling me back towards my body.

The glyph.

The clearing was wrenched away. Fionn, too, disappeared in a flash. I came upright, gasping for breath, my back to the cold stone wall of Avalin's castle room. In front of me sat a hellhound, its paws pressed against my arm.

"You saved me," I breathed.

More hellhounds gathered around the room. They must have run back down the Ley Line, to bring a warning. They'd understood my command after all.

I pushed to my feet shakily, relieved to have my real, solid sword in my hands. My body was slow to move after the weightlessness of being a ghost, but I needed to escape while Fionn was distracted. The phantom tug of the vow prompted me to say aloud, "He told me to stay while he made his new army. That's no longer an option."

The vow's pressure vanished, but it took me three attempts to cross the veil without leaving my body behind.

The connection was still tenuous, and in the end, the hell-hounds came to my rescue, flanking me on either side as Fionn's castle room became an empty field under a cloudy sky.

"Thanks," I said to the hellhounds, unable to believe I'd gone from slaughtering the beasts to owing them my life in such a short time frame. "You should probably go and wait for me somewhere else. I can't promise the mages won't attack you."

I trudged through the field towards the manor, the aches and pains of my mortal body assailing me with every step as though to remind me of what I'd missed out on when I'd shattered the cauldron. Too bad a long relaxing recovery time wasn't in the cards. Fionn was more pissed off with me than ever, and while I'd taken away his chance at building his army, he'd still managed to regain an immortal body of his own. Now, nothing was stopping him from marching out of the Vale and launching an immediate assault against the mages.

I tried to tap into my magic to boost my speed, but no response came. When I looked down, my blade's glow appeared duller than before. No wisps of magic rose to the surface, and the effect was more of a firefly than a furnace.

That's a bad sign, I thought. Had I burned myself out when I'd shattered the cauldron? I'd felt the effects ripple far beyond the clearing itself, but like when I'd destroyed the ring, I'd been too far beyond the realm of choice to consider the long-term implications.

I reached the manor's back entrance, wondering why I hadn't seen Drake yet. He'd said he'd keep an eye on me, but there was no sign of him nor anyone else. How much time had I lost? Was Vance—

I cut off the thought. No. He'd be here.

Unease trickled down my spine. More signs of abject

wrongness stuck out. Not a single glyph gleamed on the fence circling the manor, and the walls were dull greyish white, no longer shimmering with protective wards. No lights shone in the windows, and not a soul was in the garden.

All of the mages had gone.

24

Heart in my mouth, I closed the gate behind me. Who'd turned off the wards? Fionn... no, if he'd taken a detour into the mortal realm on his way to the cauldron, he wouldn't have missed the opportunity to tell me in gory detail. Someone had undoubtedly been here, though. Despite my exhaustion, I broke into a run, crossing the lawn to the manor's back entrance.

Through the conservatory, into the main corridor. Details leapt out at me. Dust on the piano. A book, lying where someone had dropped it. Dark stains on the pale wallpaper. Blood, forming a trail down to the front door.

Bodies.

"No." The hoarse cry tore from my chest as I stumbled over the limp body of Lady Penrose. One look at her injuries and all hopes that anyone had survived melted away. A gaping hole had burned through her chest, through muscle and bone and organs, and wisps of bright-green magic told me the source.

The life-drinker.

From her position, she'd tried to make a run for the back

door. Another body lay further down the hall. Lord Carlisle, his body severed nearly in two with a similar injury.

Not Vance. Please, not him. The words rang in my head like a mantra as I pounded down the hallway, leaping over another body—Lord Ellsworth—towards the room in which I'd left him.

The door to the meeting room lay in splintered pieces. Bodies were strewn on the floor.

"Vance!" I sagged against the doorway, a sob racking my chest. "No. Vance. *Vance.*"

My gaze panned over the room, over dead face after dead face. All Mage Lords, but none... none were him.

Vance wasn't here. Neither was Drake, nor Wanda either.

Vance. He'd been on the sofa, unconscious, but how many days had passed since then? How many more doors existed in this house, doors that might open to reveal his corpse? My trembling knees hit the carpet, a scream building in my chest.

A loud buzzing snapped on my fighting instincts. I leapt to my feet, my gaze landing on the meeting room table. A phone lay upright—Vance's—and the screen lit up with a message.

I forced myself to reach for it, to read the words on the screen.

If you want to see your mage again, Ivy, come to me.

"Fionn," I hissed between my teeth. *How* he'd arranged this slaughter while he'd been busy with the cauldron was a mystery only Faerie's time-warping tendencies could adequately explain, but the life-drinker had undoubtedly inflicted these wounds. One of his people had taken Vance hostage, and had probably taken Drake and Wanda as well.

I pressed the heels of my palms to my eyes. In his current state, Vance was entirely vulnerable to any depredations Fionn might inflict on him to ensure obedience from me.

Wanda had only recently recovered from an injury, while I was worn to the bone myself.

No. I won't give up on them that easily. I'd walked into Death to find Vance once before. This was no different. I wouldn't let it be.

A flash of green light outside the manor. I left the phone and drew my sword from its sheath as I ran for the door.

I screwed my eyes up in the dazzling glare of Summer magic. The glow encompassed the front lawn, and every plant seemed to bloom brighter around the two knights on horseback. Both were as pale as fresh snow and wore similar armour of silvery green inset with glittering gold gems.

"You again." I recognised the fair-haired Sidhe on the left. "Lord Raivan, was it?"

"We are here to speak to the Mage Lord," he said.

"He's not here." My voice cracked. "Thanks to Fionn. If you're on *his* side, I'll cut your throat."

"Was that a threat, mortal?" Light blazed in his eyes and heat seared the back of my neck.

"A promise." I made no move towards my own sword, though my fingers itched to ram the blade through whoever had taken Vance. "To anyone who's on Fionn's side, but I'm guessing you aren't, and that you have no idea that Lord Fionn, the Huntsman—whatever the hell he used to call himself—is on a mission to destroy the human world and conquer the Courts."

Vance's predicament had melted away most of my caution, but I clung to the little that remained, knowing that these two individuals were my one shot at getting to the Sidhe, and at finding out how to defeat Fionn.

"I have no time for your meaningless babbling," said Lord Raivan. "Hand over the ring, Ivy Lane."

He's still on about that? It took every ounce of control I possessed not to punch him in the nose. "I don't have the damn thing. If I did, you'd know, because the ring blocks all magic, including yours."

His eyes narrowed, but he didn't offer a contradiction. He knew I was right.

"What I do have, however, is a bone to pick with your people." I stepped aside, gesturing at the blood in the hallway. "Your fellow Sidhe did that. They took my partner and slaughtered the mage council."

"My people were *not* responsible," said Lord Raivan. "How dare you—"

"Your exiles." I jabbed a finger at the manor. "There are bodies in there with Summer's magic still fresh on them. Even if your Court isn't directly responsible, someone has to pay for this." When Lord Raivan opened his mouth to protest, I said, "I wish to speak to someone within your Court with higher authority. Believe me when I say that Fionn is a threat to all of us, including you, and there's no time to waste."

"She is right," said a gravelly voice. Quentin strode into view and halted in front of the two Sidhe, lifting his pointed chin. "The human is correct."

"You have a brownie?" said Lord Raivan's companion, with some surprise.

"My bond to the Colton family has lifted now the manor is undefended." Quentin addressed me, not the Sidhe. "However, I am bound to the Summer Court."

"Then go." My hands curled into fists. "Go away and let us die in peace. That's all you people want from us mortals, don't you?"

"This was never my intention." His gaze flickered to the bloodstained corridor, and his mouth tightened.

"Then what?" I burst out. "Where were you when they took Vance, hiding?"

"I was with my masters, who have petitioned the Summer

Court to speak to you on their own territory." He turned to the two Sidhe. "Ivy Lane has been granted an invitation to the Summer Court."

"What?" Lord Raivan's expression shifted to outrage. "That's not allowed. She's *human*."

"And one of your talismans did that. Look at those bodies and tell me it wasn't Summer magic that killed them.' Helpless anger warred with the need to make them understand. To defeat Fionn, I needed their help. And I needed to hear the truth of the invasion straight from the Sidhe myself, no matter the cost I had to pay in return.

"That was not our doing." Lord Raivan's mouth flattened. "I will not permit this."

"My masters insisted, and their word binds me." The brownie bowed his head to me. "I will take you, Ivy, but I must warn you that the Seelie Court is not friendly to mortals."

I gave a wild laugh. "I'll bet it's like a relaxing day on the beach compared to the Vale. I'm ready, Quentin, but I want you to promise they'll help me find Vance. I can't leave him to their mercy. I won't."

"They will," said Quentin. "The Sidhe will help you find the missing Mage Lords. And then, if it is within their power, they will aid you in defeating the Huntsman."

Doubts assailed me. The odds remained heavily stacked against me. No denial there. But I'd been given the chance to win the Sidhe's favour, and I still held a talisman of the gods. With both, I would rescue Vance, come hell or faerie apocalypse.

"All right, then," I said to Quentin. "Take me to the Seelie Court."

ABOUT THE AUTHOR

Emma is the New York Times and USA Today Bestselling author of the Changeling Chronicles urban fantasy series.

Emma spent her childhood creating imaginary worlds to compensate for a disappointingly average reality, so it was probably inevitable that she ended up writing fantasy novels. When she's not immersed in her own fictional universes, Emma can be found with her head in a book or wandering around the world in search of adventure.

Find out more about Emma's books at www.emmaladams.com.

9 781915 250568